MYSTERIES *of* **MARTHA'S VINEYARD**

MYSTERIES *of* MARTHA'S VINEYARD

Bridge Over *Troubled* Waters

JANICE THOMPSON

Guideposts

New York

Mysteries of Martha's Vineyard is a trademark of Guideposts.

Published by Guideposts Books & Inspirational Media
110 William Street
New York, NY 10038
Guideposts.org

Cover and interior design by Müllerhaus
Cover illustration by Greg Copeland, represented by Deborah Wolfe, LTD.
Typeset by Aptara, Inc.

Printed and bound in the United States of America
10 9 8 7 6 5 4 3 2 1

Defend the weak and the fatherless;
uphold the cause of the poor and the oppressed.
Rescue the weak and the needy;
deliver them from the hand of the wicked.
—Psalm 82:3–4 (NIV)

DEDICATION

To every woman who has ever known the pain of abuse,

either physical or verbal: may you find the strength to

overcome your Goliaths and to find peace in the

middle of the storm.

CHAPTER ONE

P riscilla, hurry! The ferry is going to leave without us."

Priscilla Grant looked up from her book into her cousin's anxious eyes. She shifted her gaze to the clock on the bakery wall and gasped. "Oops. Sorry about that, Trudy. Got a little lost in this book you loaned me. I think I'm going to like it."

"It's an intriguing story, for sure." Trudy rose from her spot across the table and brushed cookie crumbs from her slacks. She slung her purse strap over her shoulder. "One of the best I've read in a while. But if we don't hurry, we'll be the last on board the ferry, and you know what that means."

Priscilla tucked a lock of her chin-length hair behind her ear and shook her head. "Nope. What does it mean?" She pushed her chair back from the café table and stood, then shoved the book into her purse.

"Trust me when I say you never want to be at the back of the line on the ferry. It's all fumes back there. One time I nearly asphyxiated." Trudy pointed at Priscilla's half-full glass of coffee. "You want that in a to-go cup? I'm sure Candy will give you one."

Priscilla glanced toward the counter of Candy Lane Confectionery where the owner stood, chatting with a patron.

"No, it's all right. She's busy, and I've had enough. Remind me to order my usual next time. I'm not a fan of that new blend."

"Will do. Let's hit the road, then. We still have to swing by the museum and pick up Mildred."

"Right." Priscilla gave the clock another glance as they headed out. They really did need to hurry. Mildred was nervous enough about her speaking engagement at the Plimoth Plantation museum without their making her late for it.

Six minutes later, she turned her car into the parking lot at the East Shore Historical Museum, where Mildred, their favorite curator, stood along the edge of the sidewalk, looking more than a little anxious. Her forehead was creased with wrinkles that even her tight gray bun couldn't tug out. They served as quite a contrast to her soft, flowing skirt and blouse ensemble in varying shades of periwinkle.

As Priscilla brought the vehicle to a halt, Mildred grabbed the handle of her rolling cart, which appeared to be loaded with items from the museum.

"You got enough room in the back for that cart?" Trudy asked, as they watched Mildred struggle with the over-filled contraption.

"I think I can fit it in."

"Hope you're right. I wouldn't be a bit surprised if she has the *Niña*, the *Pinta*, and the *Santa Maria* in that thing."

"Pretty sure you mean the *Mayflower*, since it's Plimoth Plantation."

"Whatever. I was never very good with history. But I can assure you, she has some sort of costume shoved in there too."

"I'm sure you're right. She'll make it quite the production, as always." Priscilla put her vehicle into Park and jumped out to help the frazzled curator. She popped open the back of the SUV and helped Mildred heft the cart inside.

"Whew!" Mildred sounded breathless. "Thought for a minute you might have forgotten me."

"Nope. Just lost track of time, thanks to a good book. You know how it is." Priscilla closed the back of the vehicle.

"Indeed." Mildred brushed her palms against her skirt, which the island breeze had taken to whipping around her shins. "Better get this show on the road."

"Yes, of course." Priscilla gave her friend a warm smile. "We can't wait to hear you speak. In all the time I've known you, I don't think I've ever seen you in action outside of the museum."

"This is a new opportunity, and I don't mind admitting I'm nervous."

"You'll do great. I'm sure of it."

"I still can't believe they picked me to share. It's such an honor."

"If we make it on time, it'll be an honor," Trudy's voice sounded from inside the vehicle. "Let's get a move on, ladies. If we miss the ferry, all bets are off."

"Right." Just the idea sent a little shiver down Priscilla's spine. To make Mildred late for such an important event would be unforgiveable.

She climbed back into the vehicle and pointed it toward the Vineyard Haven landing. Thank goodness the ferry hadn't left yet, but cars were already inching their way on board.

Trudy groaned as she leaned back against the passenger seat. "Ugh. I knew we'd be at the back of the line. I hate it when that happens."

"At least we made it in time." Priscilla's gaze shifted to the vehicle in front of them—a large white Suburban with a *Victory for Victor* bumper sticker on the back. How anyone in Vineyard Haven could vote for that braggadocio Victor Fox for one of the island's commissioner positions was beyond her, but she decided a conversation about politics would be out of line today.

"I've got the whole day planned out, Priscilla." Mildred's anxious voice brought her back to the moment. "I have to be at the museum by ten o'clock to set up my display for my ten thirty speaking engagement. I'll speak for an hour, and then there's a special tour of the village by Jacob Lansford. You know him, right? He's an amazing historian from Boston. He's coming just for this event. I get the shivers when I think that someone as amazing as Jacob will be listening to my speech."

Was it Priscilla's imagination, or did Mildred sound even more nervous now than before? "I've never heard of him," she said. "Can't say I know that much about Plimoth Plantation, either— the men or the women. I'm ashamed to say I haven't been there yet."

"I can't believe you've lived in Massachusetts this long and still haven't visited such a famous site." Mildred clucked her tongue. "Shocking."

"Today will make up for that, and I'll have the best tour guide anyone could ask for."

"Jacob Lansford?"

"No, silly. You. You're the best."

"Humph," Mildred said and then grew quiet.

Priscilla inched her car forward, sticking close to the white Suburban in front of her. "Who's manning the museum in your absence today, Mildred?"

"No one. I put the Closed sign on the door. "

Trudy gasped. "You closed the museum? On a Tuesday?"

"Mm-hmm. That's how much this trip means to me. So let's hope we make it on board the ferry. Can you go any faster, Priscilla?"

Gracious. Priscilla couldn't remember the last time she'd seen the local historian so worked up.

"I can only go as fast as the vehicle in front of me."

Ahead of them, the line of cars began to move in unison toward the ferry. Priscilla shifted her SUV into Drive but left her foot on the brake until the time came to move forward.

"You seem awfully nervous today, Mildred," she observed. "It's not like you."

"Do I?"

"This is a big day for her, Priscilla. That's all." Trudy pulled down the visor and examined her appearance. She reached into her oversized purse and came out with a tube of bright-pink lipstick. "I just love this new Pretty in Pink lipstick from Heavenly Faces. Can't get enough of it."

"I'm just anxious," Mildred explained. "Praying that all goes well."

Priscilla nudged her car forward, taking care to keep enough distance between her SUV and the car ahead of her.

Trudy smacked her lips, shoved the tube of lipstick back in her purse, and then slapped the visor up. She pointed to the Suburban. "Hey, isn't that Betty Fox's car in front of us? I recognize the ding in the rear bumper. I heard she backed into someone at Ortmann's grocery store a couple of weeks ago. Folks said she was acting mighty strange that day."

From the back seat, Mildred cleared her throat. "If I were married to Victor Fox, I'd act strangely too. But I'm sure there's a perfectly good explanation as to why she bumped into someone, if that's what happened. I'm more curious about where she's headed today. She rarely leaves her house. She's such a recluse. Do you think she's planning to come hear me speak?"

"You did promote the event in the museum newsletter," Priscilla reminded her. "So it's possible."

"Right, though Betty's never been all that interested in history. I've only seen her at the museum a couple of times over the years, and that was when Victor was hosting some sort of to-do to garner votes. She was always dressed to the nines with perfect hair and makeup, but she looked as if she'd rather be home sipping a cup of tea and watching a documentary."

"Sounds about right," Trudy said and then rolled her eyes. "Always out for the vote, that's Victor, even when it means putting his family on the spot."

"Besides, if she wanted to come hear me speak, why not ask to ride with us? Why drive that big vehicle all by herself?"

"Maybe she's not alone," Trudy speculated. "Could be the whole Suburban is full of your adoring fans, Mildred. Maybe we'll get there, and I'll have to fight off the paparazzi to protect you as you haul your things inside and get set up."

"Gracious. I can't picture it. Little ol' me with a fan club?" The giggle that escaped from the back seat was girlish and far more relaxed than the words that preceded it.

Priscilla decided to keep the momentum going. "Tell us more about your topic, Mildred."

"I'm speaking about the role women played in the days of the Plymouth settlement. They were vital to survival back in the earliest days of the colonies. There's simply no way a man could've managed without a wife back then."

Trudy snorted. "Wouldn't say much has changed, then. Half the men I've known in my lifetime couldn't find their socks without intervention."

Priscilla couldn't help but laugh. Gary had been like that.

"Women in Plymouth Plantation were so restricted," Mildred continued. "They weren't allowed to have positions of authority. They couldn't own land or other goods."

"We've come a long way, baby." Trudy laughed.

"We sure have. Those poor women worked themselves to the bone. Did you know that only five women actually survived the first winter? And one of the deceased died of a broken heart after her husband passed away."

"Wow." Priscilla paused to think that through. Having lost a husband, she certainly knew what a broken heart felt like.

The ladies continued to chat about Mildred's topic, but Priscilla found herself distracted. Off in the distance, she caught a glimpse of a familiar man about her age walking aboard with the other on-foot passengers. She'd seen him around town, but he wasn't a regular on the island, at least not to her recollection.

"Trudy, do you remember that guy's name?" she asked. "The one with the dark hair and tanned skin—kind of a George Clooney lookalike? He's talking to the fellow in the Coast Guard uniform."

"Hmm?" Trudy looked up and glanced out the window. "Oh, yes. I think his name is Carson Fletcher. He keeps turning up around the island. I bump into him all over the place. Tilly said he came to the restaurant the other day but supposedly forgot his wallet. She covered his meal but told him not to come back. If you ask her, he's a homeless drifter. But then again, Tilly tends to speculate about folks based on what they order."

"Maybe he really did forget his wallet," Priscilla said.

"Could be. He doesn't dress like a homeless man, and he's clean-shaven," Mildred chimed in from the back seat. "I've only seen him for the past couple of months. I tried to make eye contact with him when I saw him hanging around outside the grocery store on the day of Betty's accident, but he looked the other way. I assumed he was asking people for money."

"Right." Trudy's eyes narrowed as she stared at him. "Not sure what it is about him, but I get the oddest feeling when he's around—like there's more to his story than I care to know."

"That's probably true of all of us," Priscilla said. "It's just curious that he's traveling off the island on foot, that's all. And if he was panhandling at the grocery store, wouldn't he have carried a sign or at least tried to catch your eye?"

"I guess," Trudy said. "Who knows?"

Priscilla didn't have time to ponder the idea for long, because the vehicle in front of her moved forward onto the ferry and came to a halt, leaving enough room for one more car behind it. Priscilla hated the way the interior of the ferry made her feel so confined, and she always felt a bit confused as they guided her in. She wondered if anyone had ever rammed into one of those striped posts. As she eased into the correct spot, she relaxed a bit, then slipped the car into Park.

"There you go. Everyone happy now?" she asked.

"I told you, I hate being at the end of the line on the ferry," Trudy repeated. "Fumes."

"We won't be staying in the car, so what does it matter?" Priscilla shut off the car's engine, then turned to face her friends. "Want to go on up? I'd like to find a place to sit so I can read another chapter in my novel."

"Sounds good," Mildred said. "I've brought a book as well. Thought it would calm my nerves on the journey."

"Sure hope that's not a sign that we're going to need our nerves calmed," Trudy said. "If so, I'm out of luck."

As they climbed out of the car, a loud blast sounded from the ferry, the signal that they were about to be under way. Seconds later, the ferry pulled forward into the Sound, nearly causing

Priscilla to lose her balance as it tipped to the right and then the left. She grabbed on to the hood of her vehicle to steady herself.

At that very moment, the driver's side door of the white Suburban swung open, and Betty Fox stepped out. The slender woman was dressed in casual attire—jeans and a blue button-up blouse—a little out of the ordinary for her. She carried a large handbag over her shoulder. Seconds later, the fellow Priscilla had drawn attention to approached. Carson. Was that his name? At any rate, he hovered near Betty's Suburban, then said something to her. She blanched and glanced at her vehicle. He moved along, and she reached inside the Suburban to grab a tan scarf.

"Careful, ladies," Trudy called out as the motion of the ferry caused them all to lose their balance again. "Not sure who's behind the wheel today, but we're rocking and rolling."

Betty flashed them a warm smile and then headed toward the door leading to the stairs. Priscilla followed directly behind her with Trudy on her heels. It was odd seeing Betty in jeans. Today's casual appearance was quite a contrast to her billboard photos, where she was dressed in more expensive clothing. Mildred lagged behind, book in hand.

Less than a minute later, they were swarmed by a crowd of people on the main level of the ferry. Priscilla had hoped to find a bench seat inside, but no such luck.

She glanced through one of the small round portholes to see the sights beyond: small sailboats on the water, and beyond them, the shoreline, rich with sea grasses and gnarled reeds. Quite a contrast to the goings-on inside the ferry. An older man brushed up against her as he buzzed by but never bothered to offer an apology for nearly knocking her over.

"Good grief." She did her best not to groan aloud. "This place is jam-packed. We'll never find a seat."

"There's always plenty of seating outside," Mildred said. "I brought a scarf for my hair."

"So did I," Trudy echoed. "I always seem to get stuck outside on the ferry."

Unfortunately, Priscilla hadn't thought to bring a scarf for her hair. Maybe they could find a less windy place to sit. She hoped.

Once they crossed through the café and walked out onto the deck, the breeze off the water whipped her hair all over the place. Oh well. Her gaze traveled to the small round tables with white chairs, all bolted to the deck. Hmm. Too breezy. She glanced down the side deck at the long white benches, which were also tightly fastened down with bolts. Priscilla located the perfect spot, away from passengers and partially guarded from the wind.

"Want to join us, Betty?" Trudy called as the familiar woman passed by.

Betty Fox looked back at them and shuffled her oversized designer handbag from one shoulder to the other. "Oh, maybe in a bit. I want to go inside and buy a cup of coffee. Then I have to visit the little girl's room." Her cheeks flamed pink. "Not in that order, of course."

"We'll save you a seat." Trudy plopped down onto the bench and patted the empty spot beside her.

Priscilla looked out over the railing. Sailboats dotted the water. They bobbed up and down, their sails tipping right, then left, fully submitted to the wind. Priscilla marveled at the clusters of boats, one next to the other. The whole scene looked like an oil painting, almost too beautiful to be true. Overhead, the skies stretched a brilliant blue, the clouds in wispy formations, one batch reminding her of angels' wings spread wide in praise to the Creator of it all.

The ferry shifted a bit to the right, and the morning sun hit the water with such intensity that she had to squint to be able to see.

"Ugh. Don't you hate it when that happens?" Priscilla lifted her hand to her forehead to shade her eyes. "Why didn't I think to bring a hat?"

"I'm grateful I remembered to bring my scarf." Mildred reached into her bag and pulled out a brown scarf, then wrapped it over her head.

A beautiful woman with perfectly coiffed blonde hair walked by. The shapely woman could have been a fashion model. Well, twenty-five years ago, anyway. She paused and gazed at Betty Fox, gave her what appeared to be a strained smile, then kept walking. She disappeared around the front of the ferry, and Betty took off inside to fetch her coffee.

"You know who that was, right?" Trudy fussed with her purse, finally setting it in her lap.

Priscilla took a seat next to her cousin. "She looks familiar, but I don't really know her."

"Eliza Jamison. Victor Fox's secretary. There are rumors about her, you know."

"Ah." Priscilla looked in the direction the beautiful woman had gone. "Please don't share them with me. I have this nasty habit of retaining bits of information about people, even untrue bits. I'd rather not know what the gossips are saying."

"With hips like that, I'm guessing you'll figure it out, anyway." Trudy's finely plucked brows waggled. "Let's just say that Victor has already found victory with that gal."

"Trudy." Priscilla glared at her. "I told you not to say anything. Now I'll never get that thought out of my head. And who even knows if it's true? You might be spreading false stories about the two of them."

Trudy rolled her eyes. "I do have a keen imagination, but I've picked up on all the clues. I'm just telling you, he's a man who usually gets what he wants."

"At the expense of a very sweet wife, if what you're saying is true." Mildred opened her book and leaned back against the bench. "Now, please, I want to quiet my thoughts, if you don't mind."

Priscilla wanted to quiet hers as well, but with Trudy now singing "Anchors Aweigh," she found the task very difficult. Oh well. She might as well enjoy the journey, even with an off-key soundtrack.

CHAPTER TWO

Priscilla found herself completely absorbed in her book in short order. She simply couldn't get enough of this story.

"You two are a fine pair." Trudy huffed and crossed her arms over her chest.

"What, Trudy?" Priscilla glanced up into her cousin's anxious eyes. "What do you mean?"

"I feel like the cream in the middle of a cookie, only no one's interested in me. You two have your noses stuck in those books, and you're completely missing the scenery. It's fabulous at this time of day." Trudy's voice took on a playful lilt. "The way the sun dances on the water is just remarkable, don't you think? Even the reeds at the water's edge are prettier with the sun shining on them. They remind me of a child's hair—a tangled mess."

"Sounds as pretty as it looks," Priscilla said.

"Not sure about that tangled hair part, though," Mildred chimed in and then went back to her book.

"I just love the changing of the seasons on the Sound." Trudy flung out her arms and let the breeze ruffle her blouse. "Can you believe it's the first of May already? Seems like we just came through the winter holidays."

"Agreed," Priscilla said. "Sometimes I feel like I got a four-for-one special when I moved to the Vineyard."

Mildred looked up from her book. "How so?"

"The Vineyard is one place in the summer: Filled with tourists. Bright. Happy. Warm. Buzzing with excitement. Then, in the fall, it becomes something else altogether. Crisp. Cool. Red and gold leaves dropping onto the road, and the smell of pumpkin everywhere you turn. I have to admit, the winter surprised me most. The cold was almost paralyzing at times."

"I guess I don't notice it so much, since I've lived here my whole life." Trudy shrugged. "These old bones are just used to it."

"Probably. And I'm sure I'll acclimate in time. But the springtime…" Priscilla paused. "Now we're talking about a season that reminds me why I love this island so much."

"So which Martha's Vineyard do you live on, Priscilla?" Trudy asked.

"I'll take all of them." She smiled, thinking of how happy she'd grown while living on the island.

"My favorite part of living here is the water." Trudy cast her gaze out over the Sound once again. "The Atlantic touches the shore with such gentleness, it just takes my breath away."

"You'll have to forgive me." Mildred glanced up for a moment. "Looking out at the water always makes me a little nauseous. Besides, I'm really enjoying this book."

"I read a great book the other day," Trudy interjected. She pointed at the paperback in Priscilla's hands. "This one right here. I loaned it to Priscilla so she can enjoy it too."

"Yes, I just started it," Priscilla explained. "The story has captivated me already. I'm so grateful for the loan, Trudy."

"You're gonna love it." Trudy clasped her hands together in dramatic fashion. "It's a murder mystery. The sleuth gets caught up in the investigation and almost ends up dead herself."

"Trudy, I really wish you wouldn't—"

"You wouldn't believe how chilling the story is. I found myself holding my breath. And don't even get me started on the bad guy. Talk about evil." Off Trudy went, giving away every detail of the story.

When her cousin finally paused for breath, Priscilla set the book down. No point in reading it now. She turned her attention to Mildred. "Tell us about the story you're reading, Mildred. Any bad guys?"

"A few, but not the sort Trudy was describing. This is a nonfiction book. It offers a fascinating glimpse into the history of Plymouth Plantation. Gracious, those people suffered a lot the first few years. It's a wonder any survived at all. You wouldn't believe the illnesses they faced. And the weather was awful."

"Doesn't sound like something that would hold my interest for long." Trudy's gaze shot toward the door leading inside. "I wonder what's keeping Betty?"

"Trudy, if our ancestors hadn't survived, many of us wouldn't be here today. Does that hold your interest?" Mildred rolled her eyes and went back to reading.

"I don't know why you two don't put those books down and drink in this amazing scenery." Trudy rose and walked to the railing. "Look around you, ladies! Where will you get such diversity in one glance? Water, land, air, seagulls, people, hot dogs, sodas—the ferry offers it all. I've been on this ride hundreds of times but always feel like I'm headed somewhere new, as if it's taking me away from the ordinary and toward the extraordinary."

"Would you mind keeping it down a bit?" Mildred looked queasier than before. "All this chatter is making me feel a bit ill."

Trudy pulled out her phone and started snapping photos of their surroundings. An elderly couple happened by, and Trudy engaged them in conversation. Before long, she had them both laughing. Priscilla marveled at the ease with which Trudy carried herself. How wonderful would it be to fall into such easy conversation with strangers?

She allowed the lull of the waves to draw her in. Before long, she felt her eyes growing heavy. The back-and-forth motion of the water often had this effect on her.

Trudy plopped down on the bench next to Priscilla and leaned back with a delirious sigh. "It's just so wonderful. I love it here."

"Not me." Mildred never looked up from her book. "I hate the ferry."

"For pity's sake, why?" Trudy asked.

"Confining. I feel trapped. I can't get off. And there are too many people crammed on board. I hate breathing other peoples' air. I have the same feeling about airplanes."

"Oh my." Trudy's eyes widened. "Never thought of that."

"Sorry. I'm still feeling nauseated," Mildred explained. "Do you smell that burnt grease? It's the oil they're using to cook the food. It's making me sick."

"Hey, that reminds me of the time I took my husband to a fancy French restaurant in Boston and the place nearly caught fire. The chef burned the soufflé..." Off Trudy went again.

After her overblown tale, Trudy decided to head inside to purchase bread to feed the seagulls. When she returned, she spent the next few minutes tossing bits into the sky. This, of course, led to a flock of seagulls swarming them.

"I feel like I'm in an Alfred Hitchcock movie, Trudy." Mildred put her hands over her head as a couple of seagulls swept down over them. "Do you have to do that?"

"Poor little babies are hungry."

Priscilla glanced up from her book. "They get fed all day long."

"They won't even remember how to hunt for food on their own." Mildred groaned. "Think of what you're doing to the ecosystem, Trudy."

"I'm keeping the birds well fed, that's all."

"I'd hate to think what might happen to this blouse if—" A seagull hovered dangerously low, nearly perching on Mildred's head. "Ugh! Go away, bird!" She waved her arms in an attempt to scare it away.

Trudy pulled out her phone and snapped a photo of Mildred. "Perfect! We'll use that one in your speaking portfolio." Thankfully, she ran out of bread, and the seagulls took off to the other side of the ferry.

Before long, they neared the Woods Hole landing.

"Time to get back to the vehicle, ladies." Mildred rose and tucked her book under her arm. She looked a bit green around the gills, but Priscilla couldn't decide if she was seasick or nervous.

Priscilla led the way back down to the lower level of the ferry and through the crowd toward her SUV. By the time they climbed inside, the ferry had come to a halt at the dock.

"Perfect timing." Mildred released a loud sigh from the back seat. "Now, if only the rest of the drive goes as smoothly."

"I'm sure it will." Priscilla watched as the lane of cars to their right exited the ferry. Then the cars to their left were ushered forward. Finally, it came time for her row to leave. Unfortunately, Betty's white Suburban didn't budge.

"Uh-oh. She must be having trouble getting it started or something." Priscilla wondered if she should tap her horn or get out and offer to help.

"Maybe she fell asleep at the wheel," Trudy suggested. "That would explain why she never showed up to sit with us."

"Maybe. She did look a little tired, now that I think about it." Priscilla tried to see through the vehicle's tinted back window but could not.

A few seconds later, Mildred lost her patience. "Get a move on, Betty!" she yelled, as if Betty Fox could actually hear her with the windows up. "You're making me late."

"I know how to wake her up." Trudy reached over and pressed Priscilla's horn for a long, loud honk. Up ahead, a Coast Guard official jammed his fingers in his ears and glared at them.

Priscilla mouthed the word, "Sorry!" then turned to face her cousin. "Trudy, that's not very nice."

"Well, neither is making Mildred late to her speaking engagement. You know how much she's been looking forward to this."

"That's true," Mildred said from the back seat, her words laced with nervous tension. "We're losing valuable time, and I can't afford to do that. Every minute counts."

"I can't very well drive with the vehicle in front of me at a dead halt."

The man in the Coast Guard uniform peered in the driver's side window of the Suburban, then stepped back and hollered something to a fellow worker. Priscilla couldn't quite make it out, so she rolled down her window. They were discussing Betty's vehicle. Her *empty* vehicle.

"Well, no wonder the car's not moving," she said. "There's no one in it."

"No one in it?" Mildred snorted. "Maybe she's up in the snack bar, lost in a book like the two of us, Priscilla."

"Could be."

"Surely she just lost track of time," Trudy added. "She wouldn't deliberately hold up this many people. No one would."

"There's only one car being held up—ours." Priscilla climbed out of her SUV and walked to the front of Betty's Suburban. The other ladies followed. She glanced down at the front seat and noticed a brown leather purse.

"She must be planning to come back," Mildred said. "No woman leaves her purse in an empty vehicle on purpose."

"Unless she's a victim of some sort of crime," Priscilla added, her thoughts moving in a hundred different directions at once.

"Oh dear." Mildred paled. "You suspect foul play, Priscilla?"

"Let's not jump the gun." With the wave of a hand, Trudy dismissed the idea.

Mildred pulled out her phone and checked the time. "I knew we should've taken the earlier ferry."

"It's okay, Mildred." Priscilla turned to face her friend. "I can back my car up and get around Betty's SUV. You won't be late, I promise."

"Okay." Mildred sighed and glanced back inside the Suburban. "I am worried about her, though."

"She probably just ran to the bathroom again," Trudy suggested. "Nervous bladder."

"I think we should give her purse to the officer, just in case." Priscilla reached to open the door. "Wow. It's not locked. That's strange." She grabbed the purse. As she pulled it toward herself, the contents fell out—a package of mints, a set of keys, a checkbook, and a couple of receipts from a local store.

"Shoot. Can't believe I did that." Priscilla gathered up the items and pressed them inside the purse, then stopped cold. "There's no wallet in here. Weird."

Trudy shrugged. "Not everyone carries a wallet. I often keep my money and my debit card in my bra."

"Too much information, Trudy." Mildred glanced at her phone again.

"Look at this, ladies." Priscilla pointed to the keys in the ignition. "Very odd."

Very odd, indeed. She glanced down and noticed a banking deposit slip on the floor. Oops. It must've fallen out of the purse.

She picked it up, noticing the name of the credit union and the amount of the deposit—five thousand dollars. No small change. She shoved it inside the purse. None of this was any of her business. She shouldn't have touched the purse in the first place.

Moments later, Priscilla led the way back to her SUV. She climbed in and shifted to Reverse. At the Coast Guard officer's command, she backed her vehicle up a couple of feet and then worked her way around the Suburban.

All the while, her thoughts remained fixed on Betty Fox. Where in the world had she gone? Was there more to her empty vehicle than met the eye?

CHAPTER THREE

Priscilla drove her car out of the ferry and into the packed parking lot. Sunshine streamed down overhead, a contrast to the darkened interior of the boat's hull.

"Whew. Glad we made it off safely." Mildred sounded relieved, but Priscilla's nerves would not be calmed. "Now, let's get this show on the road."

Off in the distance, Priscilla saw Eliza Jamison pull away in a bright red Corvette. Wow, what a car. Priscilla paused to let several pedestrians cross in front of her. A couple of families buzzed by, the children's chatter louder than necessary. They were followed by a young couple, arm in arm. Next came a woman in a gorgeous pink blouse with a colorful scarf over her hair. The little jewels in her sunglasses shimmered underneath the morning sun. She carried a fantastic purse, one Priscilla wished she could afford. Behind the woman, a couple of guys in their twenties were laughing and talking.

Priscilla glanced at her reflection in the rearview mirror. "My hair is frightful. I still can't believe I forgot to bring a scarf. I never seem to remember."

The pedestrian traffic cleared, and she pulled forward. Still, something nagged at her. When she reached the road, Priscilla nudged her vehicle off onto the shoulder.

"What are you doing?" Mildred's words were tinged with alarm. "We need to get going."

"I know, but my conscience won't allow it. Aren't you two the least bit curious about Betty? Maybe she's ill. Maybe she needs us."

Trudy pulled off her scarf and fussed with her hair. "I doubt it, Priscilla. She's such a loner, I can't imagine her accepting help from any of us, even if she's not feeling well."

"Still, I feel like we should offer. I'd hate to think of one of us in distress on the ferry with no one to offer assistance."

"You're going to feel pretty silly when you find her upstairs in the snack bar, eating a cinnamon roll, her nose stuck in a book."

"No, I'll feel relieved. But if you two don't want to go, I understand. I'll be quick, I promise." Priscilla unbuckled her seat belt and opened her door.

"You're really going back on board?" Mildred looked alarmed by this idea.

"Just to check on her. Won't take but a minute or two, I promise."

Priscilla took off as fast as her legs would carry her. Seconds later, she bolted past Carson Fletcher, who stood near the shoreline, cell phone pressed to his ear. Priscilla slowed her pace, hoping to get a closer look at him. For a drifter, his clothing seemed pretty... normal. Jeans and a T-shirt, not dirty or wrinkled. His hair was neatly combed. And what kind of drifter carried an expensive phone like that?

As she passed by, she clearly heard him say, "No pain, no gain," into the cell phone, followed by, "The payoff will be worth it, trust me."

Interesting. And highly suspicious.

Her radar went off as she pondered his words in light of Betty's disappearance. She wanted to stop, to confront him, but didn't have the courage. Or a logical reason. So she kept moving toward the ferry.

It took a bit of explanation for the Coast Guard official to allow her back onto the boat without a ticket, but Priscilla explained that she was an acquaintance of Betty's. "I'd like to check the places you might not have thought of," she said. "Like the ladies' room, for instance."

"Already checked it." He gave her a nod. "Nothing there."

"Right." Still, Priscilla couldn't shake the feeling that she should look in the ladies' room herself. She took off toward the stairwell, which she climbed in short order. A quick glance around the snack bar revealed a couple of teens wiping down the tables but nothing more. She walked into the restroom and peered into the empty stall. No Betty.

Just as she turned to leave, Priscilla glanced down into the trash can and caught a glimpse of something small and white. She reached down and pulled it out.

"Hmm." Nothing important after all. Just a couple of sales tags from clothing items. She held onto them, just in case they proved to be important.

"Didn't believe me, ma'am?" the Coast Guard officer asked as she stepped out of the restroom.

Priscilla shook her head. "Never hurts to double-check."

"You'll be happy to hear we've checked the men's room too. So you won't have to go in there." He quirked a brow.

"So strange. And you've looked everywhere?"

"Yes. There's no sign of her." The officer cleared his throat, probably an indication that he wanted her to move along.

A sick feeling gripped Priscilla. "Do you think it's possible she..." Her gaze traveled to the railing and the waters below. "You know..."

Creases formed between his eyes. "Was she suffering from depression?"

"I'm not sure." Priscilla wrung her hands as she considered the possibility. "There were some rumors about her husband..."

"Rumors rarely lead to suicide, ma'am. And I can assure you, one of our guys would've seen her if she'd jumped. We've got cameras all over the place."

"Right. Big Brother is watching."

"It's hardly like that. The cameras are just there for the safety of our guests. But don't fret. We'll go over the footage if she doesn't turn up."

"Do you think it's possible she got into someone else's car by mistake?" Priscilla suggested. "Just a thought."

"Don't you think she would've figured that out when she sat in the lap of the car's owner?" Trudy's voice sounded behind her.

Priscilla turned to face her cousin. "Oh, I thought you were staying in the car."

"I was, but I had to go to the little girls' room. And I thought you might want to know that Mildred is about to have a conniption. We're going to be late for her speaking engagement if you don't come right now."

"Yes, I'm coming." She followed on Trudy's heels, her thoughts tumbling. Someone had surely kidnapped Betty Fox. Or perhaps she really had decided to end it all. Maybe seeing Eliza Jamison had been the final straw.

"Penny for your thoughts," Trudy called back, her words a bit breathless as she huffed along.

"Thinking about her wallet. It's missing. Which points to a robbery."

Trudy paused to give her a knowing look. "Then why didn't the robber take her car? The keys were in it."

"I don't know. Maybe she had something important in her wallet."

"Looks to me like he took the wallet and the woman."

They arrived back at Priscilla's SUV moments later and climbed inside.

"Ladies, if we don't leave right now," Mildred said, "I'm afraid there's no point in going at all."

"I'll get you there, Mildred. I promise." Priscilla turned the key in the ignition and shifted into Drive. Then she pulled out onto the road, beyond the row of taxis, and pointed the vehicle in the direction of Falmouth. "It won't be long, and we'll be on the interstate."

Unfortunately, they met up with road construction before they ever got to the interstate, which slowed things down quite a bit. From the back seat, Mildred fussed and fussed. Priscilla felt guiltier by the minute. Why had she gone back on board the ferry?

The ladies grew silent. Trudy finally filled the awkward space with a few startling thoughts. "I keep asking myself why Carson Fletcher just happened to be on that ferry this morning."

"Oh?" Mildred asked. "Why is that?"

"I have a feeling." Trudy cleared her throat. "Not a good one. Maybe he's a reporter." She paused, then snapped her fingers. "Oh, that's got to be it! That's why he keeps turning up around the island. And have you noticed he's always on his phone? He's probably talking to his editor. Or maybe he's speaking his notes into his phone. People do things like that nowadays."

"But he couldn't possibly have known in advance that there would be a story on this particular ferry ride," Priscilla countered. "Right?"

"Maybe he did know," Trudy countered. "Think about it."

"Could be he had information about Eliza Jamison having an affair with Victor Fox," Mildred chimed in. "That would be story-worthy."

"Yes." Trudy leaned back against her seat, looking a little too smug. "We can easily deduce that he was following her to see if there would be some sort of brouhaha between her and Betty." She looked very pleased with herself. "That's got to be it, ladies. Carson Fletcher is definitely a reporter." She turned to face Priscilla. "I think you're rubbing off on me. My sleuthing skills are coming along quite nicely."

Priscilla couldn't think of a response. Trudy's assessment didn't ring true to her.

"It does make sense, now that I think about it." Mildred shrugged. "Carson Fletcher was at Ortmann's on the day Betty backed into that car."

"Maybe she was onto him," Trudy said. "Could be she got nervous and backed into that car because the reporter put her on edge. But he's the relentless sort, always after a story, so he's been following her ever since. That's how he landed on the ferry. He saw her come aboard and followed her. Probably thought he'd hit the jackpot when he saw Eliza Jamison was on board too. No doubt he's already got his article written and is turning it in as we speak."

"That's a bit of a stretch, don't you think, Trudy?" Priscilla said. "He just happened to see her get on the ferry, so he bought a ticket? Most folks order tickets online in advance, right?"

"Yes, but they can be purchased at the pier too," Trudy said.

"Where does Carson come from?" Priscilla asked. "Does anyone know?"

Trudy shrugged. "I want to say from Florida, maybe? Someplace like that."

"I wonder what brings him to the Vineyard."

"Good question. I think a lot of people have wondered. From what I can gather, he has no family, no close friends, nothing to tie him here. And it's not like he settled on the island because he had a job. For the longest time, he just wandered from place to place."

"Very suspicious," Priscilla said. "But then again, we always suspect the unfamiliar, don't we?"

Trudy's eyes narrowed. "Meaning?"

"None of us know him well enough to make a true judgment, so our suspicions go straight to him."

"I do find it odd that we are more likely to trust those we know," Mildred added. "It never seems to occur to us to suspect someone close to us. Only, if you think about it, everyone who ever committed a crime was probably trusted by those he—or she—knew."

"Never really thought about it before," Trudy said.

"I'm no good at playing detective like Priscilla here," Mildred added. "I just like to speculate."

"Wait...detective?" Priscilla laughed. "Is that what you think I am?"

"You've got good instincts," Trudy said.

"But you're a slow driver," Mildred chimed in from the back seat. "Could you pick up the pace, please? I don't want to be late."

Priscilla glanced at the dash and realized she had been driving a bit below the speed limit. "Sorry, Mildred. All of this speculating about Betty, Eliza, and Carson has me distracted."

"Then we shan't mention them again." Mildred cleared her throat as she leaned back against her seat. "All right?"

Easy for her to say. Priscilla's thoughts wouldn't stop whirling. Was Carson Fletcher really a reporter, on the hunt for a story about the Foxes? It might make sense, considering that he kept turning up around town with no other obvious reason to be there.

She found her speed slowing again as the idea took root. Oops. She'd better put the pedal to the metal, or Mildred would never make it to the museum on time.

CHAPTER FOUR

All the way to Plimoth Plantation, Priscilla's thoughts remained fixed on Betty's disappearance. She did her best to pay attention as Mildred and Trudy chatted about the upcoming speaking engagement but found her imagination roaming as she thought through Carson's strange cell phone conversation.

What sort of payoff was he referring to? What would be worth it? Maybe Trudy's speculations that he was a reporter were true. Had he somehow captured a photo of Eliza and Betty together on the side deck of the ferry? If so, was he offering to sell said photo to a major news publication? That would explain the payoff comment.

Nah, that made no sense at all. The local paper wouldn't pay him for a photo like that. Victor had the publication in his pocket. And folks off the island wouldn't care about a small-town election, so he didn't work for any of the major papers. Still, something about Carson made her feel uneasy.

"You okay over there?" Mildred asked after a long period of silence on Priscilla's part.

"Oh, yes. Sorry. Just thinking."

"If I know Priscilla, she's already coming up with a list of suspects." Trudy flipped down her visor to check her appearance. She pulled the familiar tube of pink lipstick out of her purse again and opened it. "My cousin here is wondering who kidnapped—or murdered—Betty Fox."

"You know me too well, Trudy." Priscilla did her best not to sigh. She put on her turn signal and eased the car into the right lane. "But you have to admit, the whole thing is rather strange. Women don't just disappear off of ferries every day, you know."

"I'm sure there's a simple explanation." Trudy swiped on the lipstick just as they hit a bump in the road. "Hey, watch it. Trying to make me look like a clown?"

"Sorry about that."

Trudy put the cap back on her lipstick. "Don't fret, Priscilla. Not every empty vehicle is a crime scene. By the time we get back to the island this evening, all will have been revealed. Likely her battery just died, and she walked off to call AAA."

"I hope you're right." Still, even as Priscilla spoke the words, she sensed in her gut that things would not be revealed, at least not anytime soon.

They approached Plimoth Plantation at a quarter past ten, fifteen minutes later than they had planned. Priscilla made pro-fuse apologies to Mildred as she pulled into the parking lot. "This is all my fault," she groaned. "I can't believe we're cutting it so close."

"Not entirely your fault, Priscilla," Mildred interjected. "We weren't going anywhere with a parked car in front of us." Her voice changed. Now she was all business. "Anyway, we're here now, and that's what matters."

"I'll drop you off at the front gate, then go park," Priscilla suggested. "That should speed things up a bit."

"Want to come with me, Trudy?" Mildred's voice sounded strained. "I could use your help setting up. And I still need to get into costume."

"Told you, Priscilla." Trudy grinned. "I knew there was a costume involved." She turned to face Mildred. "Happy to help. I'm not as fast as I used to be, though, so don't be afraid to leave me in your dust when we get out of the car."

Priscilla pulled her SUV up to the entrance of the museum and watched as the two ladies sprang from the car. She hollered, "I'll be right in," and then went to find a parking spot.

The task turned out to be more complicated than she'd feared. By the time she located a spot—at the far back corner of the lot—she had to sprint toward the entrance. Just as she reached the steps leading down to the main building, a text came through on her phone. She glanced down and saw Joan's name. She must be texting from work.

DID YOU HEAR ABOUT BETTY FOX?

Priscilla typed the words, WHAT HAVE YOU HEARD? Perhaps her cousin had an update.

GONE MISSING OFF OF THE WOODS HOLE FERRY.

RIGHT. WE WERE THERE. She wondered if she should take the time to add more. Unfortunately, a quick glance at the time on her phone let her know that Mildred would be taking the podium in five minutes. Priscilla shoved the phone into her purse and headed up the sidewalk toward the front door.

She paused to look at the magnificent gardens in front of her. A colorful array of springtime flowers greeted her. Any other time, she might have reached for her phone to snag some photos but not right now.

Off in the distance, she caught her first glimpse of the recreated Plimoth Plantation with its wooden buildings and quaint walkways. It was all so lifelike. She could almost imagine the early colonists moving from home to home, children laughing and playing in the background as their mothers and fathers worked to till the ground.

Then again, she could also picture them in the dead of winter, trudging through the snow to fetch medicinal herbs for a dying child. What must it have been like, to live so far away from the comforts of the life they had known before coming to the colonies?

Unfortunately, a long line of students at the ticket counter made Priscilla even later than before. She waited, her patience growing thin, and finally paid her way inside. Then she had to locate the room where Mildred was speaking. Not an easy task, especially in this mob. She approached the information desk and was pointed in the right direction.

Fortunately, she found the room, which was filled to overflowing with an enthusiastic audience. Historian Jacob Lansford invited Mildred to take her spot at the podium. Priscilla breathed a sigh of relief as she took a seat in the empty chair next to Trudy.

"It's about time." Trudy shifted in the chair as she whispered the words. "I was beginning to think you'd gone back to the ferry."

"No. Can't stop thinking about Betty, though." Priscilla looked at Mildred and studied her costume. A large ruffled collar peeked out from underneath a dark-brown button-up blouse. The fabric was sturdy. Practical. The skirt was frayed and dingy. Probably exactly what a colonist would have looked like after working in the fields. Mildred really looked the part, right down to the wisps of gray hair sticking out from under her starched white cap in haphazard fashion.

"I wanted to fix her hair," Trudy whispered, "but there wasn't time. Think people will notice?"

"They'll be too mesmerized by her topic. And it's fitting, if you think about it."

Priscilla found herself captivated too. Mildred had a way of bringing her listeners straight into the story, much like the author of that book Priscilla was reading.

She leaned back and listened as Mildred told story after story of real women who had once lived right here in Plymouth. The passionate curator spoke with authority and zeal, each tale drawing Priscilla in. She could almost imagine those amazing women as they worked to stoke the fire, to cure the meat, to darn their husband's socks. She could see them now, shearing sheep in the springtime and using the wool to craft blankets and coats. She could envision them bundling their babes in midwinter to keep them from catching pneumonia.

She leaned over to whisper to Trudy. "And I thought my life on the farm was tough."

Unfortunately, her cousin had dozed off. A snore shook the room, and folks laughed as they turned to look her way. Trudy stirred in her seat and offered an apologetic glance to Mildred, and then her eyes drifted shut again.

Mildred seemed to take it in stride. She lit into a dramatic presentation about candle making, never breaking character. Then she shared a specific story about one woman who had lived in the colony.

"Elizabeth Tilley was very young when she arrived," Mildred explained. "Just thirteen. She was taken in by the governor and his wife. Unfortunately, both of them passed away within a year."

"Can you even imagine?" Trudy must've awakened, because she whispered the words in Priscilla's ear. "Poor kid."

"Elizabeth was offered a home by the governor's manservant, a man named John Howland," Mildred explained. "She went on to marry Howland, and they had ten children."

"Whoa." Trudy spoke the word aloud, and several people turned to look at her, including one woman with a scowl on her face. "Sorry," Trudy said to the roomful of guests. "Just…ten? That's a lot of kids. I mean, who could afford to dress them and take them out for pizza?"

Never missing a beat, Mildred continued. "All of those children lived full, rich lives and went on to create more than a million descendants."

Trudy's eyes bugged, and she mouthed the word, "Wow."

"Those descendants include many famous people," Mildred explained, "including Franklin D. Roosevelt, both of the George Bushes, Ralph Waldo Emerson, and many more."

"That's what happens when you have ten children, I guess," Trudy whispered.

At that very moment, Priscilla's phone dinged. Several people in the rows ahead of her turned back to glance her way. She reached inside her bag and pulled out the phone to silence it but gasped as she read Joan's words:

FYI, FOLKS ARE SAYING BETTY MIGHT HAVE BEEN KIDNAPPED.

Priscilla shoved the phone into her purse, her heart rate skipping to double-time.

Someone had kidnapped Betty Fox from the ferry? How? Who?

And more importantly...why?

CHAPTER FIVE

Two days after the infamous trip to Plymouth, Priscilla opened her home to several local ladies. Their early evening get-together had nothing to do with Mildred's speaking engagement, though Priscilla had learned a lot—both from her friend's presentation and from the tour of the plantation that followed. No, today's gathering was of a completely different nature altogether. She'd reluctantly agreed to let Trudy host a beauty party introducing a new makeup line, one guaranteed to take ten years off every woman's face.

Naturally, many in their age group had jumped on this venture. Priscilla wasn't really a huge fan of makeup parties, but she wanted to support her cousin in this new effort. Besides, it might be fun to have the gals over for coffee, conversation, and snacks. Surely the place would be humming with chatter about Betty Fox's disappearance.

Joan was the first to arrive. She didn't look thrilled by the possibilities, but she helped herself to some cheese and crackers and settled into place in front of one of the makeup stations.

"How's the pup, Joan?" Priscilla asked.

"As ornery as ever." Joan's lips turned up in a smile. "But I wouldn't trade her for anything."

"I know you wouldn't."

"It's quite a difference, having a rambunctious younger dog after living with an older, more settled one, but I'm adjusting."

"It'll do you good," Priscilla agreed.

Tilly arrived next. The owner of the Colonial Inn and Restaurant looked anything but happy as she slipped her purse strap off her shoulder. "I won't be buying anything," she announced, her words loud and firm. "So don't even think about it."

"No need," Trudy countered. "This is all for fun. Just enjoy yourself, Tilly."

"Humph."

Tilly hung her purse on the back of one of the chairs and took a seat. "What's this I'm hearing about Betty Fox? She's gone missing?"

"Well, we suspect as much." Trudy explained the situation, and Tilly's eyes widened.

"So that's what Gail was talking about. I heard someone mention Victor's Suburban being left on the ferry."

"Funny that you call it Victor's vehicle and not Betty's, since Betty was the one driving it," Priscilla observed.

"You know how men are. They take ownership of everything." Tilly rolled her eyes. "I still remember the day Victor bought that Suburban. He paraded it through town with those big magnet signs plastered all over it, promoting himself. The car might've been for her, but his motivations were clear, trust me."

"Speaking of men, there was one on the ferry who set off our radar like crazy," Trudy added. "Carson Fletcher."

"Carson?" Tilly paused and then said the name again. After a moment, her eyes widened. "That stranger who's been hanging around town the last few weeks? Kind of a drifter? Shows up in random places?"

"Right." Trudy continued to set up makeup stations on TV trays. "I have some speculations about him."

"Oh? I just figured he was a tourist who decided to stick around." Tilly paused. "But now that you mention it, I did notice him in a store in Edgartown last week. His behavior caught my attention."

"Was he taking notes?" Trudy asked. "Speaking into his phone?"

"No. At first I thought he was working at the store, because he appeared to be shifting the merchandise around. Then I wondered if maybe he was stealing things."

"Probably just a cover for his real job," Trudy said.

"Which is?" Tilly leaned back in her chair.

"Trudy's convinced he's a reporter," Priscilla explained.

"Yep. It's more than a coincidence that he keeps turning up where Betty Fox happens to be."

"Oh my goodness!" Tilly's eyes lit up. "Now that you mention it, Betty Fox was at the store on the same day. I remember it clearly now."

"Bingo!" Trudy clasped her hands together. "Told you! Carson Fletcher is definitely a reporter, one who would do anything—and I do many anything—to get a big story."

"Anything, as in do her harm?" Tilly's eyes widened. "Is that what you suspect?"

Trudy shrugged. "He was on the ferry. So was Betty. And Eliza. And I'm sure you understand why those two names in the same sentence would be story-worthy for a reporter."

"I do." Tilly shifted her gaze to Priscilla. "The plot thickens. What sort of car did Carson drive on board? Did you notice?"

Trudy's nose wrinkled, and she stopped working on the makeup stations long enough to answer. "That's just it. He walked on board. But, for the life of me, I don't recall seeing him walk off when we arrived in Woods Hole."

"I saw him," Priscilla explained. "He was on his cell phone in an intense conversation with someone. And he was on foot."

"Lots of people walk on and off the ferry," Tilly said. "Nothing unusual there. Was he acting suspicious?"

Priscilla nodded. "Here's the strange part. I vividly remember him walking up to Betty early on and saying something to her that brought a frown to her face. It seemed odd then and even odder now, in light of her disappearance."

"Not much about this makes sense, if you want the truth of it." Tilly shrugged and started poking through the makeup samples on her tray. "I still don't want to do this, by the way."

Gail arrived next with her elderly father. "So sorry, Priscilla," she whispered as they entered the living room. "He heard there were snacks and could not be persuaded to stay home. I told him he would have to have a facial. I thought it might persuade him to stay behind. But he actually got excited about the idea. Can you imagine?"

She couldn't. But Priscilla didn't have time to think about it. "Welcome, Uncle Hugh," she called out.

"Careful, or Trudy will cover you with facial cream," Tilly threw in.

Candy Lane, proprietor at the local confectionery, arrived just as Uncle Hugh settled into the recliner on the far side of the room. Several other local ladies followed, all women Priscilla had come to know over the previous months. Though she wouldn't have planned a makeup party, she had to admit that it was fun having so many women gathered in her living room.

At six thirty on the dot, Trudy thanked them all for coming and then pointed to the makeup trays. "If you'll each take a seat behind a makeup station, we'll get started."

"Do we really have to do this?" Mildred groaned as she set down her book. "I'm nearly done with this and can't wait to see how it ends."

"They all live happily ever after, Mildred," Trudy said. "Now, let's get on with this shindig, shall we?" She turned to face Priscilla and plastered on an exaggerated smile. "Before we begin, I have a wonderful gift for our hostess as a thank-you for opening up her home for this party this lovely evening." Her gaze shifted across the room, landing directly on Tilly. "Should any of you choose to host a party, you will receive a special gift too."

Tilly snorted and crossed her arms over her chest.

Priscilla's mind reeled as she tried to imagine what she'd won.

"At the end of this evening's session, Priscilla will receive a complimentary facial, featuring our new Heavenly Faces line. She will enjoy luxurious pampering at the hands of yours truly." Trudy pointed to herself. "I'll also be using our newest facial mask as part of the treatment. It's guaranteed to make your face look years younger, erasing fine lines and wrinkles, as well as lifting and plumping."

"Great," Gail called out. "That's all I need—lifting and plumping."

Priscilla tried not to groan. Oh, brother. A facial mask? Did she really have to go through with this?

Trudy beamed with delight as she faced the crowd. "Now, let's go around the room and let everyone introduce herself—or himself," she added, looking at Uncle Hugh.

"But we already know everyone, Trudy," Joan said.

"When do we get to the eating part?" Uncle Hugh called out from his spot in the recliner. "I was promised food. You're one of the best cooks on the island, Priscilla. I'm counting on you to feed me."

Gail glanced over her shoulder at him and clucked her tongue. "Pop, quiet, or Trudy will put that facial mask on you."

He went back to reading his paper in a hurry.

Trudy cleared her throat. "Anyway, let's go around the room and make introductions, and each person can tell their favorite thing about our hostess!"

Priscilla suddenly wanted to hide behind the sofa. Instead, she sat quietly and listened as each of her friends and family members said lovely things about her. Joan loved her smile. Gail was a fan of her bravery, coming to the island all the way from Kansas. Several of the other ladies commented on what a great friend she was.

Candy loved her generous heart and her ability to spread cheer. Mildred was mesmerized by Priscilla's curiosity and sleuthing skills. That last one really caught Priscilla off-guard. If only Gary could have lived to hear all this.

She didn't have time to absorb the sweet comments, though, because the party was off and running. Trudy started by instructing them to use the skin cleanser cloths.

"This is the part I hate," Tilly said with a groan. "You ladies are about to see me stripped down to my natural self."

Trudy laughed. "I hope not, Tilly."

"My face, silly. I never go out in public without makeup on, so you gals will have to promise to never share what you've seen here, once I removed my makeup with this cleanser."

They all took a vow of silence and promised not to post photos of any bare-faced friends on social media.

Priscilla scrubbed her face with the cleansing cloth. To her right, Gail scrubbed her face clean as well.

"I still can't get over the fact that Betty Fox just...disappeared." Gail pinched her eyes shut and wiped them down. "I don't know what to make of it."

"Well, I do," Uncle Hugh piped up from his recliner. "Victor's sly as a fox. I guarantee he's behind it."

"He offed her?" Tilly asked, her word choice a bit more blunt than Priscilla might've expected.

Uncle Hugh shrugged. "Not so sure about that, but let's just say he was ready for a newer, younger version and leave it at that."

He grumbled something under his breath about Eliza Jamison, but Priscilla couldn't really make it out.

"Yeah, I think we all know what that means," Gail whispered.

"Ladies, please . . . let's stick to topics related to makeup," Trudy instructed. She swiped a lock of her platinum hair out of her face and dove into a lecture about the benefits of clean pores.

It didn't take long, though, before the conversation shifted back to Betty and Victor Fox.

"Have you seen all of those *Victory for Victor* signs around Tisbury?" Joan asked. "They're everywhere. I can't escape them."

"Yeah." Priscilla offered what felt like a lame shrug. "I don't know how to put my finger on it, but there's something about the guy that just rubs me the wrong way."

"Eddie Haskell."

"Huh?" She gave Joan a curious look.

"Don't you remember Eddie Haskell from *Leave It to Beaver*? The boy who always said things like, 'How lovely you look today, Mrs. Cleaver' or 'My mother said to thank you for the recipe you gave her. It was the most delicious chicken she ever ate.'" Joan pursed her lips. "You know. Eddie Haskell."

"Right, right. I remember him. Kind of a—"

"Hypocrite," Tilly said. "I remember that character well. Two-faced. Said one thing in front of the parents, but as soon as their backs were turned, his true self came out."

This certainly got Priscilla's attention. "You're saying Victor is two-faced?"

Across the room, Uncle Hugh started snoring. This got a laugh out of everyone.

"Oh, girl, you don't know the half of it." Joan clucked her tongue. "Truth be told, Betty probably doesn't know a quarter of it." She paused and appeared to be thinking. "Or maybe she does."

"Speaking of not being who you claim to be, it's time to start putting on makeup," Trudy said. "Primer and foundation, ladies!"

They went to work with the primer first. It felt soft and silky on Priscilla's skin. Then she used a few dots of the ivory foundation, smoothing it into her skin. "Not bad," she said, as she studied her reflection in the mirror.

"I like the feel of this stuff, Trudy," Tilly said as she smoothed the primer into her skin. "Velvety. So soft to the touch."

"It's truly heavenly, isn't it?" Trudy beamed. She lit into saleswoman mode again and began telling them the benefits of the Heavenly Faces products.

Priscilla didn't mind. It was rather fun to see her cousin filled with so much zeal over a new venture. She knew what that felt like, of course. That same sense of wonder and excitement came over her every time she felt stirred to solve another mystery.

Like now, for instance.

CHAPTER SIX

Trudy walked the women through the benefits of the Heavenly Faces primer and foundation while they applied it to their skin. Her sales techniques were stellar. She must've been practicing for days. Either that, or she was working off of some sort of script she'd memorized.

When she finally paused for breath, Priscilla jumped in. "I do hope you'll forgive me for taking the conversation back to Victor, but I have a few questions."

Trudy set the bottle of primer down on the coffee table. "What about him, Priscilla?"

"Well, forgive me if I sound naive. I'm still pretty new to the island, so I don't have the benefit of knowing the history. If he's really such a hypocrite, why do so many people vote for him? That part doesn't make sense to me."

"Why, indeed?" To her left, Tilly worked dabs of foundation into her soft, wrinkled skin. "I've been asking myself that question for years. And yes, time after time, he gets himself reelected. Victor has served every position a person can think of, from head elder at the Presbyterian church, to head of the spring parade, to the art festival, to commissioner. He's been in campaign mode from the day I first met him thirty years ago. Of course, back then he wasn't a politician. He ran a car lot. Did you know that?"

"No." Priscilla shook her head. "I didn't."

"He's a natural-born salesman." Tilly folded her lips inward, and the wrinkles around her lips disappeared. "And I'll be honest, if I hear the words *Victory for Victor* one more time, I might hurl."

The other ladies all nodded in agreement, a few vocalizing their similar thoughts on the matter. Several even voiced complaints about the way Victor paraded his beautiful young secretary around town.

"You can blame the men." Uncle Hugh's groggy voice sounded from the recliner. "He's got most of the fellas in the local men's clubs bamboozled into thinking he's the best man for every job. Never cared for him, myself. I can see right through him."

Priscilla stared at her skin in the mirror, noticing how smooth and even it looked. Wow. "I've just noticed that he doesn't ever quite look people in the eye."

Candy looked up from her makeup application. "But where I come from, we call that discernment. You're picking up on spiritual cues, Priscilla. You've got a good inner eye."

"Speaking of eyes, let's move on to eye color." Trudy gave further instructions, and before long the ladies were applying eye shadow, liner, and mascara that Trudy called the Heavenly Lift. Priscilla had to admit that her lashes did look longer and fuller with this stuff on.

About the time they finished that portion of the makeover, Joan looked Priscilla's way. "I agree with you that Victor isn't who he claims to be. I've always felt something was off. I get that 'wolf in sheep's clothing' feeling when I'm around him."

Mildred joined in, her eye makeup a bit too heavy. "I suspect Betty would say that too—if we could find her."

"Are you saying Victor is somehow responsible for her disappearance?" Priscilla asked.

Mildred shrugged. "Don't know. But I'm suspicious, for sure."

Priscilla found herself distracted. Her marriage to Gary had been wonderful. Mostly. But there were still things she hadn't shared with others, even her own daughter. Things she had struggled with, tucked far into the recesses of her heart. Loneliness, when her husband worked long hours. Insecurity, when she looked at the women around her who were prettier, better put together. Maybe every woman had secrets she'd rather keep to herself.

Surely Betty Fox had secrets. And she'd kept them hidden in deep, dark closets, it seemed.

"I tried to get to know Betty." Candy never looked up from applying her mascara as she spoke. "I was in the parking lot at the grocery store, about to back out. Suddenly I felt a bump. She'd rammed right into me."

"I heard about that," Priscilla said, "and saw the dent in her bumper when we pulled into the line at the ferry landing. Her vehicle was right in front of mine."

"Ah." Candy glanced up. "She apologized, but she was really distracted as she did. Thank goodness there was no damage to my car, but she sure dinged up her bumper."

"And never had it fixed," Mildred observed. "Don't you find that strange? Victor always puts his best face forward. I'd think he would've fixed that bumper right away to avoid having people ask about it. Odd that he let it go."

"He's got bigger issues to deal with right now." Candy shrugged and went back to working on her lashes. "Maybe he didn't even notice, you know? Some men don't."

"They'll notice if you put on this amazing new blush and lip liner," Trudy said, still sounding stiff and professional. "He'll never look at you the same way again. Guaranteed."

"You mean he'll never give me a 'why isn't my dinner on the table?' look?" Candy asked. "If so, I'm in." She grabbed the blush and started dabbing her cheeks. This got a laugh out of everyone.

"Men don't always notice the things we do," Trudy said. "I bought some new clothes a couple of months ago and hung them in the closet. I've been pulling them out one piece a week or so, to see if my husband notices. He did ask about the blue blouse. I told him it'd been hanging in my closet for ages." She giggled. "I'm surprised he noticed at all. As I said, most of the time men are clueless."

Priscilla continued to work on her cheeks and lips until she was happy with the outcome.

"Wow, Priscilla." Gail gave her a little whistle. "Where have you been hiding?"

"What do you mean?"

Gail pointed at the mirror. "Look at yourself, girl. You're a beauty queen."

Priscilla's heart fluttered as she glanced at her reflection. "Far from it." Still, she did notice the difference. This makeup was better than most she'd tried.

Trudy walked her way to see the results. "Amazing, Priscilla. It's hard to deny the radical transformation the Heavenly Faces line has made in your appearance."

"Gee, thanks a lot." Priscilla did her best not to roll her eyes.

"No, you know what I mean. You were always beautiful, but these new products just enhance what God gave you."

Priscilla had to admit that she did look younger.

When all of the ladies had finished their makeup, they decided to take photos.

"Now do I have your permission to put your photo on Facebook, Tilly?" Trudy asked as she snapped a picture of Tilly looking lovely and much younger in the new makeup.

"For pity's sake, yes. I don't mind a bit, now that I look like this." Tilly continued to stare at her mirror. "This stuff has magical powers."

"It does, indeed," Trudy said. "And you can buy the starter kit today—all of the products we sampled and more—for a mere $199.99."

Tilly's eyes widened.

"No way," Mildred said. "Not happening, even if this stuff has magic properties."

"Oh, it does. It really does." Trudy paused. "Now it's time for the biggest transformation of all." Trudy gestured for Priscilla to join her at the front of the room. "Our hostess is going to enjoy a luxurious facial mask, administered by yours truly."

She handed Priscilla a couple of makeup remover wipes, which Priscilla used to wipe off all of the amazing makeup she'd just applied. Before long her face was clean and shiny, without a hint of color other than what God had given her. She took a seat in front of the crowd, and Trudy worked to apply the mask, a white pasty substance.

"You will notice, ladies, that this has a lovely almond scent. I personally believe heaven is going to smell like almonds. Apparently, the owners of the Heavenly Faces line believe that too." She continued to apply the mask. Priscilla enjoyed the feel of Trudy's fingertips as they worked their magic across her cheeks, chin, nose, and forehead.

A couple of the ladies in the room turned the conversation back to Victor and his secretary. Several speculations, though vague, were made. Priscilla certainly got the point. Most of the women were convinced that Victor Fox and Eliza Jamison were carrying on an affair behind Betty's back.

Or maybe to her face. Maybe she just got tired of being made to look the fool and took off to start a new life. Things like that happened all the time, didn't they?

Once again, Priscilla lost herself to her jumbled thoughts. If Carson hadn't played a role in Betty's disappearance, maybe Eliza Jamison had. She was on the ferry too, wasn't she? Very interesting.

Minutes later, the mask began to harden around the edges. Trudy rattled on about the purpose of the mask, but Priscilla found herself growing sleepy.

Until noise from outside the house jarred her.

"What's going on out there?" Trudy glanced toward the window. "Sounds like you've got company."

"Heavens, I hope not." Priscilla rose and made her way to the window. She peeked out, then gasped. "Oh, I totally forgot. Teresa is going to bring her tour groups around on Saturdays, but she told me she had a special group that could only make arrangements for this evening. She's calling it a sunset tour. I told her it would be fine just this once. Can't believe I forgot."

She could have kicked herself. Poor Teresa probably had to park a block away, what with all of the cars in Priscilla's driveway.

The sound of voices grew louder. Priscilla watched through the window as nearly a dozen people converged on her property. Young. Old. People in their middle years. They were all smiling, laughing, and talking as Teresa led them toward the lighthouse to begin her tour.

Uncle Hugh rose and walked to the front door. "Sounds like we're under attack. Do I need to get my gun?" He swung the door wide, and Jake bounded through it.

"Jake, come back!" Priscilla called.

He kept running, his red and white fur billowing in the breeze as he headed straight for the tour group. Great. Now what?

Priscilla turned to face her friends, her thoughts a bit twisted as she tried to figure out how to handle this. "I promised Teresa I wouldn't let him annoy the guests."

Sure enough, the dog took to yapping outside. Why hadn't she put him in his kennel with guests coming and going?

Priscilla groaned. "Sorry to interrupt, but give me a second, ladies. I've got to go fetch him before he causes any more trouble."

Trudy put her hand up. "But, Priscilla, don't you think you should—"

She didn't take the time to let her cousin finish the sentence. With the dog carrying on, Priscilla had little choice but to go out and bring him back inside.

CHAPTER SEVEN

Priscilla sprinted toward the tour group, apologies flowing like water. "I'm so sorry, folks. This sweet fella thinks he's part of the tour, but don't mind him. We're going back inside now."

As Priscilla drew near the group, Teresa's eyes widened. Not that Priscilla blamed her for being startled. Teresa would never want to bring a tour group back if Priscilla couldn't get this dog under control. She took hold of his collar and shushed him.

Teresa was usually very chatty, but her silence threw Priscilla for a loop. She held tight to her dog's collar and tried to keep him still.

"Well, I should get back inside. I've got company." Priscilla took a couple of steps toward the door. The tour group members watched her so closely it made her a bit nervous. "C'mon, boy." She led Jake toward the front porch. "Let's go."

Teresa gave her a little nod, the edges of her lips turning up in what almost looked like a smile.

"Thanks for stopping by," Priscilla said to the group. "Enjoy your tour." She reached the porch and knelt next to her dog to give him a talking-to. His tail wagged merrily.

A car drew to a halt in front of her house. She glanced up to see a familiar Coast Guard vehicle. Her heart skipped a beat as

Gerald O'Bannon, captain of the local Coast Guard station, stepped out, dressed in uniform. She gave him a little wave, keeping one hand on Jake's collar as she rose.

The handsome captain took a few steps in her direction, the creases in his brow growing more pronounced as he drew near.

She smiled, trying to hold on to the dog's collar. "Gerald. Nice to see you. Sorry about Jake."

"Good to see you too. And don't worry about him. He's not bothering me." Gerald gazed at her with such intensity that her heart rate quickened. Gracious. A woman could get used to being looked at like this.

Or not. He continued to stare at her face, the edges of his lips curling up in a suspicious grin. After another moment, things began to feel a bit awkward. She wasn't sure what, if anything, to say.

"Um, Priscilla," he said after a moment, "do you mind if I ask you a question?"

"Ask away. I'm an open book."

"Okay. What's that"—he pointed to her face—"that...white stuff?"

She snapped to attention as the realization set in. She felt her cheeks grow hot as her hands flew to cover her face. "Oh, Gerald! For pity's sake, why didn't you say something? You were just going to let me stand here with this cleansing mask on my face and say nothing." She peeked through her fingers at him. "Good gravy."

"I'm saying something." He chuckled, and his hazel eyes narrowed as he examined her face from a different angle. "And thanks for answering my question. Where do I go to get one of those? I might want to consider it for Halloween. Looks like an inexpensive alternative."

Priscilla did her best not to groan as she responded. "Very funny. But, to answer your question, you can purchase this—for a limited time only—in my living room. Trudy is in there right now, trying to sell us on her new beauty products—the Heavenly Faces line. I seriously doubt this is inexpensive, though."

"All that white fluff does make it look heavenly, but I won't say this particular model shows off your face to its fullest advantage, so I guess I'll save my pennies. Thanks all the same."

"You're a laugh a minute." She punched him on the arm and turned back toward the house. "Now to deal with the fallout from this. I'm sure Teresa and the folks on her tour are laughing themselves silly."

"Tell them you're providing a new stop on the tour, complete with ghosts. That'll shake 'em up. And then let them know they'll be charged double for the entertainment value." He flashed a smile that warmed her heart.

"No way. Then they'll expect to see me in makeup and costume every time." As she spoke the word *costume*, Priscilla's hands immediately went to her neckline. "Oh, no! I'm still wearing the apron." Now the people from the tour would really think she was nuts.

"That bright shade of pink is perfect with your pale complexion." Gerald chuckled, and she groaned.

Could this day possibly get any worse?

"I stopped by to tell you we're expecting an incoming storm. Bad one," he said.

"Ugh."

"Yes, and after that incident with the lightning strike a while back, I thought you might want to keep an eye on the area around the lighthouse. Don't want to see another fire."

"Me neither." She didn't particularly want to see another storm of that intensity, either, but she couldn't exactly stop that from happening, now could she? "Hey, while I have you here, can I ask you a question?"

"Sure. The longer I get to gaze upon this face, the better. I'm getting some ideas for how I can go incognito, should the need arise."

She punched him again. "I'm wondering—and forgive me if this is gossip—but I'm wondering if you've heard anything about Victor and Betty Fox."

His smile faded at once. "Other than the part where she's gone missing, you mean?"

"Well, I'm referring to their relationship. Have you ever heard anything about how he treats her?"

"Ah." Gerald's gaze shifted to the ground. "I've picked up on a few cues and have heard some things from the guys who work with him in his inner circle."

"Like what?"

"Nothing specific."

She brushed her hair behind her ears. "I see. Well, rumor has it their marriage is troubled."

"Lots of marriages are troubled." His mood seemed to darken a bit, and she wondered if he might be thinking of his ex-wife, Cathy. Over twenty years had passed since she walked out on him, but the pain still rose to the surface on occasion. Priscilla had observed it in his eyes.

"True," she said. "Not everything is as it seems publicly. I know that."

"Right, but wives don't just run away. I'm more inclined to suspect foul play."

"A lot of folks—and by folks, I mean the ladies in my living room right now—are saying that, well, he's been seen around town a lot with his secretary. If he's been wanting to drop wife A to acquire wife B, then perhaps things are not as they seem."

Gerald's eyes widened. "Well now, if it's coming from the ladies at the makeup party, it must be true. Just like anything you read on the Internet."

She fought the temptation to roll her eyes. "I know, I know, it's just gossip. But sometimes, if you're really listening, you can glean information, even from folks with loose lips."

"So, slick-talking Vic is having a fling with his secretary, and you suspect the two of them have done away with his wife to clear the road for them to marry?"

"I never said that...exactly. Just saying the notion has come up in conversation."

"And you don't think it would be strange to pull off something this high profile during a political season when the eyes of everyone in the community are on you, and you're trying to win the favor of the people?"

She sighed. "I hadn't really thought it through, but now that you mention it, the timing would be a bit odd."

"Look, I'd be lying if I said the thought hadn't entered my mind. I see how he is with women—such a schmoozer."

"Schmoozer?"

"You know. Slick. He's that way when it comes to campaigning and seems to be that way around the ladies as well. Those kinds of guys turn me off every time. I just don't understand how people can keep falling under his spell."

"Same here. He gives me the creeps. Why would people vote for someone they couldn't trust?" Priscilla paused and watched the seagulls swoop around the tour group as several tossed bread pieces into the air. "It's so strange that we're pointing fingers at Victor. Yesterday I'd made up my mind to figure out what Carson Fletcher was doing on that ferry."

"Carson Fletcher?" Gerald paused and appeared to be thinking. "Oh, right. I met him at the bakery one afternoon. Seems like a nice guy. He's a suspect too?"

"You know me better than that. I'm not naming suspects."

"Yet." He gave her a knowing look.

"It's just that the ladies also think Carson has some sort of hidden story, that he's an elusive figure. Maybe even a reporter. Trudy's got some interesting notions, trust me."

"Speaking of elusive figures, are you sure you don't want to go back inside and wash that stuff off?" He pointed to her face. "It's starting to crack. I'm having a hard time watching you talk, because I half-expect it to snap."

"Good grief. How is it possible I keep forgetting I've got this on?" Her hands went to her face once again. "Yes, I'm going inside. I would invite you in to keep Uncle Hugh company, but Trudy would probably talk you into buying makeup for your daughter or some such thing."

"I'm good at saying no, even to the most persuasive among us." He grinned.

"Pretty sure you'll have a hard time turning Trudy down."

Gerald shrugged. "Guess we'll just have to see, then. But I love a good challenge." He stared at her with such intensity that Priscilla had to wonder if he was talking about makeup at all.

CHAPTER EIGHT

The makeup party lasted longer than expected, what with so many women ordering the kit and signing up to sell the products. Trudy was delighted, of course, and Priscilla—though embarrassed about what had happened with the cleansing mask—was tickled that the evening had come off without a hitch.

Uncle Hugh was the only grumbler, but he settled down after they fed him several yummy snacks and a ham sandwich. Gerald came and went without purchasing a thing for his daughter, though he did promise to share the good news about the Heavenly Faces makeup line.

After her guests left, Priscilla found herself growing sleepy. She decided to head to bed earlier than usual. There would be plenty of time to clean up her messy living room in the morning.

After brushing her teeth and dressing in a cool nightgown, Priscilla climbed into bed. She leaned back, and her eyes fluttered closed. Moments later, the strangest sensation came over her, as if she'd climbed aboard a boat that rocked back and forth.

When her eyes grew heavier, she could almost picture the waves of the Sound pressing against the hull. Priscilla allowed the gentle pull of the waves to draw her into a dreamlike state. In that instant, she was transported to the side deck of the ferry once again. Trudy sang "Anchors Aweigh." Mildred sat nearby, her nose buried in a book. Off in the distance—through a porthole—she caught a glimpse of Betty Fox crying.

The dream shifted, and Priscilla felt the waves tossing with more vengeance. Overhead, storm clouds loomed. Trudy's song shifted to a funeral dirge, and Betty Fox emerged, dressed in elaborate funeral attire, and walked to the railing of the ship. Eliza Jamison watched it all, eyes wide, an evil smile on her face. Carson Fletcher watched too, scribbling notes into a notepad. Priscilla sprinted from her spot on the bench, ready to offer a word of comfort. Only, when she reached the railing, Betty was gone. She had disappeared into thin air.

Priscilla awoke with a pounding heart. She was shocked to see glimpses of sunlight through the bedroom window. Had the dream really lasted all night? From his bed in the corner of her room, Jake let out a little growl, as if sensing her unease. She drew in a few long breaths to steady her nerves.

"Just a nightmare, boy." She rubbed her eyes and sat up.

Jake approached the side of her bed and placed his nose on the mattress. She reached down to stroke his head. Dogs always seemed to know when to show up. They had an innate sense of caregiving in them.

Priscilla rose and made a quick trip to the bathroom, her thoughts firmly affixed on the dream. Clearly, Betty's disappearance had affected her more than she realized. How did a woman simply disappear over the railing of a ferry with no one noticing? And why was Betty dressed in funeral attire? What was she mourning? The loss of something—or someone—dear?

As she walked back toward the bed, Priscilla found herself wide awake.

"Now what, boy?" She glanced down at the dog, who hovered at her side. "Breakfast? We didn't really have much of a dinner last night, did we?"

His tail wagged.

Priscilla headed toward the kitchen, trying to remember snatches of the dream, which was fading rapidly. Perhaps that was for the best. She would rather remember Betty in her lovely blue blouse and tan scarf.

A niggling concern crept over her as a memory took root. Priscilla walked back into the bedroom to fetch her purse. She shoveled through the various items—a comb, coin purse, package of gum, a program from last Sunday's service—until she finally found the tags at the bottom.

The first tag was for a multicolored scarf, purchased at a local store. The second for a pink blouse, size medium.

They couldn't be connected to Betty Fox. She had definitely been wearing blue. And her scarf was tan. Still, Priscilla couldn't let go of the idea that the clothing tags might hold a clue.

She glanced at the clock on the wall: 7:45 a.m. Trudy would be awake. Priscilla reached for her cell phone and called her cousin.

Trudy answered, sounding as bubbly as ever. "Oh, Priscilla, wasn't last night wonderful? I had the best time ever. Thanks for letting me host the party at your place."

"Happy to be of service." Priscilla quickly explained the reason for her call, giving all the details of the dream that she could remember, followed by what she knew about the clothing tags.

Trudy's tone changed at once. "What do you think it means, Priscilla?"

"I'm not sure. I just wanted to confirm that when we saw Betty on the ship, she was wearing a blue blouse."

"Gorgeous blue, perfect for the springtime. I remember thinking that. It had pretty little birds on it, if memory serves me right."

"That's what I remember too. A blue blouse and jeans. Just regular, ordinary jeans."

"Why are you asking?"

"I just had this weird flashback to getting off the ferry and seeing a group of people crossing the street. One of them had on the prettiest pink blouse. It caught my eye, because I loved the design. Very flattering."

"So?"

"I'm just wondering if that pink blouse is the same pink blouse once attached to this tag." She gave it a closer look. "Someplace called the Perfect Fit."

"Ooh, I know that store. It's in Edgartown." Trudy's voice sounded more animated. "They have sizes for all women in there—from the largest to the smallest." She paused. "I'm always looking for an excuse to shop, Priscilla. Want to take a quick trip over there?"

"This morning?"

"Sure. Why not? We can show the tag to the owner, Marcia, and see if she remembers the buyer."

"Are you sure you're up for it? Aren't you exhausted?"

"Exhausted? Me?" Trudy laughed. "I'm energized! Just give me time to shower and put on some makeup."

"Same here."

"I'll pick you up around nine thirty," Trudy said. "What a perfect week this is turning out to be! I booked three parties, signed up two new distributors, sold nine hundred dollars in product, and now I get to go shopping!"

Priscilla couldn't help but laugh at her cousin's glee. She ended the call and headed to the bathroom to shower and get ready for the day. Then she added lipstick and mascara and took the dog outside for a quick break. Afterwards, when Priscilla realized she'd somehow overlooked breakfast, she headed to the kitchen to toast an english muffin. Jake looked on longingly. She filled his bowl with dry food and checked the water level in his other bowl.

"I won't be gone long, boy." She gave Jake a pat on the head. "You hold down the fort until I get back, okay?"

His tag wagged merrily.

Trudy pulled into the driveway moments later. Priscilla opened the passenger side door of Trudy's car and climbed inside.

"Long time no see." Trudy's smile brightened. She checked her appearance in the rearview mirror, then ran her fingers through her platinum hair.

"Thanks for picking me up." Priscilla buckled her seat belt.

"Really, it's my pleasure." Trudy backed the car out of the drive, and they pulled out onto the main road.

Priscilla glanced back at her property. Underneath the shimmer of the morning sun, the place looked magnificent. "I just love the cottage in springtime, don't you?"

"Hmm? What?" Trudy was focused on the road.

"The white shutters seem even whiter. The flowers in the garden are blooming. It's all so beautiful."

To their right, they passed a gorgeous clapboard home with a white picket fence. Priscilla couldn't help but sigh once more. "It's this island, I tell you. It has won my heart, right down to the design of the homes and yards."

"Prettiest place on the planet."

"Yes. I've heard of white picket fences all my life. They're kind of like..." She paused to think through the rest of the sentence. "The American ideal. You know?"

"I guess." Trudy still seemed a bit distracted as she rounded the next bend.

"People always say they want to live in a 3-2-2 with a white picket fence. They want to raise perfect children in an ideal environment."

"Well, the Vineyard is a pretty ideal environment. You have to admit that." Trudy worked her way around the bend in the road and came to the first of many stop signs. Traffic was thick for a Friday morning. Hopefully it wouldn't be like this all the way to Edgartown.

"For sure." Though Priscilla did find it odd that so many strange things kept popping up in such an idyllic place. Martha's Vineyard was both lovely and intriguing.

Trudy carried on and on about the makeup party as she crossed the island toward Edgartown. By the time they arrived at the shop, Priscilla knew far more than she cared to about beauty products. Still, she enjoyed her cousin's zeal.

Trudy pulled her car into the parking lot of the cutest little store, which was all decked out with gingerbread trim. They got out of the car to walk inside. As they rounded the corner to the front of the shop, Priscilla stopped cold.

"Trudy, look." She gestured to a man standing on the side of the road near the shop. "That's the man from the ferry. Carson."

"Sure is. Wonder what he's doing over here in Edgartown."

"Maybe he really is a drifter. He shifts from village to village." Still, as Priscilla observed his clothes again, she had to admit he didn't dress like she would imagine a drifter would. He had on ordinary clothing, like any other man would wear. Something about his movements, though, seemed very suspicious. He seemed far too interested in the shop's exterior.

She gasped as he pulled out his phone and took a picture. "Oh! Did you see that?" Why would he take a picture of the outside of a store? Was he planning to come back later and rob the place? Yes, surely he was scoping out the store for a hit. Or maybe Trudy was right. Maybe he really was a reporter, sniffing out a story.

"He's kind of like the character in the new scary movie that just released." Trudy's words came out as a hoarse whisper. "You know the one? They keep playing the commercial on TV."

"No. I'm not into scary movies."

"Me neither, but I keep hearing about this one. It has this weird guy who just keeps popping up here, there, and everywhere. He teleports from one place to another. I think he comes from the future to kill people. And he can move around from place to place in an instant, just by snapping his fingers."

"Good grief. Are you telling me that Carson has teleported himself from one end of the island to the other?"

"No. Maybe he has a car. But he walked on board the ferry, right?" Trudy paused. "So maybe he doesn't have a car."

"Lots of people walk on board the ferry to save money. It's a fraction of the cost to cross the Sound without a vehicle."

"True."

Priscilla watched him out of the corner of her eye and wondered if they could get past him to enter the store. "He seems to be scoping the place out," she whispered as they eased by him.

"Told you he was a reporter," Trudy said.

"Maybe. But why this place? Betty Fox isn't here."

"That we know of."

"Surely not." Priscilla paused. "Do you think we should tell the owner that she's being watched?"

"Definitely," Trudy agreed. "Or I could just call the police right now. They'll come if there's any suspicious behavior."

"It's not really suspicious, I guess. He just keeps staring at the building."

He took one final picture, gave them a nod, and then headed down the sidewalk. Very strange, indeed.

CHAPTER NINE

A bell jingled as Trudy opened the door, and a clerk greeted them with a vibrant, "Welcome to the Perfect Fit!"

"Thank you." Priscilla gave the woman with dark-brown hair and gorgeous olive skin a smile. "Cute place. Can't believe I've never been here before."

"Happy to have you now." The woman's brown eyes creased around the edges as she welcomed them inside.

Priscilla hated to alarm her but felt she must tell her about Carson. "Did you know there was a man outside taking pictures of your store?"

"Pretty sure he's a reporter," Trudy threw in.

"Wow." The clerk's brow wrinkled as she glanced toward the storefront window. "Really? Well, a lot of people take pictures because of the gingerbread architecture. They go all over Edgartown taking pictures of the buildings. That's what we're known for. So I'm not too worried. We get a lot of that around here. And it might be good for business if he is a reporter, you know?"

"True." Priscilla glanced toward the window. Still, something about all of this didn't add up. There were too many questions surrounding Carson Fletcher.

For the first time, she wondered if, perhaps, he was trailing her, as well as Betty. The very idea gave her the creeps.

"Is your mama working today, Claire?" Trudy asked.

The young woman shook her head. "No, she's away on a business trip. But she'll be excited to hear you came back and brought a friend, Trudy. By the way, I wanted to thank you for the sweet card you sent. I sure appreciate your prayers." She turned her attention to another customer who wanted to pay for merchandise.

"Prayers?" Priscilla asked.

"Long story," Trudy replied. "I'll fill you in after we've shopped. Marcia, the owner, always runs the best sales when the seasons change."

She headed toward the clearance rack at the back of the store, but Priscilla found herself drawn to a rack of bright springtime blouses near the front. She kept an eye out for anything in a lovely shade of pink. Maybe she could match the blouse to the mysterious tag she'd found on the ferry.

Priscilla was captivated by several blouses, but none were pink. Still, she might have to try a few of these on, though the prices were a bit higher than she had expected. No wonder Trudy had ventured to the sales rack at the back of the store.

A few moments later, Claire approached, her arms loaded down with empty hangers. "You doing okay over here? Need any help?"

"These shirts are beautiful. I'm finding a lot to look at."

"Thanks. We pride ourselves on carrying items you won't find in other stores." Claire's smile broadened. "In fact, that's why my mother isn't here today. She's meeting with a new designer in

New York. Before long, we'll have even more beautiful items to choose from." She paused. "Want to try something on, maybe?"

"Yes. I mean, no. I mean, I was looking for a particular blouse. In pink. It had embroidery on it, I think. Let me show you the tag."

"Sure. Just let me carry these hangers to the back, and I'll be right with you." Claire disappeared and then returned moments later, arms empty. "Now, what have you got for me to look at?"

Priscilla reached in her purse to pull out the tags and handed them to the young woman, whose brow wrinkled as she looked them over.

"So you *have* shopped with us before."

"No." Priscilla shook her head. "I haven't."

"But you bought these items..." Claire looked genuinely confused.

"No. I didn't buy them at all. The tags came from a trash can on the ferry. I'm just trying to find out if this tag is for the pink blouse I'm thinking of."

Claire's right eyebrow elevated. "I see."

"I know, it's weird. I don't usually go rummaging through trash cans for clothing tags. And I'm not sure these tags have anything at all to do with, well, anything." Priscilla sighed. "Honestly? It's kind of a long story, but let me simplify: I saw a pink blouse on the ferry that I really liked, and this tag was in the trash can in the ladies' room on board. The tag says it came from this store, so I was wondering if it's from the same blouse I saw. That's all."

Claire nodded. "I'll have to get on the computer and see which blouse this is. Will you give me a moment?"

"Sure. I'll keep looking. Maybe I'll stumble across the same blouse. I'd love to have one, myself. If it's the blouse I have in mind, it certainly caught my eye."

Trudy appeared with several pairs of slacks in hand. "Such a great sale, Priscilla! I'm going to try these on. Did you have any luck with the tags?"

"The clerk is checking now."

"Sorry Marcia isn't here. She would know right away, I'm sure."

"I'll take whatever I can get."

"Well, Claire is great too. The apple doesn't fall far from the tree, you know. Though I am a little surprised to see Claire working. She's been ill for several months now."

"Oh?" That was surprising.

"Systemic Lupus," Trudy whispered. "It's hit her kidneys. She's been through chemo over the past several months, but I don't know that it's done much good."

"Poor thing." Wow. Maybe it would be a good idea to make a few purchases here, if for no other reason than to lend moral and financial support to the friendly sales clerk.

A couple of minutes later, Claire reappeared with one of the tags in hand. "I'm sorry, it appears we're out of that particular style at the moment. Would you like me to order one for you? I can have it in a week or so."

"That would be great." Priscilla didn't particularly need a new blouse, but she felt she needed to give this shop her business as a show of support. "Now, can I ask you question?"

"Sure."

She took out her phone and pulled up a picture of Betty Fox from Victor's website. "Does this woman look familiar?"

Claire took the photo and gave it a closer look. "Hmm. I mean, sort of. I don't know her, but I think she's been in the store a time or two."

"Do you have a way to look up prior sales to see if she happened to purchase that blouse?"

Claire paused and appeared to be thinking. "We do have a record of all sales, of course, but tracking items to particular customers will be tough unless she paid with a credit card. Do you know if she did?"

Priscilla shrugged. "I honestly have no idea. I'm grasping at straws here. If she purchased the blouse, it might've been with cash. I doubt she would've wanted the purchase tracked."

"Sounds intriguing."

"Very." Priscilla reached into her purse and came out with a receipt from Ortmann's grocery store. "Can I give you my number? If your mom comes in, could you ask her if she knows Betty Fox? Maybe she would remember the sale, if so."

"I'll tell her you were here and will ask about the blouse."

"Thank you. I greatly appreciate it."

Priscilla wanted to say more, but a gorgeous green blouse with purple flowers was calling her name, and she felt led to answer.

CHAPTER TEN

After heading home from the Perfect Fit, Priscilla decided to tackle some spring cleaning tasks. She cleared all of the knickknacks from the various tables and shelves and grabbed a dustcloth, ready to get to work. Just as she reached for the dusting spray, a knock sounded at the door. *Ugh.* Perfect timing.

She crossed the living room to open the door and was puzzled when she saw who stood outside. Tony McClaren, Victor Fox's chief opponent for commissioner. She'd only met him in person a couple of times, and he seemed nice enough, but what was he doing at her house?

"Mrs. Grant." He offered her a warm smile, then extended his hand. "I hope you don't mind that I stopped by unannounced."

"Um, well..."

"If I'm interrupting, please let me know. I was hoping to have a few words with you."

"I was just about to dust, so you'll find things a bit scattered, but I don't mind if you don't." She did her best not to sigh. Why did visits like this always come at the most inopportune times? "Would you like to come in?"

"Sure. And thanks. I won't stay long, I promise. Just a quick visit, is all."

Priscilla was counting on that. She pulled the door a bit wider, and he stepped through. She couldn't help but stare at the tall, stately man as he entered. He was handsome, with salt-and-pepper hair and soft blue eyes. In many ways, he reminded her of Gary. Of course, Gary rarely dressed in a suit, and certainly not an expensive one like the tailored number Tony wore.

"How can I help you, Mr. McClaren?" She gestured to the sofa, and he took a seat, looking completely at ease.

"Call me Tony. Please." The edges of his lips tugged up in another smile, this one more playful than the last. His eyes sparkled, and his gaze lingered on her a bit longer than she might have expected. Gracious. Was he flirting with her? "I confess I've sought you out, Mrs. Grant."

Okay, now she really felt uncomfortable. She cleared her throat and said, "Priscilla."

"Priscilla." He flashed another warm smile, and she noticed his teeth were perfectly white. The contrast against his tanned skin was appealing. "I have Teresa Claybrook to thank, actually."

"Does this have something to do with her tours?"

"Not at all. She's just a good judge of people, and she says you're the real deal."

"Real deal?"

"I'm in the middle of a campaign, as you know. I understand from Candy Lane down at the confectionery that you are considering voting for me." His gaze remained on her face.

"Yes. I think you'll do a fine job as commissioner." *Certainly better than Victor Fox.*

"Thank you. I hope the other voters agree. I must confess I'm not skilled in the art of persuasion, like my opponent is. He seems to have a way with words."

"You can say that twice and mean it."

"Yes." Tony cleared his throat. "Well, he's polished. We'll leave it at that. And he seems to have hit a nerve with women."

"In a good way or a bad way?"

"Hard to tell, I guess. Ever since my wife passed away, I've been doing my best to figure out how to appeal to the opposite sex." His cheeks flamed red. "I did not mean that at all the way it sounded. I was just speaking as a candidate."

"I understand." She offered a comforting smile, and he seemed to relax a bit.

"I just meant to say that getting the female vote is awkward for me. I know what makes guys tick. I know the issues that matter to them, especially in Vineyard Haven, because many of them have been in the same clubs and organizations with me most of my adult life. But women…" He shook his head. "They're a mystery, one I don't believe I'll ever solve."

She laughed. "We'd probably say the same thing about men, if that makes you feel any better."

Fine lines formed around his eyes as he smiled. "Yes, I suppose so." He paused and then released a slow breath. She could read the concern in those beautiful blue eyes. "I was hoping, Mrs. Grant, that you would come on board not just as a supporter, but as a helper to my campaign."

"Helper…how?"

"Though you're relatively new to the island, the ladies have certainly taken to you. You're a leader. I saw the work you put into the fall festival. I've been watching as you opened your home, your property, to Teresa's tour groups. You're a go-getter, and I like that." He shrugged. "To be honest, I need that."

"Need what?"

"I need someone who can tell me the issues that matter to women in Vineyard Haven. Someone who can guide me, as it were."

"Surely you have people for that, Mr. McClaren."

"Tony. And no, not really. I mean, I have Tilly's input. She's been great. Her work at the inn puts her in touch with lots of people. And Mildred often gives me advice. And Teresa, as I said. I value her opinion very much." He paused and appeared to be thinking. "Your cousins offer great advice, as well."

"Sounds like you have quite a team."

"Yes, and I'm thrilled to have them. But the team needs to grow even more as we get closer to the election, and I have the strongest sense you would be a great asset." His soft smile captivated her. "According to Teresa, you've got a level of—what would you call it, discernment?—that other people don't have."

Funny, that he should use that word. Did she really have as much discernment as folks seemed to think, or did they just perceive her that way?

"I don't think you're as easily swayed by my opponent's personality as some people around here," he said.

"That's true. Definitely not."

"Good." His words softened even more. "At any rate, please think about it. And pray about it too, of course. I know you're a praying woman, a churchgoing woman. I sit a few pews behind you at Faith Fellowship."

Had he been watching her? She struggled to find the words to respond, finally settling on, "I'll pray about it, Mr. McClaren."

"Tony." He rose and extended his hand. "Thank you for considering this, Mrs.—Priscilla. I will be so grateful to have your input, should you decide to help. And I promise not to tax you."

"Tax me?"

He chuckled, and those gorgeous eyes took to sparkling. "I meant, I promise not to take advantage of your time. I can't promise you won't pay taxes. That's out of my hands."

They laughed together. As the laughter faded, Priscilla noticed he still had hold of her hand. She withdrew it and smiled. "Well, I make no promises, but I'll pray about this. And thanks for stopping by, Tony."

"No, thank you."

She walked him to the door. When she swung it open, Priscilla was stunned to find Trudy standing on the other side, holding a box labeled *Heavenly Faces*.

"Oh, I . . ." Trudy's cheeks turned crimson. "Sorry to interrupt. When I got home from our little shopping excursion, I saw that your makeup order had arrived, Priscilla."

"Wow, that's fast."

"Yes, they have twenty-four-hour shipping. Just one more reason I love to sing the praises of Heavenly Faces." Trudy cleared her throat. "Anyway, I rushed it right over. I thought you'd be eager to have the goodies before the big day tomorrow."

"Tomorrow? Big day?"

"The parade in Edgartown. Remember?"

"Oh, right." Priscilla gestured for her cousin to enter. "Come on in, Trudy. Please."

Her cousin stepped through the door, hands still firmly holding the large box, but her gaze never left Tony McClaren.

He offered one last nod as he stepped outside. "Priscilla, thank you for considering my proposition."

Trudy's eyes widened.

"If you have any questions, don't hesitate to call." Tony reached into his pocket and came out with a business card. "Then again, that's my public line. Let me give you my cell number." He pulled out a pen and scribbled on the back of the card. "Call anytime."

Something about the twinkle in his eye as he said "anytime" made her heart flutter a bit. She thanked him for his visit, then closed the door behind him.

Time to face the music. Priscilla turned to find her cousin staring at her.

"Um, what was all that about?" Trudy set the makeup box on the coffee table and placed her hands on her hips.

With the wave of a hand, Priscilla tried to appear dismissive. "Nothing, really. He just seems to think I can be of help with his campaign."

"And he chose you because...?"

"From what I gather, I have Teresa to thank for this. And Candy too. She must've told him that I'm voting for him."

"Lots of people are voting for him."

Priscilla shrugged. "He said it's because I'm new to the island and less likely to be swayed by personalities. I'm more open-minded."

"He's hoping you're open-minded, all right." Trudy giggled. "But I sincerely doubt he's hanging around for your vote."

Priscilla could hardly believe Trudy would imply such a thing. "I don't know why you would say that. I haven't done a thing to lead him on."

"I didn't say you had."

"Nor am I interested."

"He does have lovely hazel eyes."

"They're blue." Priscilla wanted to clamp a hand over her mouth the minute she spoke. She'd fallen right into Trudy's trap.

"So you've noticed those beautiful blue eyes. And I suppose that gorgeous perfectly combed hair didn't sway you, either. Or that expensive suit. Or his broad shoulders. Not that I've noticed any of the above." Trudy released an exaggerated sigh. "He is awfully handsome."

"Yet another reason he would never be interested in someone like me." Priscilla brushed her palms on her slacks. "I'm just ordinary. Plain. A farmer's wife. I'm not dating material for a man like that, trust me."

"Dating material? So now you're thinking of going out with him?" Trudy's eyes widened. "Then I'm just in time with the new makeup. We'll doll you up, and he won't be able to resist."

Priscilla shook her head. "How do you do it, Trudy?"

"Do what?" She batted her overly made-up eyes and offered a shrug of innocence.

"Move conversations forward the way you do."

"Just a gift, I guess." Trudy laughed. "Look, I'm all over this idea of pairing you up with a handsome man. I know what the other cousins are saying. They would like to see you with Gerald O'Bannon, but I say we give the Coast Guard a run for their money. If there was ever a fellow in Vineyard Haven who could catch a woman's eye, it's Tony McClaren. If you don't believe me, just ask Teresa Claybrook."

"Teresa?"

"She's had her eye on Tony ever since his wife passed away a little over a year ago, but don't ever tell her I said that, okay? Point is, he's a handsome guy who could catch any woman's eye." She winked. "If you get my drift. But the makeup will help, for sure."

"Trudy!" Priscilla shook her head. "I'm not a teenager trying to get a date for the prom."

"I know, I know. And I'm half-kidding, Priscilla. He's a handsome devil, is all."

"He doesn't seem at all devilish to me."

"Right. He's a great guy, and he's running a good campaign. I'm sure he would be happy to have you in his corner, because you would have a lot of sage advice. You're very discerning."

There was that word again. Right now, Priscilla didn't feel very discerning. She did, however, feel a little irritated.

"Well, I need to be on my way." Trudy was suddenly all business again. "My car is filled with products that need to be delivered. All the women in Vineyard Haven will be singing the praises of Heavenly Faces soon. Thanks for your order, cousin. Heavenly Faces are happy faces!"

She bounded toward the door, and Priscilla waved goodbye as Trudy headed off on her way to other customers.

When she closed the door, Priscilla's thoughts shifted back to Tony McClaren. He was handsome, no debating that fact. And he was charming too. A woman could easily be swept in by his welcoming smile and comfortable demeanor.

Thinking of Tony made her think of Victor Fox. And thinking of Victor made her think of Betty.

Priscilla suddenly wondered if, perhaps, Tony McClaren had ulterior motives for his visit today. Did he know that she was interested in figuring out who was responsible for Betty's disappearance? Had he, by any slim chance, played a role in her disappearance?

Just the idea of it sent a shiver down Priscilla's spine. Perhaps Tony McClaren wasn't quite who he'd made himself out to be. She would certainly have to pray for discernment before agreeing to help him with his campaign, that was for sure.

CHAPTER ELEVEN

Even after sleeping on it, Priscilla still hadn't made up her mind whether or not she would help Tony McClaren with his campaign. Her ongoing concerns about Betty Fox's disappearance kept her distracted.

On the morning after Tony's visit, she drove to Edgartown to meet family and friends for a local parade to celebrate what was known as Pink and Green Weekend. This special weekend celebrated both spring and Mother's Day, offering an abundance of events—everything from a prom to a dog show to a variety of brunches. She could hardly wait.

Martha's Vineyard was vibrant at this time of year. Truly vibrant. There was an electricity of sorts that traveled from village to village as the various gardens burst forth with springtime foliage. Priscilla found herself more distracted than ever by the brightly colored flowers everywhere. Heirloom roses, peonies, larkspurs, and hydrangeas bloomed in abundance, capturing her imagination. Wildflowers galore filled empty fields, as if begging for visitors. The whole place had a lovely storybook charm.

Minutes later, she gathered with her cousins and several other friends along one of the main streets in Edgartown to watch the parade. Gail stood beside Priscilla and opened an umbrella over their heads to shade them from the sun.

"How are you enjoying your first spring on the island, Priscilla?" Gail asked.

"I feel like I spend half my time nearly driving my car off the road because I'm so overwhelmed by all of the flowers, and the other half mesmerized by how beautiful the water looks this time of year. The sky even seems bluer."

"It is bluer. Not thick and murky like in wintertime."

"I've decided springtime is my favorite season here. Everything is so fresh and new. It's almost as if you can smell the changes in the air. I'm not sure how to explain it, but it brings about such a hopeful feeling, like change is possible, even for someone like me, who's been stuck in winter for so long."

"We're called a summer colony for a reason," Gail explained. "The island teems with people from June through August, but people don't know what they're missing in the springtime."

"I'm so in love with the smells of spring that I can hardly contain myself. Just the other day I was taking a walk with Jake, and we found ourselves on the edge of my neighbor's lawn, admiring their flower beds. It was all I could do not to traipse across their grass and sniff those flowers up close. Wouldn't that have been a sight?" She laughed.

"This is my favorite time of year, for sure." Gail smiled. "Have you been by to see Joan's gardens?"

"Yes. Remarkable. I don't know how she does it. And my place is really springing to life too. I was out watering the garden before everyone arrived for the makeup party."

"Makeup party." Gail shook her head. "What will Trudy come up with next?"

"I'm surprised she hasn't put a Heavenly Faces float in the parade."

Gail chuckled and then grew more reflective. "I do love the Pink and Green Parade. It's always a hit with folks young and old. This is your first time to see it, right, Priscilla?"

"Right. I've heard such wonderful things about it. I'm so glad that bad storm that Gerald warned me about missed us. I would have hated for the parade to be cancelled."

"It's a local favorite, and not just for the residents of Edgartown. Folks come from all over the island. The food vendors are awesome too. Remind me later to take you to the BBQ wagon. You'll love it. And the seafood truck has the most divine crab rolls. Better than Tilly's, even."

"Sounds yummy, but don't let Tilly hear you say that."

"Never!" Gail laughed. "I know better than that."

"Ooh, the parade is starting!" Joan's voice sounded behind them, and Priscilla moved over to make room under the umbrella. "Do you hear the music? That's the regional high school marching band. They've been exceptional this year. Won several competitions."

"Where's Trudy?" Priscilla raised her voice above the incoming band.

"She's going from customer to customer, asking how they like their new beauty products."

"I'm a fan," Gail called out.

Priscilla had to admit she was too. The makeup made her feel younger, prettier. Every woman needed that extra boost.

The band marched by, followed by several fun floats representing various businesses, not just in Edgartown but all across the island. With so many people gathered around her, Priscilla got the full effect—the cheers of those in attendance, the smell of fish frying in the background, the colorful banners on the various floats.

Next came the classic cars. "Wow, look at that, will you?" Joan pointed at a blue Bel Air. "I haven't seen a car like that since I was a girl."

Behind the Bel Air came a red Triumph sports car, then a yellow Ford truck from the 1950s. Priscilla's favorite? A gasoline truck from the 1950s. After that came a 1955 teal Ford Thunderbird.

"I feel like I've traveled back in time," Priscilla called out above the cheers from the crowd. "These old cars are so much fun!"

A gorgeous black convertible approached, and she caught a glimpse of the man in the passenger seat. Tony McClaren. He glanced her way, and his smile broadened when he saw her. He offered a boisterous wave. She responded in kind, albeit not with as much vigor.

"I'm not sure I understand why our Vineyard Haven candidates are in a parade in Edgartown," Priscilla observed. "Seems odd."

"Not odd at all," Gail countered. "Folks from all over the island participate." She paused. "But I do find it strange that Tony McClaren is still running such a strong campaign, now that Victor's wife has gone missing."

"I was just thinking the same thing." Joan turned to face them. "I would've guessed he would wait until after she turns up to kick it into high gear."

"Right?" Gail shrugged.

"I talked to Teresa about all of that," Joan said. "She's been helping out in his campaign office a lot. She's the one who advised him to move forward. No point in losing momentum now. So that's his strategy."

"I still find it odd that Betty disappeared right in the heart of the political season, don't you think?" Gail's nose wrinkled. "That's just a weird coincidence. If it's a coincidence at all, I mean."

Priscilla's antennae went up immediately. "Are you saying that Victor's opponent might have something to do with this?"

Joan shrugged. "Not necessarily. I just find the timing odd, you know? Right in the heat of the battle, one of the opponents loses a spouse."

"I guess. I hadn't thought about it that way before. But goodness, 'losing a spouse' sounds so final. Have you heard something new, Joan?"

"No." She pushed her short brown hair out of her face. "Sorry to be so dramatic. I don't know why I processed my thoughts out loud like that."

"Speaking of loud . . ." Gail pointed to a red Corvette coming down the street, horn blaring. She raised her voice to shout, "Do they have to be so obnoxious about it?"

"Trying to get the attention of everyone within earshot, I guess," Priscilla shouted back.

"I dare say people off the island could hear them coming. Who is it, anyway?"

"Let me guess!" Trudy's voice rang out from behind them, and Priscilla turned to discover she had joined them. "Victor Fox."

Sure enough, Victor was in the passenger seat of the convertible. To Priscilla's surprise, Eliza Jamison was behind the wheel, eyes locked on the road ahead. Victor waved at his adoring fans, and many in the crowd cheered.

"Wow. He's campaigning, even with his wife missing?" Joan shook her head. "That's awful."

"The show must go on!" Trudy hollered over the noise of the crowd. "You know how he is."

Priscilla was learning, all right. What kind of a man would parade himself through town when his wife had just gone missing from the ferry? A man who was trying too hard, perhaps?

The car made its way past them, and the noise dimmed.

"Thank goodness that's over." Gail removed her fingers from her ears. "I get nauseous just looking at that man."

"Me too," Priscilla said.

"I don't know how Betty stayed married to him, anyway," Trudy said. "I really don't."

Gail shrugged. "Most of the women I know who are married to political types are either A, proud of their husbands and doing all they can to promote him, or B, ready to tell you all of the reasons they wish their husbands would retire and buy an RV. I don't know any who just fall silent."

"I've known her for years," Joan said. "I've tried a hundred ways from Sunday to talk to her, but Victor always shows up and turns the attention to himself."

"Same here," Mildred added. "The one and only time I engaged her in conversation, she kept glancing at the clock on her phone, like she was counting the minutes or something. Then a text came through from her husband. I saw his name pop up on the screen. She was visibly shaken. Tossed the phone in her purse and said, 'Sorry, I've got to run. Need to get home.'"

"So strange," Priscilla agreed. She turned her attention to the next float, one representing the Vineyard Haven garden club.

Trudy held out a bag of popcorn after the float rolled by. "Hungry, anyone?"

Priscilla took a few nibbles of popcorn as the parade continued. When it ended, the streets overflowed with folks trying to make their way to the food trucks. She followed her cousins as they headed to the Meat Wagon BBQ truck. The smell of food drew her like a magnet. It didn't take much to make her hungry these days. The various delicacies on Martha's Vineyard were like a beacon, calling her name. If she wasn't careful, her cousins would have to roll her home.

It took a while to get through the line at the BBQ truck, but Gail was right. This food was mouthwatering. As they ate their meal, Gail asked Priscilla her thoughts on the parade.

"It was great. I loved all of it." She paused. "Well, not all of it. I still can't believe Victor Fox would hit the campaign trail with his wife missing."

"Right?" Gail took a bite of her sandwich. "And it's not like he needs to campaign very hard, anyway. He's got this election in the bag. Just like last time. And the time before. You know?"

"So he's a perpetual winner? Why is Tony even bothering, then? And why are all of you working so hard to get him elected?"

"We just feel bad for the underdog," Gail explained.

"And none of us like Victor's politics either," Joan added. "It's not just the man himself. I don't like what he's doing to our town."

"Tony's the right man for the job, and I plan to work for him until he takes office," a familiar voice said behind them. Priscilla turned to discover Teresa had joined them.

"Did you ask Tony McClaren to pay me a visit, Teresa?" Priscilla asked. "He stopped by my house the other morning."

"I'm the one to blame." She shrugged. "He's looking for support, and you're such a good judge of character. I knew you couldn't possibly be voting for Victor."

"I'm not, but neither was I interested in—"

"I'm in Tony's campaign office a couple of days a week right now. I would love for you to join us."

Priscilla sighed. This was a losing battle.

"You'll be a great addition to his campaign." Teresa waved and then headed off to meet up with Tilly Snyder. "See you soon."

"Well, isn't this interesting?" Joan's eyes widened. "I'm not surprised Teresa's working for Tony. Anyone who's been paying attention could tell you she's set her sights on him. But why would she handpick you, Priscilla? It strikes me as odd."

Priscilla shrugged. "I'm clueless."

"You gonna do it?" Trudy asked. "I say go for it. I'll still take Tony over Victor any day. I question Victor's motives." Trudy nibbled on a french fry. "Among other things."

"Hmm." Priscilla paused. The idea of Trudy questioning his motives did put things into perspective.

"Is anyone who he—or she—says he—or she—is? Don't we always just put our image out there for the masses to see?" Trudy pointed at the photo of a smiling Victor Fox on the side of the food court area. "Airbrushed."

"Yeah, I guess." Priscilla wiped the BBQ sauce from her fingers.

Trudy's eyes narrowed to slits as she stared at the poster of Victor. "Give me a vulnerable, flawed candidate any day. I don't trust a guy who appears to be perfect. Anytime I see an airbrushed photo, I just want to use some of my Heavenly Faces eyeliner to paint some freckles on him. Make him more real. Flawed."

"So Victor's not real."

"We can only tell you what we've learned from years of knowing and watching the guy, Priscilla." Gail shrugged. "To me, he comes across as polished. Slick. Perfect suit. Perfect hair. Perfect home. Perfect..."

"Wife?" Priscilla asked.

"Exactly. And did you ever see Betty when she wasn't perfect? Her hair, makeup, clothes...she was already very well put together. But it never seemed to match her quiet, shy personality."

"Why are we speaking about her in the past tense?" Trudy asked. "It's scary."

"Sorry." Gail dabbed her lips with a napkin.

"We're all thinking it," Joan said. "Just not saying it. But you're right that she hasn't always been the typical politician's wife, Gail. I rarely saw her in public, now that you mention it."

"Exactly. Because, like most women, the interior doesn't match the exterior. Maybe she was afraid she would ruin his image once people realized how shy she was. Or maybe he kept her away from people so they wouldn't see the truth."

"Which is?" Priscilla asked.

"That he's a different man when the cameras are turned off. That the smile fades and the slogans disappear, and the real man emerges." A troubled look came over Gail as she spoke.

"You've been watching too many made-for-TV movies," Trudy said. "Sounds like they're starting to rub off on you."

"Maybe. But I do have a certain amount of discernment too, you know. I can tell things about people. Pick up on nuances."

"Not me." Trudy shook her head. "If an ax murderer smiled at me, I'd fall right into his trap. I'm always ready to believe the best about everyone, even the bad guys." She paused. "I guess that's how I get taken advantage of so often. I can't even be mean to telemarketers when they call. Trust me, that's how I end up spending money on things I don't need."

"Like makeup?" Gail asked.

Trudy's mouth fell open. "Bite your tongue."

The cousins dove into a conversation about telemarketers, but Priscilla only heard half of it. She couldn't stop thinking about Victor Fox's campaign. How could he go on as if nothing had happened, even though his wife was missing? Her thoughts shifted to the local police. Surely they had information on Betty's whereabouts by now. She would have to seek out April Brown at the Tisbury Police Department for a private chat. In the meantime, she had one more question.

When Trudy paused for breath, Priscilla took advantage of the moment. "Trudy, did you notice that Betty looked emotional that day on the ferry? I almost mentioned it at the time, but I thought perhaps she just wasn't feeling well."

"I noticed her eyes were swollen, but I figured it was from allergies."

Gail rubbed her nose with the back of her hand. "Yeah, allergies are terrible this time of year. I've been on a daytime antihistamine for weeks now."

"Me too," Joan added.

"I just thought it was odd that she didn't talk much," Priscilla explained. "It added to my suspicions that she'd been crying in her vehicle as we pulled onto the ferry. I never like to talk to people when I'm worked up, either."

Gail gave her a thoughtful look. "I have a hard time picturing you worked up, Priscilla. You're on an even keel all the time."

"Trust me, in the months after Gary's death, I was a mess. Ask my daughter. Rachel will tell you that I completely fell apart."

"As any woman would."

"I went through every emotion a person can feel. So yes, I understand being worked up. And I still say Betty had been crying."

"A man like Victor would give a woman plenty to cry about." Trudy nibbled on another french fry. "Just saying."

More speculation, of course. No one, as of yet, had proven that Victor was having an affair. Or mistreating his wife. Or running an aggressive campaign. All the chatter about him so far was just that—chatter.

But if Betty's red-rimmed eyes that day on the ferry were any indication, someone had given her plenty to be sad about. And Priscilla wouldn't stop until she knew who—and why.

CHAPTER TWELVE

After wrapping up lunch with her cousins, Priscilla happened to catch a glimpse of Tony McClaren across the crowd, talking with Teresa Claybrook. He looked Priscilla's way, then headed right for her. Uh-oh.

"Incoming politician," Trudy whispered. "I think he's coming to talk to you, Priscilla." She nudged Priscilla with an elbow and then winked.

Priscilla couldn't help herself. She pinched her eyes shut and then promptly opened them again. Yep, he was still there. And Teresa was following closely on his heels.

Tony greeted them with an authentic smile. "Ladies. Good afternoon."

"Hi, Tony." Trudy offered him a warm smile and scooted over so he could sit between her and Priscilla. "Join us."

Ugh.

Priscilla made room for him, and he squeezed into the spot. She had to admit he did smell good. That cologne he was wearing reminded her of something Gary tried once. It hadn't suited him, but on Tony it seemed like a match made in heaven.

"I've been sharing the good news about my new makeup line, Heavenly Faces," Trudy said. "We have a wonderful cleansing mask for both men and women. Would you be interested?"

"I—well…" Tony looked flustered.

Trudy began to describe the benefits of the mask, but Tony managed to shut her down in a hurry. "No, thanks. I'm still not sure why you ladies feel the need to wear makeup. Isn't the point of living on an island to be relaxed? Natural?"

Trudy shook her head. "Trust me, if you saw me 'natural,' you would run screaming from the room."

"I don't know about that. I think women have natural beauty and don't need the added enhancement." He turned his gaze to Priscilla, and she felt her cheeks grow hot. "Have you given any more thought to my proposition, Priscilla?" he asked, his eyes sparkling.

Priscilla's cheeks grew even warmer. "As I said earlier, ladies, Tony has asked me to help with his campaign, to bring in the women's vote. I've been giving it some thought. And praying, of course."

"I thought Priscilla would be perfect for the job." Teresa's smile looked a bit strained. Odd. Perhaps because no one thought to offer her a place to sit? Too late now. They couldn't squeeze in one more if they tried all day.

"The women do all admire you," Trudy said. "And you're a hard worker."

"See? Told you so." Tony offered a smile so warm, Priscilla almost found herself lost in it. "So what do you say? Want to help a guy out?"

Out of the corner of her eye, Priscilla saw Gerald O'Bannon approaching with his grandson, Max, who bounced up and down, clearly delighted with his surroundings. "What's going on over here?" Gerald asked. "Someone throw a party and forget to invite us?" His gaze shifted back and forth between Priscilla and Tony.

"Awkward," Trudy whispered.

This time Priscilla wished she could do the elbowing, but Tony was between her and Trudy. She turned her attention to Gerald. "Just talking politics. Want to join us?"

"No, thanks. Not my forte. I'd rather talk about ways to improve life on the island." His eyebrows elevated mischievously. "See what I did there?"

"I see." Tony did not look amused. "Well, think about it, anyway, Priscilla. I still think you're the right person for the job." He rose, gave them a nod, and headed off to talk to others in the crowd. Teresa took off after him.

Gerald looked at Priscilla. "Clearly, I interrupted. Sorry about that."

"No. On the contrary, you came just in the nick of time." She rose and stepped over the bench. "Can I join you and Max? Please? I need a diversion."

"Of course. We were headed to the ice cream truck. I promised this guy he could have a treat."

"Sounds good." She turned back to her cousins. "Do you gals mind?"

"Of course not." Gail gave her a warm smile. "Have fun."

Priscilla walked with Gerald toward the ice cream truck, his hand tightly clutched by his young grandson's. After a couple of moments of awkward silence, Gerald cleared his throat.

"I'm tempted to ask what Tony McClaren was referring to, but you'll notice I'm not asking."

"Yes, I can see you're not asking."

"And you're not telling."

More silence passed as she chose her next words. "He seems to think I can help sway female voters to choose him over Victor, so he has asked me to join the campaign."

"Ah. He handpicked you?" Gerald's jaw twitched. "I see how it is."

"He says I have discernment."

"You do. You're a very discerning woman."

"Would I be showing lack of discernment if I did help him out?"

"Not saying that. I'd rather see Tony win the election than Vainglorious Victor. I'm just fascinated that he set his sights on you."

"It's not like that, Gerald."

"Hmm."

Max pulled his hand loose and bolted ahead of them. Gerald took off after him. Seconds later, they stood in front of the Dribbles & Bits ice cream truck, the youngster bouncing up and down as he tried to pick out flavors. Priscilla did her best to put Gerald's concerns out of her mind. He clearly didn't like the idea of her working with Tony, but why?

Gerald ordered cookies and cream for Max, then chose chocolate for himself.

"What's your pleasure, ma'am?" he asked Priscilla.

"I've always been a fan of Rocky Road."

"One scoop or two?"

"One, please."

He turned back to the vendor. "One scoop of Rocky Road for the lady." He paused. "No, make it two. I'm trying to win the female vote."

Priscilla couldn't help but laugh.

When she got her ice cream cone, he gestured toward a nearby seating area. "Let's sit awhile, okay?"

"Sure."

Before they could take their seats, a couple of the local police officers happened by. Priscilla recognized one of them as police chief Hank Westin. With him was Officer April Brown.

April greeted Priscilla with a smile. "What did you think of the parade?"

"I loved it." Priscilla paused.

"But?"

"I was surprised to see Victor Fox in the parade. I would think..." Her words drifted off.

"I know, I know." April rolled her eyes and glanced toward Hank. "We were saying the same thing." She sniffled and reached into her pocket for a tissue. She blew her nose and sighed. "Sorry. I can't seem to shake this cold."

"Might be allergies," Priscilla suggested. She turned her attention back to the case. "I'm assuming you've already questioned Victor?"

April nodded. "Yes."

Hank cleared his throat. "And, as you know, that is confidential information."

"Of course. But there was obviously no reason for you to hold him, or he wouldn't be here today, shaking hands and kissing babies."

"Haven't seen him kiss any babies, but I get your point," Hank said. "And no, we had no reason to hold him. He wasn't on the ferry."

"He was in his office, working," April added. "And his last interaction with his wife—if what he's saying is true—was positive. So he seems flabbergasted."

"But not too flabbergasted to campaign."

"Right." April reached back into her pocket for the tissue, which she used to wipe her nose. "We're working on some other leads, though, so there's a lot to plow through."

"Other leads?" Priscilla licked her ice cream cone, which had started to drip in the late-morning sun. "You mean Carson Fletcher or someone else?"

"Carson Fletcher?" Hank glanced at April and then back at Priscilla. "Don't think I know that name. You have some reason to suspect a man named Carson Fletcher?"

"No, I—well... it's just an impression based on gossip, I suppose. So, Eliza Jamison, then?"

"We've spoken to Eliza," he said. "She's one of many we're chatting with."

Tony walked by. He gave Priscilla a wave and flashed a big smile. She returned the wave, then shifted her gaze back to April. "What were we saying?"

Gerald cleared his throat. "We were talking about suspects in Betty's disappearance."

Priscilla noticed that April and Hank seemed to be watching Tony closely. "Is he on your list?"

The police chief gave her a knowing look. "Now, Priscilla, you know I can't divulge that information."

"Well, I need to know for a particular reason."

"Tony has asked Priscilla to help with his campaign," Gerald said. "He's hand-selected her." Something about the way he said those words struck Priscilla in the heart. Was Gerald jealous?

"Hmm. I see." April looked at Priscilla, a thoughtful expression on her face. "This is just a suggestion, Priscilla, but do you think it's possible Tony is showing an interest in you because he's heard of your reputation and wants to persuade you of his sterling character?"

"An interest in me?" Priscilla's heart suddenly felt like lead. "Is that what you think? He just stopped by to ask for my help with his campaign, that's all. He wants a woman's point of view."

"Right." April did not look convinced, and something about the way she said the word made Priscilla nervous. And a little irritated.

"First of all, I haven't taken Tony's attentions to be anything other than business-related. Second, is he a suspect in this investigation, or am I missing something here?"

Creases formed between April's brows. She pulled Priscilla aside, away from the others, and lowered her voice. "Priscilla, he's Victor Fox's chief opponent. Victor's wife is missing. No one knows if she's dead or alive. There's been no ransom note, no evidence of foul play, but we still believe her disappearance is linked to this election. We don't want to leave any stones unturned, so of course we're looking at him."

"And what have you found?"

"We're not at liberty to say." April's gaze shifted to Tony, who had approached a table filled with locals. "This is an ongoing investigation."

"So you really think Tony might have kidnapped her—or arranged for her kidnapping—to cast his opponent in a bad light? If so, it might rebound on him. People might just give Victor the sympathy vote."

"Which is why we're also looking at Victor as a suspect," April said.

"Ah. So maybe he arranged all of this to draw attention to himself?"

"I'm just saying we're exhausting all possibilities, which means we're watching both men." April shifted her weight. "And just for the record, we know Tony was at your place yesterday. Thought you might want to know that."

"Gee, that's comforting. Great to know I'm being watched. Does that make me a suspect too?"

"Don't be silly, Priscilla." April cleared her throat. "We know you were with Mildred and Trudy that morning on the ferry. We've already talked with them."

"This is starting to feel less like a friendly conversation and more like an inquisition."

"Not at all." April's lips tipped up in a slight smile. "Hey, I see the draw. Tony's a handsome guy. And he is widowed, you know. Just saying."

"Why does everyone keep bringing that up?" Priscilla groaned. "Let me get this straight. You're suggesting I should start dating Tony McClaren because he's widowed and has beautiful eyes? Is that it?"

April's smile vanished. "Well, when you put it like that..."

"Because I'd say that a kidnapper or murderer—even a handsome one—wouldn't make a terrific soul mate."

"This conversation got complicated in a hurry." April's laughter came out a bit strained.

"I'd say." Priscilla squared her shoulders. "You've given me a lot to think about. If anyone believes, even for a moment, that I might be compromising this investigation in some way, I won't try to help Tony win the women's vote."

"On the contrary. I love the idea of you working with Tony. You can keep a close eye on him for us. It's win-win. And if he's innocent, all the better."

"Well, terrific. Now you want to use me to trap a kidnapper. Should I really try to help him win the election, or would that defeat the purpose?"

April sighed. "This conversation isn't going at all the way I pictured."

"Imagine how I feel." Priscilla felt something wet and gooey on her hand. She glanced down and realized she'd forgotten all about her ice cream, which had melted all over the place.

Gerald approached and handed her a napkin. "Here you go. Saw it happening. Didn't want to interrupt—again—but decided I'd better come to the rescue."

He was so good about sweeping in to her rescue these days, wasn't he? Yes, Gerald O'Bannon was a great guy.

And Tony McClaren?

Well, he was a handsome guy who might—or might not—be associated with Betty Fox's disappearance. And now, it appeared, she would be working with him to win an election. Wasn't that just peachy?

CHAPTER THIRTEEN

Priscilla didn't mean to spy on Eliza Jamison but simply couldn't help herself. When she saw Eliza walk out of a local bed-and-breakfast the following Monday morning, followed moments later by Victor Fox, she couldn't look away. Why had the two of them been in the B&B together? And where were they headed now, in separate cars?

Stranger still, why was Victor driving the white Suburban? Hadn't the police impounded it?

Priscilla eased out of the grocery store parking lot and into the lane behind Eliza's red Corvette. What sort of secretary drove a Corvette, anyway? Clerical workers didn't make that kind of money, did they? Not that it was any of Priscilla's business. But wasn't this the car Victor had used in the parade? Suspicious. Maybe he'd purchased it for Eliza as a gift. That would explain it. If that turned out to be the case, it cast further suspicion on them both.

Priscilla followed at a distance, hoping Eliza wouldn't notice her. The beat of a song coming through the radio distracted her, so she turned it down. Weird, how music could prove to be such an annoyance when she was hot on the trail of a suspect.

Was Eliza a suspect? She could be. She and Victor could be having a secret rendezvous to discuss what they'd done to Betty.

Priscilla reached for her cell phone to call April at the police department. Just to bring her up to speed, of course. The officer answered on the third ring with a brusque, "Hello?"

"Sorry to bother you," Priscilla said, "but I have some information that might prove interesting."

"What is th-th-that?" April released a loud sneezed followed by a sigh. "Sorry."

"I'm sorry you're still not feeling well. I just wanted you to know that Eliza Jamison and Victor Fox have been spotted together."

"Priscilla, they were spotted together two days ago at the parade. She was driving the car, remember?"

"Well, this is a much more compromising place I've spotted them at."

"And where's that?" The police officer turned her attention away from the call and started talking to someone in the room with her. She returned after a moment. "What were you saying?"

"They were coming out of a B&B just now and left in separate cars. And he's in the white Suburban Betty was driving that morning on the ferry. Only he's had the bumper fixed now. Don't you find that suspicious?"

"Suspicious that a man would have a dent in a bumper fixed?" April paused to blow her nose. "Not at all."

"Why didn't he have it fixed when his wife was driving the vehicle? Why now?"

"Priscilla, I have no idea. But it's not at all suspicious to me."

"You know Eliza was on the ferry that morning, right?"

"Of course we know."

"Oh, right." Priscilla paused and watched as both vehicles ahead of her turned into the parking lot at City Hall. "Looks like they're going back to work now. She's still with him. Well, in separate cars, but with him, otherwise."

"She's Victor's secretary, Priscilla. It makes sense she would be with him."

"At City Hall, sure. But at a B&B?"

"We suspect they have more than a working relationship. But even that doesn't point to kidnapping. Or murder."

"You think Betty was murdered?" This was certainly news to Priscilla. "What have you discovered?"

"Priscilla, stop. You know I can't share any more. We know that Betty went missing. We went over that Suburban with a fine-tooth comb."

"You checked under the floor mats?"

"Yes." April sneezed once more.

"And in the wheel wells?"

"Yes. There's nothing in that vehicle, Priscilla, other than the purse. And we found nothing suspicious in the purse."

"So Betty vanished into thin air. And Eliza—who looks really terrific in this cute outfit, by the way—just happened to be on the same ferry that morning."

"We're looking at everything, Priscilla. Now, let me go so I can do my job. It's what they p-p-pay me to—a-*choo*!"

"Right." Priscilla pulled into a parking spot and kept a watchful eye out for anything suspicious.

"People from Martha's Vineyard travel on that ferry every day," April added. "Nothing unusual about that."

"Unless one of them happens to be a kidnapper. Or murderer."

"I need to get back to work, Priscilla. Call if you happen to notice anything else. Oh, and let me know if you decide to help Tony with his campaign. I'm curious to see what he has up his sleeve. Your input will be helpful."

"Right, I will. And I hope you get to feeling better, April."

"Just a springtime cold. I'll live."

Priscilla decided to head to Tony's office right now. He worked in this same building, after all. Why not kill two birds with one stone? Visit Tony and swing by Victor's office.

Tony seemed thrilled to see her. Those gorgeous blue eyes of his sparkled as he received the news that she would be available to help with his campaign. "You're going to be a great asset, Priscilla." He took her hand and gave it a squeeze. "I really mean that. I'm especially keen on having you come up with new brochures we can hand out to the various women's organizations in town. Would you be interested in that?"

"Of course. I'll be happy to help."

"Again, I'm thrilled to have you on board."

She withdrew her hand. Something about Tony still seemed iffy to her, but if working for him would nudge the investigation forward, she was all for it.

As she left his office, Priscilla passed Victor's door. She opened the door and saw Eliza Jamison at the front desk. The pretty secretary looked up as she entered. "Can I help you?"

"Yes, I'd like to visit with Mr. Fox, please." What Priscilla would say when she saw him, she had no idea. But she would come up with something. Maybe she could ask him about the dent in the bumper. Let him know that she had seen his wife on the ferry. Offer encouragement. Tell him she was praying for Betty. She was, after all.

"Do you have an appointment?" Eliza's words jarred Priscilla back to the moment.

"Um, no. Sorry." Priscilla glanced over the secretary's shoulder and saw the computer screen—displaying someone's bank account.

Eliza quickly shifted the computer screen away and faced Priscilla. "He's not feeling very well this morning, I'm afraid. I'm not sure he's up to seeing anyone."

Interesting, in light of the fact that he'd spent the night at a B&B. He should be well rested.

"It's not really business-related," Priscilla explained. "I was hoping to speak with him about his wife's disappearance. I was on the ferry that morning and happened to be in the car behind hers."

"Do you have information about his wife that might be helpful?" Eliza's eyes widened. "Maybe you should go to the police. They're still gathering evidence, I believe."

Was it Priscilla's imagination, or did Eliza's hands begin to tremble as the word *wife* was spoken? "Not really information. I would just like to speak with him, if you don't mind."

"As you can imagine, Mr. Fox is very distressed right now."

Sure he was.

"The police have been coming and going, and filling him in on the details of their investigation. Until Mrs. Fox is safely home, Victor will have nothing to say to people outside the family. I'm sure you understand."

Interesting, that she switched from calling him Mr. Fox to calling him Victor.

"I understand he must be tormented right now, what with his wife being gone. But I have some questions—and perhaps some observations—that might be of interest to him, should he want to talk. I'll just leave you my phone number." Priscilla looked around for a piece of paper and noticed a stack of sticky notes. She pulled one off and scrambled in her purse for a pen. "He can call me any time. As I said, I was right there." After she scribbled her number, Priscilla looked up at Eliza. "But, of course, you already know that, since you were on board that day too. I believe we passed on the side deck, in fact."

"Yes." Eliza straightened the desk calendar, her fingers running across the various dates. "I was on the ferry." She shifted her gaze to Priscilla. "Headed to see my mother in Falmouth. Not that it matters, but that's where I was going. She's been battling cancer, and I want to spend all the time with her I can."

Priscilla softened at once. "I miss my mom terribly." A little sigh followed. "Enjoy your mother while you have her, Eliza. Don't let a day go by without letting her know how loved she is."

Eliza's shoulders slumped forward as she physically let her guard down. "Thank you for that reminder. I will enjoy every moment, though I hate seeing her in such pain. It's gut-wrenching."

"She needs you now more than ever."

"Right. I'm trying to put together a plan to help her now. She deserves the very best." Eliza walked to the front of the desk. Her expression didn't seem quite so cold. "I'll tell you what—I'll ask Mr. Fox if he might be willing to give you some time. No promises, though. And just so you know, he's in the lunch room at the back of the office, so it'll take me a few minutes. You might as well take a seat."

"I'll be right here waiting. Thanks again."

Eliza left the room to fetch Mr. Fox, and Priscilla eased her way around to the side of the desk to check her appearance in a mirror on the wall. As she did, she caught another glimpse of the computer screen, which Eliza had turned sideways. The bank statement displayed on the screen belonged to Betty Fox. And in it—lots and lots of money.

CHAPTER FOURTEEN

Unfortunately Priscilla never got to meet with Victor Fox. He was inexplicably called out of the office, or so she was told. On the following morning, she felt compelled to do a little research online. She called Mildred to see if she could utilize the museum's files, since they had access to ancestry sites and newspaper records from days gone by. Mildred agreed. An hour later, Priscilla was settled in at the curator's computer, browsing ancestry sites and trying to piece together some of her data.

"What are you thinking, Priscilla?" Mildred asked.

"Well, I realized that I don't know much about Victor Fox at all. I have no idea where he came from, what his life was like before. Do you?"

"He's been around a long time, but I honestly don't know his background, now that you mention it. He didn't grow up here. I do remember that, because the first time he ran for office, he ran against the guy who was my senior class president. That was kind of an issue between them, that Victor was an outsider."

"And still Victor won." Priscilla sighed. She couldn't figure out how he always managed to pull off a victory.

"For one thing, he's a member of several men's clubs around town. You know the kind—they're always doing great things for the community. He nudged himself up the ladder in several of those and won some of the men over. Then, of course, he started convincing them to back him for commissioner."

"I see. And they went along with it because he made a good leader?"

"I suspect he's strong-arming them, but not in the usual ways. From what I can gather, he's a master manipulator. He really takes the time to work on people's minds, to make them think he's the ideal candidate. And all of that schmoozing is working for him. People are falling into it and getting stuck."

"And that, my friend, is how you get elected." Priscilla sighed. "I've always hated politics. This certainly doesn't boost my confidence."

"Well, I don't hate the process and certainly believe we need good representation. Emphasis on the word *good*." Mildred smiled. "But there are often bad eggs in the bunch. Now, where were we?"

"Learning more about Victor's past." Priscilla continued searching the ancestry site and soon stumbled across something fascinating. "Look at this, Mildred." She pointed at the screen.

"What is it?"

"According to this file, Victor Fox was married in 1977."

"1977?" Mildred squinted. "That's over forty years ago."

"Right." Priscilla paused to think it through. "Have he and Betty been married that long? She doesn't seem old enough to make that a real possibility."

Mildred shook her head. "No. She's only in her early fifties now, if my guess is right. He's a bit older, though, obviously."

"So, a first wife, maybe?" Priscilla did a bit more digging and finally got the answer to her question. "Bingo. Wife's name was Jerilyn."

Mildred blinked. "Wow. I had no idea."

"According to this site, the marriage license was issued in the state of Pennsylvania."

"Did they divorce or something?" Mildred asked.

"I'm clueless, but I do see that he married Betty in 2001. The question is what happened to Jerilyn—and when."

"Here, let me help." Mildred shooed Priscilla out of the chair and took over. "Let's see if we can find divorce records for Victor Fox." Several minutes later, that search came up empty. "One more thing to try." Mildred went to work again, this time searching for a death record for Jerilyn Fox.

She found it right away.

"Wow." Priscilla leaned over her shoulder and read the information. "So she passed away in 1997, also in the state of Pennsylvania."

"Far away from Martha's Vineyard, which explains why none of us knew about her." Mildred continued to scroll. "I don't see any information about how she died, but I do see that they had children."

"Oh, wow. They did?" This certainly intrigued Priscilla.

"Mm-hmm."

"So we know that she died, but we don't know how. How do we find out something like that?" Priscilla asked.

"We go to a different source." Mildred scrolled through records of Pennsylvania newspapers from 1997. Unfortunately, her task was interrupted when a visitor entered the museum. "Sorry, Priscilla. I need to get back to work. I'm still on the clock. Keep looking, okay?"

"Will do." Priscilla took the seat once again and continued to enter Jerilyn Fox's name into search engines, this time in newspaper records. She was just about to give up when something came up. In fact, more than one thing. She found three separate articles—including one from a small-town newspaper where Jerilyn had grown up.

Priscilla could hardly believe what she was reading. Victor's wife had a story, but nothing like she might have imagined. In her mind, Jerilyn Fox had passed away from cancer or maybe a car accident. But like this? It certainly brought an added twist to an already complicated story.

Mildred entered the room a few seconds later and walked to the computer. "Find anything?"

"Did I ever. Mildred, look at this." Priscilla pointed at the screen. "Tell me what you think."

The museum curator skimmed the article, and her eyes widened. "Oh, my. Jerilyn slipped and fell in the shower?"

"Looks that way. In their home, according to this article. Broken neck. She passed away immediately."

Mildred reread the article. "I guess it's not all that suspicious, Priscilla. People slip and fall in the bathroom all the time. My elderly neighbor broke her right hip just two weeks ago trying to get out of the tub. It happens."

"Sure, it happens. To older people. To people with physical conditions. I just find it odd that wife number one died and wife number two disappeared. The first is only suspicious in light of the second, you know?"

"Definitely."

"I guess we have to figure out if it's just a coincidence or foul play."

Mildred pursed her lips and then released a sigh. "Sooner or later he's bound to give himself away. Don't you think?"

"I'm not so sure, to be perfectly honest. He's a skilled actor."

"How will we ever know if he killed his first wife?"

"I'll have to research her death."

"But how?"

"Not sure." Priscilla glanced at the clock on the wall and gasped. "I hate to do this, but I have to leave. I promised Tony McClaren I'd work at his campaign office this afternoon."

Mildred looked stunned by this news. "You're working for Tony now?"

"Volunteering, not a paid position." Even talking about it felt awkward.

Mildred's brows elevated mischievously. "Well, he is a handsome man. I can see the draw."

Priscilla flinched. "Why does everyone say that?"

"Say what?"

"That I'm spending time with him because he's handsome. He happens to be running against a man I would never vote for. I'm just throwing my support behind the better candidate."

"Who happens to have really great eyes," Mildred said. "Not that I've noticed."

"You sound like Trudy."

"Well, there's a first. I don't know that I've ever sounded like Trudy before." Mildred laughed.

"For what it's worth, Teresa Claybrook got me into this."

"Teresa? I'm surprised to hear that. She's had her eye on Tony for a while now."

"So I hear. But, for whatever reason, she convinced him I need to be helping out."

"She knows a good thing when she sees it. Seriously, Priscilla, you'll be great at this. You've earned the respect of so many women around the island in the short time you've been here. And sometimes"—Mildred paused—"sometimes it's good to get a fresh perspective. That's probably the main reason Teresa thought of you. You come at this from a fresh, new perspective."

"I suppose so." That explanation made sense, anyway.

Priscilla left the museum and headed to her car. Her cell phone rang, and she glanced down at the unfamiliar number. She answered with a hesitant, "Hello?"

"Priscilla, Tony here. I wondered if you would be interested in meeting me for lunch at the inn. Today is clam chowder day, and it's my favorite."

"Ah." She hesitated, not knowing what to say. "I thought I was supposed to be working at the office today."

"I decided it might be good to sit a while and just talk through some ideas Teresa and I came up with. How does that sound? Bring a notepad so you can take notes. We'll brainstorm ways for you to help. I'm sure we'll come up with a great many things."

"Sure. Will Teresa be joining us?"

"No, she's got other work to do at her office." He paused. "Have you eaten yet?"

"Well, I had breakfast a few hours ago, but clam chowder does sound good."

"Perfect. Want to meet me there, or should I swing by and pick you up? I'm fine, either way."

Swing by and pick her up? He was getting a little too familiar.

"I'll just meet you there, Tony." Priscilla tried to sound firm, but her voice quavered. "See you in a few minutes."

"Can't wait."

He sounded like he couldn't. Either he was genuinely excited about working with her, or he had something else up his sleeve. Did he know she was trying to figure out what had happened to Betty Fox? Was he overcompensating in some way after, say, kidnapping Betty? Priscilla's imagination went into overdrive as she pondered the possibilities.

Still, she headed to the Colonial Inn to meet Tony, as promised. April would want whatever information Priscilla could glean, and she would do it all with her shoulders squared. She walked into the restaurant and was greeted by the smell of seafood. Suddenly she could hardly wait to eat.

Tilly met her at the door. "Just one today?"

"No, I'm meeting someone."

"Gerald?" Tilly grabbed a couple of menus. "If so, he won't need one of these." She lifted the menus. "He's practically got it memorized."

"Not Gerald."

"Well, those cousins of yours have it memorized too." Tilly led the way toward the tables.

"Not one of the cousins."

Tilly turned to give her a curious look, but Priscilla found herself distracted by a woman seated at the first table. She stopped and smiled. "Eliza."

Victor's secretary looked up at her, eyes widening. "Oh, hello again."

"Great to see you."

"You too."

An awkward pause followed, and Tilly gestured toward a nearby table.

"Just leave the menus, if you will," Priscilla said. "I'll be there in a minute." She lingered at Eliza's table, working up her courage. "Do you mind if I ask something?"

Eliza shrugged. "Sure. Whatever."

Priscilla took the seat across from her so she could lower her voice. "I'm just curious how long you've worked for Mr. Fox."

"Since 1998."

"Ah. Did you know about his first wife?"

Eliza's eyes grew wide. "Know about her? Yes, of course. He came to the island right after she passed away. I started working for him when he was still mourning her loss."

"So you realized he was a widower, then?"

"Of course. But he and Betty got married two or three years later. Why do you ask?"

"It's just so sad. He lost one wife, and now he's lost another."

"Ah." Eliza's gaze shifted to the window, as if she found this conversation too much to handle. "Yes, very sad, I'd say."

"And so tragic how she went—falling in the shower like that."

Eliza faced her. "From what I understand, it really broke Victor's heart. I honestly believe her death was a trigger to make him, well, the man he is today. The hardest part was watching how he blamed himself. He was still going through that when I met him. He was very different back then from the man you see now."

"Better or worse?" Priscilla asked.

"Just different."

"But he blamed himself for his wife's death?" This certainly got Priscilla's attention. "Why?"

"From what he told me—and mind you, this was years ago— his wife Jerilyn struggled with chronic rheumatoid arthritis. She often battled to get around, due to joint pain."

"Oh, that's awful. I had a friend back in Kansas with RA."

"Yeah. It can be debilitating. Anyway, he was called away on business. The accident happened when he wasn't there to help her. Trust me when I say that he's blamed himself a thousand times."

"I didn't realize he was gone when the accident took place."

"Yes." Eliza shook her head. "Can you imagine hearing about your spouse's death while you're out of town and can't even be there for your children?"

"But the kids were home?"

"Sadly. That's how he found out. His daughter called him. From what I understand, they were all devastated. I don't know that the kids ever recovered, and I know Victor didn't." Her expression shifted. "As I said, it caused changes in his...personality." Judging from the expression on Eliza's face, she wanted to say more but didn't.

"Naturally." Priscilla paused. "Do the kids still live in Pennsylvania?"

Eliza's brow wrinkled. "How did you know he lived in Pennsylvania? Did I mention that?"

"Oh, I—well..." Priscilla drifted off. "I seem to remember something like that. Hasn't he talked about that in his campaign speeches?"

"To answer your question, both kids live in the Philadelphia area. Monica works at the Franklin Institute, and David is an accountant."

"Interesting. So neither went into politics." Priscilla paused. "Did Victor and Betty have children?"

"No. By the time they married, his kids were already in their teens. And she has a daughter from a previous marriage too, so maybe they just thought they had enough kids already. And like I said, he was never quite the same after he and Betty married. I—well..." Her words faded.

"She has a daughter? Would you happen to know her name?"

"Sure. Keeley. She used to live in Manhattan. She works as a designer of some sort. I don't really know the details. Sorry."

She'd just started to ask Eliza another question when the door opened, and Tony walked in.

"Ladies." He flashed a bright smile.

Eliza turned her attention to her menu. No doubt she felt awkward, meeting up with her boss's opponent. Priscilla thanked her for her time, then followed Tony to their booth. They settled in, and Tilly came by to take their order. Tony chose the clam chowder, and Priscilla opted for catfish. The conversation started out as campaign talk but morphed into a heart-to-heart about the woes of single life.

"I keep thinking about Rene," he said, his eyes taking on a faraway look.

Priscilla took a sip of her sweet tea and then asked the obvious question. "Your wife?"

"Yes. She would have loved every minute of this campaign. She was a social butterfly. Always loved being out around people. I dare say she would have had more fun campaigning than I'm having." He paused. "I'm not saying I'm not enjoying it. Just saying it would've been more fun if she could have walked this road with me."

"Of course. And I'm sure she would have been very proud of you, Tony."

"Yes, that's what I keep reminding myself. Every time I get in a funk or think I'm not making a difference, I just ask myself what

Rene would say." He laughed. "I knew her so well. She would have quoted that verse from Galatians: 'Let us not become weary in doing good, for at the proper time we will reap a harvest if we do not give up.'"

"Well then, there's your answer. Just keep plowing forward with Rene in mind."

"Trust me, that's exactly what I'm doing."

Still, he didn't look very encouraged. It sounded like Tony was feeling lonelier than he'd let on after the death of his wife. Hopefully Priscilla could get this conversation back on track before he fell down a well of despair.

She managed to shift the conversation back to campaigning. Before long, Tony was all smiles again and excited about the road ahead. Now, if only she could figure out some way to sneak out of here before somebody saw them and got the wrong idea.

CHAPTER FIFTEEN

The next morning, she rose early, dressed, and took Jake out for a longer-than-usual walk. The poor dog was long overdue for some time outside. He bounded ahead of her, headed for the pier to the west of her cottage.

"Slow down, boy. I'm not as young and spritely as I used to be." This was especially true in the mornings. Growing older wasn't for sissies. It seemed like everything took longer these days, even preparing herself for the day ahead.

Her thoughts shifted to Victor's first wife, Jerilyn. Struggling with RA could be grueling. This Priscilla knew firsthand, having walked her mother through it years ago. How awful, to struggle to get around. It was tough enough just going through the normal aches and pains associated with getting older.

Jake tugged on the leash and pulled ahead, his pace increasing. "Hold up, boy. I don't want to fall." She finally managed to slow him down as they reached the bend in the road. To her left, a beautiful home loomed, large and welcoming. The landscape drew her in, as always. She marveled at how so many of the homes, like this one, hugged the shore. Some, from just the right angle, almost looked as if they hovered over the water, magically rising from the depths.

A glance to Priscilla's right revealed a brilliant view of the harbor—complete with sailboats and other small fishing boats. Rib-
bons of early morning sunlight danced on the water, showing off
the vibrant colors. What a brilliant display of God's handiwork.
She wished she could spend a few quiet moments on the dock
with her legs hanging over the water below. In that quiet spot, she
would find time to reflect, to ponder life's complexities. To pray.

"Why not?" she said, though no one but Jake could hear.
"Want to walk on the pier, boy?" He yapped his answer. His wagging tail was all the convincing Priscilla needed. "Okay, then."

He bounded toward the water's edge, tail wagging.

"Careful, boy," she yelled. "Don't get—" She didn't have time
to add the word *wet* before he dove headlong into the reeds.

Oh, well. She'd just hose him down at the cottage. He deserved
a good time.

She made her way through the tall grasses to the edge of the
dock, then walked the length of it, finally sitting when she reached
the end. There, she pulled off her worn sandals and dangled her
toes in the chilly water, her gaze traveling to the various species of
waterfowl off in the distance—black ducks, bluebills, even Canada
geese. She watched them at play, her heart full as the morning sun
warmed her face.

Bliss.

The salty air wrapped her like a warm blanket. Funny how you
could practically taste the salt on the tip of your tongue. In all her
years as a Kansas farm wife, she'd never dreamed such a thing possible. Even on her visits to the island as a child, she hadn't noticed.

Now, though? Now she picked up on every nuance, savored each detail, much as one would study a butterfly emerging from its cocoon.

She pulled her phone out of her pocket and pulled up the Bible app, ready to spend some time in the Word before praying. The scripture of the day felt completely appropriate: *Finally, brothers and sisters, whatever is true, whatever is noble, whatever is right, whatever is pure, whatever is lovely, whatever is admirable—if anything is excellent or praiseworthy—think about such things.* She stared at the familiar verse from Philippians as if reading it for the first time.

Priscilla pondered those words at length, fully allowing her heart to be touched by the Lord. Then she began to pray—at first aloud, but then silently as the geese in the distance took to vocalizing. She lifted up her daughter, Rachel, and her cousins. Then she focused on Betty Fox. Her prayers increased in intensity as she interceded on her behalf.

Lord, I don't know if she's still alive or if someone has hurt her in some way. But, Father, I ask You to shelter her and give her peace, no matter where she is. Protect her from those who would do her harm.

Even as she thought the word *harm,* Priscilla's thoughts shifted to Victor. He was ruthless. This she had learned from watching him campaign. But had he done something to his wife? Had Eliza? Would "the other woman" get rid of her so she could have the man she loved? Stranger things had happened.

Priscilla thought back to her marriage to Gary. Things hadn't always been perfect, but they had settled into a routine, one that became familiar and comfortable. Sure, there were things she would have changed if she could. What marriage didn't offer opportunity to adapt? But thinking about Betty—wondering if her marriage to Victor was anything like he portrayed it on the billboards around town—made Priscilla grateful she'd had the real deal.

Not that she could prove Betty and Victor's marriage was troubled. Still, that annoying concern gripped her every time she saw a photograph of the two of them together. The sadness in Betty's eyes was palpable, the forced smile on Victor's face not quite believable. Something in those photos spoke of another reality, one hidden away from the public.

But what did that mean, exactly? Was Victor some sort of monster, capable of hurting his wife? Had he—like the husbands in made-for-TV movies—hired someone to do her in? Or was he genuinely missing her right now, wondering and worrying about where she was?

Priscilla's ponderings shifted to Carson Fletcher. There were still so many lingering questions about the stranger. Was he a reporter in search of a story, as Trudy suggested? If so, he had found one in Betty's disappearance. Did he have something to do with her disappearance somehow? Priscilla shivered, just thinking about it.

Finally, her thoughts turned to Tony McClaren. He seemed genuine enough. He was still hurting from the loss of his wife. Surely he hadn't played a role in doing away with his opponent's wife, not when his emotions were still so fragile. Right?

Before she could give it much thought, the phone rang. It startled her, and she nearly dropped it. When she finally got control of it, she noticed her daughter's number.

Priscilla answered with an exuberant, "Rachel!"

"Mom? How are you?"

"Fine. Hanging out at the pier. Just having my prayer time."

"Sounds great. Sorry to interrupt." Rachel paused. "So what's this I hear about you working on a political campaign?"

"Where did you hear that?" Priscilla shifted the phone to her other ear.

"I follow Trudy on Facebook. She posted something about how you and the cousins are all working for someone running for commissioner."

"Right. I'm helping put together brochures. We're trying to bring in the female voters."

"Wow, Mom. I'm impressed. I've always known you felt strongly about your political beliefs, but this is the first time I've seen you get involved like this."

Priscilla paused to think about her daughter's words. "Well, on the farm, we were just too busy. I didn't have the free time. These days—"

"You're free and easy?" Rachel laughed. "I'm looking forward to those days. You wouldn't believe how crazy things are at work right now." This led to a lengthy conversation about her job. Though Priscilla didn't have a clue about half the things Rachel referred to, she loved the lilt of her daughter's voice, the up and down movement as she shared the highs and lows related to her workplace.

When she'd run out of work-related things to talk about, Rachel shifted gears. "Hey, Trudy also posted something about a woman disappearing from the ferry. What's all that about?"

"Wife of a prominent politician."

"Whoa. Did someone push her overboard?"

"No idea."

"Maybe she was kidnapped or something. Stuff like that happens all the time. Innocent, unsuspecting women dragged into other people's cars. Could've happened like that."

"Right. The police are looking at every option."

"And you?"

"Me?"

"C'mon, Mom. I know you. According to Trudy, you were on that ferry when it happened. If I know you—and I do—you're already trying to figure this out. Am I right?"

Priscilla paused. "You're right. But don't worry. I'm not going to get in over my head."

"Isn't that what you said last time?" Rachel laughed. "But speaking of people getting in over their heads, Trudy is selling makeup now? Is that really true?"

"Oh, it's true. The products are really good, so I bought some."

"Just promise me you won't start selling them. If so, I'll feel compelled to buy some, and I really can't afford that right now."

"Trust me, I have too much on my plate to take on a sales job."

"And yet you had plenty of time to volunteer to help someone running for office." Rachel paused. "He's got nice eyes, by the way. I looked him up."

Priscilla groaned. Behind her, she heard the crunch of tires against gravel. She turned to discover a white Coast Guard SUV had pulled up to the curb. Seconds later, Gerald emerged. He gave her a little wave, then stepped onto the pier to join her.

"Rachel, I have to let you go. Gerald just got here."

"Does he know about this guy you're working for?"

"Of course."

"Okay, just curious. Love you, Mom. Talk to you later."

They ended the call just as Gerald approached. Priscilla started to stand, but he stopped her.

"Don't get up on my account."

She settled back down. "What brings you here this early in the morning?"

"I wanted to bring you up to speed on something." Gerald walked to the edge of the water and looked out over the harbor. "You know, this place always has a calming effect on me," he said after a few moments of peaceful silence. "It's left a lasting impression."

"Me too." She turned to look up at him and was unable to hide the smile that crept up as she saw the twinkle in his eyes. It turned out he hadn't been looking at the harbor at all but rather at her. Or had she just imagined that?

Her face warmed, and she turned back to face the water. "I do believe Martha's Vineyard has cast its spell on everyone, even me."

"I'm so glad you're here to stay." The edges of his lips turned up in a smile.

"Not everyone wants to stay on the island, though. Betty Fox didn't."

"You have reason to think she disappeared of her own accord?" Gerald looked surprised by this notion. "What makes you think that?"

"Oh, it's just one of the many thoughts tumbling through my brain this morning. I've been thinking a lot about how people aren't always who they claim to be. It boggles my mind to know that some folks carry on hidden lives—pretending to be one thing, but they're really someone altogether different." She paused, and her mind shifted back to Victor Fox. "It's just such a foreign concept to me."

"It should be a foreign concept to you, Priscilla. To all of us. We learn, as children, to trust. We're never taught to suspect others of being double-minded. Unfortunately, we have to learn those lessons the hard way."

"I guess. It stinks, though."

The air between them grew thick with silence.

"I'm starting to figure you out, Priscilla," Gerald said after a while.

"Oh?"

"You don't just get involved in these cases because you're drawn toward the mysterious. You get involved because you care about people." His smile grew bigger. "And that's an admirable trait, in my book."

"Thank you, Gerald. And yes, most of the time I just can't stop worrying about the people involved. Maybe I care about this situation with Betty because I feel there's more to her story than people know."

"I wouldn't be a bit surprised. Public persona and private reality are two completely different things."

"Yes. But based on personal observation and comments I've heard from others, she never seemed very happy." Priscilla paused. "You know what I mean? She didn't fit the mold of the typical politician's wife."

Gerald shrugged. "Look at the presidents and their wives. Several haven't fit the mold, either."

"Maybe that's the problem," Priscilla countered. "We get this idea in our heads that someone in the public eye has to be beautiful. Or social. Or engaging. And then along comes someone who is none of those things."

"I think Betty Fox is nice-looking."

"Oh, I didn't mean that. I think she's lovely. I just mean that she's not the sort to host a soiree or campaign publicly. She's a very quiet person."

"A recluse, even," he observed. "That's my take on her."

"Which makes me wonder if she finally just snapped and ran away from home." Priscilla shrugged. "Which leads me to something else that's been bothering me."

"What's that?"

"I caught a glimpse of Betty's bank account."

"What? How?"

"Eliza Jamison, of all people, had it up on her computer when I stopped in Victor Fox's office. It was a local account, and nothing seemed terribly strange about it—other than the fact that Eliza was looking at it—but I have this niggling concern that I'm over-looking something."

"Like what?"

"I wish I knew. Maybe she was secretly socking away every penny her husband gave her for groceries or gas into that account, knowing she'd one day bolt. Some women do that, you know. They save up until they have what they need to start a new life. There was a lot of money in that account, Gerald."

"Yes, but you just said that Eliza had access to that account, which means Victor did too. I'm not saying that's unusual. Secretaries, especially ones like Eliza, who have training in account-ing, often help the boss's family with their personal finances."

"Yeah. My dad's secretary doubled as our family's CPA every year," Priscilla concurred. "She was really good."

"Right." Gerald nodded. "I would venture a guess that Eliza was simply checking that account to see if there had been any activity on it. In fact, I'd be willing to bet the police have checked that account too. If any monies have been removed, then Betty's out there somewhere, tapping into it. If the account hasn't been touched, then there's a greater chance of foul play. See?"

"Of course." That made perfect sense. All of her concerns washed away as she thought it through. "Gerald, thank you for helping me. I've had so much internal wrangling over that bank account, you have no idea. I just wish I could've taken a closer look at it to know if there have been any withdrawals. It would ease my mind to know she's still out there. I've had this weird theory that she simply skipped town. But trust me, I have plenty of other ideas that contradict that one."

"So do the police. That's why I stopped by, to update you on one of the people they've been interviewing."

"Who is that?"

"Carson Fletcher. And I think you're going to be glad you're sitting down when you hear what I have to share."

CHAPTER SIXTEEN

"Carson Fletcher?" Priscilla motioned for Gerald to sit beside her. "What about him?"

"I know why he's on the island."

"Is he a reporter after all?"

"Nope. Not even close."

There went that theory. Trudy would be disappointed.

"I happened upon him at the Colonial Inn while having lunch," Gerald said, "and the next thing you know, he was spilling his story. Did you know he has a daughter who lives here?"

"Wait...what? He does have family on the island? That contradicts what I've been told."

"He does. His daughter is in her midtwenties. She works on the island. It turns out Carson didn't even know he had a daughter until a couple of years back, when an old girlfriend reached out to let him know."

"Then why is all this top secret? If he came to the island to meet her, why wouldn't he let people know that?"

"From what he explained, her mother is a prominent business owner."

"What sort of business?" Priscilla asked, more curious than ever.

"Shop owner, I think. Well-known in the community. So broaching the subject was difficult for her, I guess."

Priscilla paused as the realization set in. "Oh, I see. The gossip."

"Exactly. From what I can gather, her husband raised the little girl as his own. So no one knew the truth, that the child had a different father from her younger siblings."

"Crazy."

"The police still haven't fully absolved him, though. Hank told me that Carson didn't purchase a ticket to board the ferry that day."

"Did you ask Carson about that?"

"No. I didn't want to interrupt a perfectly friendly conversation to poke my nose into his business. Didn't seem appropriate."

"Right. I see your point."

"Anyway, there's no record of an online account for him, so we know he didn't get his ticket in advance."

"But I saw him with my own eyes."

"Yes, and there's footage of him on board as well. The whole thing is baffling."

"Wow. So he was on the ferry, but without a ticket. And he has a daughter on the island." Priscilla paused. "What about the girl's mother? What do you know about her—other than the fact that she's a business owner, I mean."

"I think she's more embarrassed than anything. No one knew she had a child before she married. She left her past behind when she came to the Vineyard. And you know how people on the island are about their images."

"Squeaky clean. But we're already seeing with Victor Fox that not everyone—or everything—is as it seems."

"People like to put their best foot forward," Gerald said. "We see what people want us to see and no more. They don't let us in to the icky stuff. No pictures with moles or warts or double chins."

"It's even more exaggerated these days with social media," Priscilla added.

"True, but as a rule, folks have always cared about impressing others. That started long before social media even existed. Husbands and wives always wanted to make their marriages look perfect, even before they were able to capture their date nights in photos to be posted online."

"Things are worse now, though, you have to admit, so I guess I can see why Carson's ex-girlfriend was too afraid to let others know about her past."

"Agreed."

"Things are definitely more exaggerated in the twenty-first century. If a husband brings the wife roses, she posts a picture and sings his praises." She paused. "For the life of me, I can't remember the last time anyone brought me roses."

"But if someone did, you'd post a picture of them?"

"Yep. And I'd probably break down and cry too."

"Which just proves my point. We share the things that bring joy and the moments that are flattering to those we love. That's how life is, whether we like it or not. Maybe we're all just in denial. Maybe we don't like to admit that life is riddled with flaws, imperfections. That relationships are hard. That kids go astray. That our bodies change over time."

Priscilla sighed. "In happier news, the new makeup I'm using helps with that. They have a great toning and tightening line."

"Whatever that means. My point is, when we brag about how great our lives are—when we pretend to be flawless—maybe we're really trying to convince ourselves that it's true."

"Only, of course, it's not."

"Our situations might not be as complicated as Victor and Betty's, but we've all got dirty linen hidden away."

She thought about the foundation she'd just purchased from Heavenly Faces, how it covered imperfections. When she really thought about it, that was what folks did every day. They slathered on foundation and covered up the imperfections so that people could only see what they wanted them to see. Nothing more, nothing less.

"I'm not saying we should air our dirty laundry," Gerald continued. "But every now and again, we should do a few reality checks. Maybe a day without makeup, something like that."

"Bite your tongue."

"Or maybe a photo of the kitchen after baking. Something that shows the reality of our lives—the imperfections."

"Okay, fine. You go first." She jabbed him with her elbow.

"I might," he said. "I might take a picture of myself first thing in the morning, before I shave. Wouldn't that be something?"

"I'm sure you look fine in the morning."

"It's clear you do." His gaze lingered on her for a long moment until she felt uncomfortable.

"Well, I should probably get back inside. I've got some work to do today."

"Work?"

"Yes." She nodded. "I'm helping Tony McClaren with his campaign. Coming up with ideas to draw in the female vote."

"I don't even want to go there. I wouldn't know where to start."

"Well, I'm going to start on the Internet. Going to do some research. But I'm a little nervous about what I might find if I start researching the topic of women voters. There are some radical women out there with far different views from my own."

"Yes. Just glean what you can and toss the rest. You'll do great, Priscilla. You always do."

She lost herself in his warm smile, and the flattery felt nice too. In fact, she felt so good about it that going inside the house to work suddenly didn't feel important at all.

CHAPTER SEVENTEEN

Friday morning, Priscilla agreed to meet Gail and Uncle Hugh for breakfast at the historic inn. She decided to head into town a little earlier than they had planned. She could have a cup of coffee before her cousin and uncle arrived. She might even have two.

Priscilla entered the restaurant and gave Tilly a nod.

"Back so soon?" her friend asked.

"Yes. Meeting Gail and Uncle Hugh this time."

"I'll put you in a booth near the window."

"Thanks." Priscilla settled in and ordered her coffee. Gail wasn't set to arrive for another twenty minutes, but Priscilla wanted to use this time to plan the rest of her day.

Unfortunately, someone else had other ideas.

When the words, "Well, good morning!" sounded to her right, she looked up to discover Tony had joined her. Great.

"You coming into the office today?" He brushed a piece of lint off the lapel of his perfectly pressed suit. "I want to go over the text you wrote for the brochures."

"Sure. I'll come in."

"Great. Teresa and I both loved what you wrote. We just want to add a line or two and then figure out how to merge the text with the graphics. I really feel like having you there is making a difference." He gazed at her with disconcerting intensity.

Thank goodness Tilly approached to take their orders. She gave Priscilla a curious look. In fact, her gaze traveled back and forth between Tony and Priscilla so many times that the whole thing began to feel rather uncomfortable. Not that Tony appeared to notice.

"I'll have a hungry man breakfast with toast. Over-easy on the eggs, if you don't mind." He gave Tilly a warm smile.

"Got it. What would you like, Priscilla?"

"Yes, go ahead, Priscilla," Tony said. "Breakfast is on me. Consider it a thank-you for all you've done for me."

Priscilla wanted to cover her face with the menu. No doubt her cheeks were as red as the bottled ketchup at the end of the table. Instead, she released a calculated breath and smiled. "Thank you. I think I will. I hope Gail and Uncle Hugh won't think I'm rude for ordering before they get here, but I'm starving."

"I wouldn't think they would care," Tony said.

"Great, because my stomach is growling. I'm in the mood for an omelet." She faced Tilly. "Ham and cheese, please. With onions."

"Sure you want to go for the onions?" Tilly gestured to Tony with her eyes.

"I want the onions. And more coffee, please. Just keep it flowing."

"Omelet with onions. Coffee. Any toast?"

"No, thanks."

Before Tilly could step away, Tony was already talking business. Well, for the first minute or two, anyway. Afterward, he
shifted gears and started talking about his home, which—according to him—was on the outskirts of Vineyard Haven. Priscilla had
never been there before, so she couldn't quite keep up as he
described the beautiful scenery around his home and the deck that
ran along the backside of his house.

"You've got to come and see it, Priscilla. I've got the best view on
the island." He paused and then gave her a tender glance. "Next to
your place, of course. Misty Harbor beats every other spot on the
island for its views. I wouldn't mind coming over for another look,
in fact."

Oh my. Was he fishing for an invitation? Unwilling to allow
the conversation to shift in that direction, Priscilla went back to
talking about the campaign.

"Here's what I've decided you should do to garner the votes of
more women."

"What's that?"

"Women don't like to be sold on anything. Period. Don't get
all salesman-like when you give speeches."

"Got it. No sales."

Her thoughts shifted back to her most recent conversation
with Gerald, about how people always tried too hard to appear
perfect. "And for pity's sake, admit your flaws. I'm not saying you
need to share all of them publicly, but don't come across as
perfect."

"Trust me, I'm the furthest thing from perfect." He seemed to lose himself in his thoughts, and Priscilla found herself wondering what he was fretting over.

Tilly arrived with Tony's coffee cup, which she placed on the table and then filled. "If you want my vote," she said, "then tell me how you plan to deal with traffic issues during tourist season. It gets crazy in the summertime."

"Okay. So, kill the salesman, don't appear perfect, and fix the traffic problems. Got it." A boyish grin followed. "Anything else, ladies?"

"Yes." Tilly's eyes narrowed to slits. When someone asks you a direct question, don't dance all around it and dodge answering it. I hate it when politicians do that."

"Be direct. No dodging, no spin." He chuckled.

Priscilla found herself relaxing. In spite of her earlier reservations about Tony, he seemed to be a good man. Surely he would be a better commissioner than Victor Fox.

A couple of minutes later, Gail arrived with Uncle Hugh at her side. She took one look at Tony McClaren, and her eyes widened.

"What is this, a party?" Uncle Hugh grumbled. "I thought we were having breakfast with Priscilla."

"We are, Pop." Gail glanced at the table, which was filled with plates from Tony's big breakfast.

"It's okay. I'm almost done, anyway." Tony took a few more bites and then rose. "Gotta get back to the office. Lots to do.

See you later, Priscilla." He offered a warm smile and then took off toward the cash register to pay their bill.

"Well, that was interesting." Uncle Hugh slid into the spot where Tony had been sitting. He glanced down at the uneaten toast and picked up a piece. "Mmm. Just how I like it. Crispy." He took a bite.

Gail slid into the spot next to her father. She didn't say a word, but Priscilla could sense the questions running through her cousin's mind.

Priscilla managed to turn the conversation away from Tony McClaren and onto the weather. Before long, they were all gabbing about the goings-on on the island. Relief flooded over Priscilla.

Just as they finished up their meal, Gerald showed up. "Sorry to interrupt."

"No interruption." Priscilla smiled, happy to see him. "What's up?"

Gerald gestured to the spot next to Priscilla. "Do you mind? I have something I need to share that might interest you."

"Sure. Have a seat."

He sat, and she nudged herself farther down the bench. "I just wanted to let you know that my daughter's friend is a Realtor. She happened to mention that Carson Fletcher rented an office space from her."

"Rented an office?" Gail's eyes widened. "So he's planning to stay?"

"Sounds like it. The Realtor said something about an investment firm."

Uncle Hugh snorted. "Hey, at least it's not a restaurant. Tilly would flip if Vineyard Haven added another eating establishment. She's already fuming at that new seafood place near the ferry landing."

"Trudy will be disappointed to hear that he's not a reporter," Gail said.

"I meant to tell her the other day," Priscilla said. "It completely slipped my mind."

"So you've known, Priscilla?" Gail's eyes narrowed to slits.

"Yes, he's got quite a story, in fact. He's got a daughter here on the island."

"Wow, that's certainly news."

"Having a daughter is news?" Uncle Hugh snorted again. "I should get a headline in the paper, then. I've had one for..." He paused. "How old are you again, Gail?"

"Pop." She elbowed him. "Don't go there."

Uncle Hugh shrugged and took another bite of toast.

"There's more to Carson's story." Gerald gestured for Tilly, and she arrived with a cup of steaming coffee. "He's apparently got money, according to my friend. So all of those speculations about him being a drifter are definitely false. He wasn't hanging around to beg for coins on the street corner. He's well-off."

"Wow." Gail shook her head. "Was I ever wrong about him, then."

"It just goes to show, you can't judge a book by its cover," Priscilla said. "We were wrong on every count. He's got family on the island, and he's a businessman, not a reporter."

"Shame," Uncle Hugh said. "If he was a reporter, he could do a write-up about me having a daughter. We could be a front-page story."

Gail groaned.

"From what I gather, he was looking for a place to set up shop for some time," Gerald explained.

Priscilla found this fascinating. "But why wander around like a drifter?"

"He wasn't wandering around," Gerald explained. "He was just helping out in various places."

"So he wasn't stealing merchandise?" Gail asked. "There goes another of Trudy's theories. Maybe she's not such a great sleuth after all."

"Let's leave the sleuthing to Priscilla, shall we?" Uncle Hugh took another bite of Tony's toast, then leaned back.

"There was another story going around that Carson was serving as caretaker on someone's houseboat," Gerald added. "It turns out he owns that houseboat. He plans to stay there through the summer."

"Wow." Priscilla was dumbfounded by all of this.

"Yes." He took a swig of his coffee. "It didn't take much research to figure out that Carson is prominent back in Naples, Florida. He's kind of a big deal in his town, especially known for his generosity with folks in need."

"I'm just floored by this." Priscilla couldn't get over it, in fact.

"Me too. But there's more. His wife passed away a year ago from breast cancer. From what I read online—one can learn a lot from obituaries—she passed very quickly. Anyway, there were no children listed among her survivors." Gerald leaned back against the seat and took another drink of his coffee.

"Wow. So finding out he had a daughter here must have been the blessing of a lifetime for Carson."

"No doubt."

The conversation shifted to the upcoming election, but Priscilla couldn't stop thinking about Carson. As it turned out, her first instincts about him had been wrong. Dead wrong.

Or were they? In spite of Gerald's news, she still had persistent doubts. There was more to Carson's story, and she was determined to figure it out.

CHAPTER EIGHTEEN

Priscilla worked hard to put together a plan to help Tony reach out to female voters. By Tuesday morning, she'd created the perfect brochures—just the right colors, approach, and wording. If this didn't sway the ladies of Martha's Vineyard to vote for Tony, nothing would. And it didn't hurt that she'd put a picture of him— with those gorgeous blue eyes—front and center.

Now, to figure out how and where to distribute them. Door-to-door canvassing would be a good idea, but she would have to leave that to other campaign workers with more time on their hands. In the meantime, she dropped off several hundred brochures at Tony's campaign headquarters, then took off toward Candy Lane Confectionery to leave several there, stopping only to fill her tank with gas at a local station on the way.

As Priscilla drove down the narrow, winding road toward the bakery, she found herself captivated once again by the beauty around her. The whole island was springing to life, each day more beautiful than the last. The vibrant green leaves on the various trees hung over the road like a canopy.

In her rearview mirror, she noticed a sports car, a snazzy blue number. It must be nice to have that kind of money. She slowed and put on her signal as she approached the road leading to the bakery. The sports car followed closely and turned when she did. With all the suspicions in her head, the idea of being this closely followed made her nervous.

"Don't be silly, Priscilla," she said to herself. "Who's getting paranoid now?"

She approached another turn and glanced at the mirror to make sure the car didn't follow her this time.

It did.

Hmm.

She stayed on the road until the turnoff to the bakery. As she pulled into the parking lot, Priscilla was relieved to see the sports car zoom on by. So much for letting her nerves get the best of her.

She parked her vehicle, got out, and walked inside Candy Lane's, carrying the brochures.

Hovering in the air over her was the luscious smell of coffee, mingled with cinnamon and sugar from the various pastries. The bakery case lit the senses with its colorful goods—muffins, cookies, cupcakes topped with sprinkles and chocolate drizzle—and so much more. *Mmm.* She loved coming here, especially when fresh baked goods were just coming out of the oven.

Priscilla looked around the crowded room, her gaze finally landing on Candy, who stood behind the counter near the coffeepots. Perfect. Now to ask if she could leave the brochures. Surely Candy wouldn't mind.

Priscilla approached the counter and greeted her friend with a happy, "Hello."

Candy looked up and grinned. "Long time no see."

"I know. I've been really busy."

"Yes, I heard you were helping out with McClaren's campaign."

"Who told you that?"

"Trudy, of course. I hope you're not mad at me for giving Tony your name. He was looking for someone to help, and you seemed like the perfect candidate."

"I don't know about that, but I've done my best." Priscilla gestured to the stack of brochures she was carrying. "Can I leave these here for folks to pick up?"

"I guess." Candy picked up a brochure and looked it over. "You designed these?"

"I did. I'm helping him come up with ways to reach out to female voters."

"Putting his photo on the front was the best way." Candy paused, and her gaze lingered on the picture. "Those eyes."

"Yes, I know."

"They're enough of a draw." Candy smiled. "But don't tell Beau I said that. He has a bit of a jealous streak." She took the brochures and walked over to a small desk near the door, where she placed them for patrons to take. Then she turned back to Priscilla. "And he's certainly the more likeable candidate, as we've established. But this morning's article in the *Vineyard Gazette* did take me by surprise. Had me questioning him, even."

"Article in the *Gazette*?"

"Yes. Henry Braswell interviewed him. I take it you haven't seen the paper, then?"

"Not this morning."

"Henry asked him specifically about Betty Fox's disappearance, and Tony alluded to troubles in the Fox marriage."

"Oh, I see. I'm a little surprised by that. He's done a great job of staying out of it, at least publicly."

"I was surprised too." Creases formed between Candy's brows. "His words certainly cast a bad light on Victor, that's for sure. He painted him as a rogue. A cheater. Said he wouldn't trust the fellow in a room alone with any woman on the island."

"Whoa. Strong words. I mean, folks are probably all thinking that, but to come out and say it? Bold."

"I thought so too. But people are taking him seriously, especially in light of the fact that Betty Fox has been gone for two weeks." Candy paused. "The whole thing is very strange, don't you think?"

"I do. Trust me. I've spent way too much time already trying to figure it out, but I keep coming up empty. Plenty of suspects, but I can't get a handle on which one might be responsible."

Candy leaned in close, lowering her voice as she spoke. "I noticed Eliza Jamison with him that day at the parade."

"In the red Corvette?"

"Yeah. She's his biggest advocate. You rarely see one without the other."

"Could you say the same thing about his wife?"

Candy looked perplexed. "What do you mean?"

"Were they together a lot? Was she his biggest advocate? Did people see them as a team? I haven't been on the island long enough to get to know her, but you know everyone, Candy. You would've noticed if something was amiss. I know you."

"To be honest with you, if not for Victor's billboards, I'd barely be able to pull together an image in my mind of what Betty Fox looks like. I saw her so rarely. She never came in here, that I can recall. Now that you mention it, I do find that rather strange. She was the wife of a prominent politician who made the rounds to every business."

"Ugh. We're speaking about her in past tense again." Priscilla sighed. "I keep doing that."

"It's all just so strange. Women don't just disappear off of ferries every day."

"I just wish I'd known her better, is all. Then maybe I'd be in a better place to speculate. I still feel pretty new to the island."

"Not that new." Candy gave her a smile so warm it lifted Priscilla's spirits immediately. "I'd say you're a permanent fixture around here."

"Permanent, eh? Hoping I'll stick around?"

Candy's expression shifted, the smile fading. "You're not thinking about leaving, are you?"

"No, no." Priscilla laughed. "I'm not going anywhere."

"Well, good." The sparkle returned to Candy's eyes. "Because I, for one, would be devastated if you took off."

"Like Betty did."

Candy leaned in close. "You think she ran away from home?"

Priscilla shrugged. "I wish I knew." Through the window, she caught a glimpse of a blue sports car driving by. A familiar blue sports car. The same one that had followed her to the bakery.

"Something catch your eye?" Candy leaned toward the window and peered out.

"Yes." Priscilla watched as the car disappeared around a curve in the road. Then she turned to face her friend. "Do you ever get the feeling that someone is watching you?"

"Yeah, every day. Customers by the hundreds. But that's a good thing, I guess."

"No, I mean, do you ever get that eerie feeling that someone's tracking you?"

"Are you being serious or kidding around?"

"Completely serious. That sports car was right behind me as I drove here. It made me nervous."

"You're sure they're following you? Maybe they're just lost." Candy paused. "Or maybe they heard how great my cranberry scones are and wanted to find my bakery. Could be something that simple."

"Those scones are pretty remarkable." Priscilla smiled. "Speaking of which..."

"Yep. Just pulled some from the oven a few minutes ago. You hungry?"

"No, but that's never stopped me before." Priscilla laughed and followed Candy to the bakery counter to purchase one of the yummy cranberry scones. She'd just paid for her treat when the door to the bakery swung open, and Trudy and Joan entered. They made straight for the counter, deep in conversation.

"Well, hello, Priscilla." Trudy smiled the moment she saw her. "I see you're wearing your new Heavenly Faces blusher. It's perfect for your facial structure."

"I love it, thanks."

"And the eye makeup is lovely too, though I think you went a bit too light with the liner."

Priscilla shook her head. "I'm not one for heavy eyeliner. As you've probably noticed, I don't spend a lot of time fussing with makeup."

"Ooh, you don't know what you're missing. If you'll just reconsider and join me as a distributor for Heavenly Faces, I'll make a cosmetics lover out of you yet."

"No thanks, Trudy."

"Yeah, I know." Her cousin put a hand up in the air. "You're far too busy these days helping *Tony McClaren* with his campaign."

"Time for a change of subject." Joan reached inside her purse and pulled out a five-dollar bill. "We just stopped in for one of Candy's new cupcakes. It's cookie butter flavored, and I hear it's divine."

"Cookie butter? What's that?"

Candy looked up from her spot behind the counter. "Oh, you know, Priscilla. Cookie butter. It's mashed up Speculoos cookies in a buttery texture. Kind of like peanut butter, but not. They sell it on the peanut butter aisle, though. On a whim, I added some to my brown sugar cupcakes, and the result was fabulous. I put some in the butter cream too. It's perfect."

"I'd never heard of it until today," Trudy interjected. "Joan's been rambling on about it all morning long. I like my cookies in a package, not from a jar."

Candy laughed. "So say you now, but that's just because you haven't tasted cookie butter yet. It's got this yummy warm spicy flavor—a little nutmeg, lots of cinnamon, even a hint of clove."

"Okay, okay!" Trudy reached inside her purse for her wallet. "You've totally won me over. A cookie butter cupcake it is."

"Make that two," Joan added.

Candy pulled a couple of cupcakes out of the case and set them on small plates. "They're best with a cup of chai tea. Just saying."

Priscilla fought the temptation to buy one. Though it sounded delicious, she'd rather eat her cranberry scone.

"Well, we might as well sit awhile and visit," Joan said. "Unless you've got someplace to be, Priscilla."

"Nope. No place at all." She gestured to a table near the counter, and they all sat down to enjoy their treats.

No sooner had they done so than the door to the bakery opened, and Eliza Jamison walked in.

CHAPTER NINETEEN

I think one of your suspects just walked in the room, Priscilla," Trudy whispered, her gaze riveted to the bakery door.

"*My* suspects?" Priscilla shook her head. "I'm not a cop."

"But you're putting together a list of people who might be linked to Betty Fox's disappearance, right?" Trudy gestured with her head toward the door, where Eliza Jamison stood.

"Welcome to Candy Lane Confectionery!" Candy's voice rang out from behind the counter.

"Thank you." Eliza spoke to Candy, but her gaze shot to Priscilla. She gave her a quick nod as she passed by.

"She looks as nervous as a long-tailed cat in a room full of rocking chairs," Trudy whispered. "Don't you think?"

Joan shot a warning look Trudy's way. *"Shh."*

Priscilla did have to admit that Eliza looked a bit unnerved. Priscilla did her best to veer the conversation in a different direction, though she watched out of the corner of her eye as Eliza ordered a cupcake and took a seat by herself at a corner table.

"I hate eating by myself in public places." Joan's words came out low and filled with compassion. "It's so uncomfortable. And I get a little lonely."

Priscilla shrugged. "It bothered me more in the first year after Gary passed away, but I'm getting used to it now."

Trudy took a bite of her cupcake. "I have to tell you ladies that I've been converted. This cookie butter frosting is truly one of the most delicious things I've ever put in my mouth. If I could smear it on every food item I eat today, I'd be a happy woman."

"Agreed." Joan took a taste of hers. "I think I have a new favorite." She glanced Priscilla's way. "Want a bite?" She held up her plate.

"Maybe a little one." Priscilla took her fork, pressed it into Joan's cupcake, and took a bite. "Wow." The combination of sweetness and spice was just right. "Next time I'll order that." She glanced Eliza's way just as the secretary lifted a cupcake to her lips. "Looks like Eliza's enjoying it too."

"What's not to love?" Trudy took another bite. "But watch yourself, Priscilla. Before long, you're going to be besties with all of your suspects."

"What do you mean?" Priscilla took a sip of water and leaned back in her chair.

"You're already cozying up to Tony McClaren, and I don't think he's been cleared yet, right?" Trudy gave her a playful wink. "Not saying I blame you. He's *GQ* material, that one."

"Trudy. I've gone over this with you before. I'm just helping him with his campaign." Priscilla gestured toward the desk near the door. "If you don't believe me, check out the brochures I brought in. Take a few to hand out to the ladies in your Bible study."

"I'm just teasing you, Priscilla. Don't take it so hard. But after that article in the *Gazette*, I'm not sure the ladies will vote for him, anyway. He was kind of hard on Victor."

"Since when have you cared about anyone being hard on Victor Fox?" Joan looked perplexed by the very idea.

"Just saying. He wasn't very nice, and the ladies in my Bible study like nice." Trudy took another bite. "I thought Priscilla might want to know what people are saying about her man, now that this newspaper article has come out."

"Her man?" Joan looked at Trudy and then Priscilla. "What am I missing here?"

"Absolutely nothing." Priscilla wanted to say a few more things to Trudy, to explain that her relationship with Tony was purely business, but decided not to go there. She knew her cousin was mostly teasing, and this would only escalate if she continued to fan the flames. Instead, Priscilla opted to shift the conversation once again, this time to the weather.

When they finished their sweets, Joan brushed crumbs from her lap. "Sorry, ladies, but I have to roll. I've got a fitness class at the gym."

"And I've got a Heavenly Faces party at Tilly's house tonight," Trudy said. "She's going to end up being my best distributor yet." She shot a glance at Priscilla. "Unless you change your mind and decide to join us. Once this sleuthing is behind you, I mean."

Priscilla shook her head. "I can see myself as a great many things, but beauty consultant is not one of them." She dabbed her lips with her napkin. "It was great hanging out with you ladies. I need to get home. Jake is probably itching to get out."

They said their goodbyes, and Priscilla made a pit stop at the ladies' room before heading out to the parking lot. By the time she got to her car, her cousins were long gone. She was supposed to go back to the campaign office, but after hearing about the article in the *Gazette*, she felt hesitant. Was Tony up to no good? Had he planted that story on purpose, to cast Victor in a negative light?

Eliza walked out of the bakery and headed to her red Corvette, which happened to be parked next to Priscilla's vehicle. Eliza glanced her way, a nervous expression on her face. Priscilla offered a wave, and Eliza took a few steps in her direction.

"I saw you in there, sitting with your cousins. I . . . well, I was alone. Seems to be happening a lot lately."

A wave of guilt washed over Priscilla. She and her cousins had been talking about Eliza, sharing their thoughts about her possible role in Betty's disappearance. Never once had it occurred to her to invite Eliza to join them.

"I've had a hard time reaching out to people lately," Eliza explained. "It's almost like I'm being shunned or something."

"I—I'm sorry, Eliza."

She wrung her hands, then looked Priscilla directly in the eye. "Can I ask a favor?"

"Sure."

"Would you come and sit in my car for a minute so we can talk? I would feel safer there."

"I—I guess so. I was going to head back to Tony's campaign off—" She stopped short. "Anyway, I have time. No problem." She walked around Eliza's sports car and got in on the passenger side. As she settled in, she found herself mesmerized by this amazing, expensive vehicle. How had the humble secretary afforded such luxury?

Eliza got in the driver's seat and set her purse aside. Her hands trembled as she rested them on the steering wheel. "Priscilla, I'm terrified to tell you this, but I feel like I can trust you."

"You can trust me, Eliza." *Then again, if what you're about to tell me is evidence, it might be used against you. Just saying.*

"People have the wrong idea about Victor and me." She turned to face Priscilla, and Priscilla noticed tears in her eyes.

"Oh?"

"You wouldn't believe me, Priscilla, but there are actually people out there who think that Victor and I are...well, a couple." She shivered, and her eyes clouded over. "As if I could, for even a minute, look at that man as anything other than what—or who— he is."

Okay, this certainly wasn't what Priscilla had expected, and it seemed to contradict Eliza's description of Victor that day at his office.

"People think I would be interested in a man like that? They don't know me at all. And they certainly don't know him. No woman—not even his own wife—could stand to be around him for long. He suffocates people."

"Wow." Priscilla paused. "I must admit, I'd heard the rumors about the two of you."

"And believed them to be true?" Eliza sniffled. "Folks have done a bang-up job of spreading the word. And I suppose that's why I'm shunned. People must think I'm trying to replace his wife. I'm not, I assure you. That's the last thing I'd want to do."

"I don't really know you or Victor well enough to judge. I'm just saying I'd heard the rumors, is all."

"You can wash them right out of your mind. They're completely false."

"Good to know." Priscilla wondered about so many things, but one in particular. "So about that day on the ferry..."

"Please don't tell me you suspect me of somehow hurting Betty. I've already been questioned by the police."

"No, not really. I mean, the idea crossed my mind, but it only flitted through. It didn't linger for long."

"I was going to see my mother, as I said. Mom has been so sick. And I had no idea Betty would be on that same ferry, but when I saw the Suburban, I knew it was providential."

"What was providential?"

Tears sprang to cover Eliza's lashes. "I finally had an opportunity to talk to her apart from Victor. He couldn't control the situation."

"What do you mean?"

"I needed her to know that what she'd heard about us wasn't true. It was never true. You have to believe me. I couldn't have an affair with Victor Fox, even if he wasn't married. He's the last man on the planet I'd get involved with, trust me. I've done my best to keep his image perfect, just like he's forced me to do, but I'm reaching the breaking point. I just can't do it anymore."

"But..." Priscilla wanted to say something about seeing Eliza's car at the B&B, but she didn't know how to broach the subject.

"I looked for her on the ferry that day but didn't see her in the snack bar. I walked around the deck but didn't see her there, either. It was so strange. I watched her get out of her car, but she disappeared into the crowd, and it was almost as if she just vanished."

"*Suspicious* is more the word I had in mind."

"Yes, I guess so. And the police seem to think I had something to do with it. If only they knew the truth."

"Which is?"

"That I wanted to tell Betty I understood her plight, that I was sick and tired of her husband trying to manipulate and control me, just as he'd done to her all these years."

"Manipulate and control you?"

Eliza burst into tears. She couldn't seem to get control of herself. When she was finally able to speak, her words came out in gasps. "I—I—I just couldn't t-take it anymore, Priscilla. It started so innocently, but over the years Victor has given me no privacy at all, no opportunity to make decisions for myself... nothing. I'm a puppet, and he's the string-puller. It became obvious to me that he was doing the same thing to her. And I was so afraid she would never escape. I was afraid of the same thing myself."

Priscilla felt her breath catch in her throat. "So, forgive me, but I have to ask."

"Ask what?"

"On Wednesday of last week, I happened to be driving by the B&B as you pulled out."

"Yes?"

"And Victor pulled out right behind you."

"Right." Eliza's eyes grew wide, and she clamped a hand over her mouth. "Oh, Priscilla. You thought..."

"Well, you were coming out of a B&B at the same time."

Eliza began weeping once again. Priscilla wondered how—or if—she would ever get things calmed down to continue the conversation.

CHAPTER TWENTY

Eliza finally paused for breath. She wiped her eyes, leaving a streak of mascara on her upper cheek.

"I can see why you might have assumed that—why anyone might assume that—but I assure you, my reason for being at the B&B that morning had nothing to do with Victor whatsoever. In fact, I was really angry when he showed up, which is why I stormed out. If you were watching, you probably noticed that I was in a hurry."

"I did notice. That's the same day I stopped by your office to see about meeting with him."

"Oh, right." Eliza paused and then shook her head. "I was at the B&B because I was trying to figure out a long-term care solution for my mom."

"What?"

"I told you she has cancer, right?"

"You did."

"She's about to be placed on hospice. They're willing to come to her home, but she lives in Falmouth. I can't get to Falmouth every day. And she can't move in with me, because I live in a small duplex with bedrooms on the second floor. She can't navigate stairs, and the living room is too small for a bed. So I got to thinking about Anna's place. The B&B has beautiful rooms, and they're not terribly expensive. I've known the owners for years. In fact, the owners know my mom too. Anna's mom was my mom's roommate in college."

"Wow, small world."

"Right. I thought maybe she would give me a monthly rate that would be cheaper than a nursing home. Mama could stay in a room that felt like home and have all of her meals prepared while hospice came and went. I could keep my job and..."

"And still see her every day, overseeing her care."

"Yes." Eliza brushed away tears. "That's it."

"So why did Victor show up at the B&B? Just to check up on you?"

Eliza groaned. "He called me while I was meeting with Anna. Said he wanted me to come into the office early to type up a new campaign speech. I told him that I would be in the office at the usual time, but he wouldn't take no for an answer. Apparently, he tracked my phone to the B&B. He was happy to find me there, but trust me when I say it had nothing to do with romance or intrigue. He was collecting on a debt."

"A debt?"

"Anna had been strong-armed into promising a donation to the campaign, but she changed her mind when Betty went missing. Victor was keen to pay her a visit to smooth things over. And he thought—strange as it might sound—that if I was there, she might be more inclined to give."

"And was she?"

"Yes." Eliza sighed. "I honestly don't know how he does it, but Victor can squeeze blood out of a turnip. He manages to get money from anyone who glances his way. It's an art form, trust me. I didn't get that money-making gene."

"Me either. My sales abilities are sadly lacking, and I'm fine with that. But let's go back to the part where you said he tracked your phone."

"Right. It's so stupid, I know. He has this app on all of our phones—mine, his, Betty's—that helps him track where the other person is at all times. It's like I'm always being watched. I hate it."

"Can't you turn the app off?"

"The phone is on his account. They all are."

"So if his wife went missing and has her phone with her..."

"That's just it. She didn't take her phone." Eliza's eyes grew wide. "It's sitting on her bedside table. I know because he told me. This is just one more reason I'm convinced she felt threatened by him."

"Makes sense."

"Priscilla, in some bizarre way, I think he loves her. That's why he keeps such tight reins on her. Every aspect of her life is under the lens of his microscope." Eliza shuddered. "But living like that is awful, I assure you. I'm sure what I've gone through is nothing in comparison to what Betty has faced all these years. And there's something else he does, but I'm afraid you won't believe me. Maybe I really am going crazy."

"What do you mean?"

"Every once in a while Victor does this thing where he'll deny saying something he said, or something will disappear, and he'll say it was never there in the first place. He really messes with my head. He tells me I imagine things that never happened or never existed."

Priscilla was horrified. "That's terrible! How can he get away with that?"

"So you believe me? You don't think I"m crazy?"

"Not at all." Priscilla shook her head. "It's just so hard to believe someone could be that cruel."

"Just one more question," Priscilla asked after a moment's pause. "Did you have your phone with you on the ferry that day?"

"Yes, but I didn't care if Victor knew where I was going. He's known about my mom for weeks now. I decided to talk to Betty because we might never be in a situation like that again—both of us alone and away from him. Does that make sense?"

"Of course. But you never got to talk to her."

"No, I lost my courage and headed back to my car. I didn't even realize she'd gone missing until later on. My car was ahead of hers in line, you see. I just drove off the ferry and went straight to my mom's place to check on her. I didn't have a clue until I started getting text messages from Victor an hour or so later. It shook him up that she took off like that. Like I said, he kept close tabs on her."

"Do you think there's any chance he knew what happened and just acted like he didn't? In other words, do you suspect he had something to do with her disappearance, Eliza? Did Victor Fox hire someone to kidnap or even kill his wife? If so, why?"

Eliza's eyes widened. "He's a horrible man, Priscilla, but even I—the person who knows him best, outside of Betty—would be stunned to hear he was capable of that. I'm not saying he didn't. Anything is possible. But I can't think of a motive."

"With people who are manipulative and controlling, getting to the motive can be a lot tougher."

"True."

"This is off the subject, but I couldn't help but notice Betty's bank account was open on your screen that day I came into the office."

Eliza's eyes widened. "Victor would flip if he knew you saw that. Ugh."

"I didn't mean to snoop." She paused. "Or maybe I did. I was just wondering if she had tapped into that account since she went missing."

"We've checked it every single day, as per the police's instructions. That's why it was open. That particular morning, I thought I saw a transaction, but it ended up being an automatic debit for her car insurance. So, no. Nothing. She hasn't used her debit card or any of her credit cards, either."

"Which leads us to believe the worst." Priscilla sighed. "I think I've been holding out hope that she would turn up."

"You and me both." Eliza shuddered. "You don't know how badly I wish I'd intervened in some way."

"Do you really think it would've made any difference if you had spoken to her that day, Eliza?"

"That's the million-dollar question, I suppose." Eliza released a slow breath. "I'm glad I didn't say 'million dollars' in front of Victor. He'd be hitting me up for a donation. And heaven knows

I've got nothing to give." She sighed. "Look, I wish I didn't have to work for him. But I need the income to take care of Mom. Such a conundrum, I tell you. But most things in life are, aren't they? Nothing's easy, to my way of thinking."

"You're right about that." Priscilla opened her door. "I'm glad we had this little chat. You've opened my eyes to much, Eliza. And best of all, I'm glad we've spoken, because you seem like the sort of person I could be friends with. Once all this election stuff is behind us, let's have lunch."

"Thank you." Eliza's eyes brimmed with tears once more. "I would like that. Very much."

Priscilla's heart suddenly ached for her. She rested her hand on Eliza's arm. "I really appreciate you, Eliza. Thank you for opening up. And just for the record, I think the B&B is a great idea for your mom."

"Me too."

"Just promise me one thing. Start looking for another job."

Eliza shrugged. "If Victor loses the election, I'll be out of a job, anyway."

"True. But be looking now. You never know where God might take you. Maybe He's got a fresh start for you. You know?"

"I do." She nodded. "And thank you for that encouragement, Priscilla. I appreciate it more than you know."

"Don't give up." Priscilla gave her new friend a compassionate smile. "There's always hope as long as your fishing line is in the water."

"What?"

Priscilla laughed. "Oh, sorry. That's just something my husband used to say. He was always coming up with things like that."

"I think I like it." Eliza's lips curled up in a half-smile. "And just for the record, I'm keeping my line in the water. Surely there's a great catch out there somewhere."

"Yep. He's out there all right." Even as she spoke the words, Priscilla wondered if they might be true for her someday as well. Not that she had time to think about such things, not with the investigation zigging and zagging all over the place. Right now, she just needed to stay focused on the task at hand.

She eased out of the passenger seat, heart filled to overflowing for her new friend. As she got out of the car, Priscilla thought of one more question. It was probably none of her business, but one little thing had been bothering her, and she wanted to get to the bottom of it.

"This car, Eliza…" She swept her fingers along the passenger side door. "It's really something."

"It's fabulous, isn't it?" Eliza got out of the car and brushed her hand over its top. Her eyes filled with fresh tears. "It was my brother's."

"Your brother's?"

"Yes. He passed away two years ago. He was my only sibling. This car was his pride and joy. It's old and needs constant repair, but I keep it because it's the only piece of him I have left. I know it's odd, but I've fallen in love with these older model sports cars. It's probably psychological. I'm fascinated by them because I know my brother was. It's a way to keep him alive, I guess."

"Oh no. I'm so sorry to hear that. You've been through so much."

"I have." Eliza sighed. "Mom was diagnosed with cancer less than a year after he passed. If I didn't know any better, I would say the grief opened her up to the cancer. That probably doesn't make sense, though."

"I don't know. Our bodies do seem to respond to stress differently. How did he die?"

"He was a police officer in Boston. He was working a scene and things got...complicated. He was trying to save a woman and a little girl from an abusive husband, and ended up right in the middle of their..." She couldn't seem to finish the sentence.

"He died trying to save someone else." Priscilla paused and wondered what advice Eliza's brother would have given her, had he known she was in a twisted relationship with her boss.

"The whole thing is just so ironic," she said after a couple of moments' silence. "Betty and I are seen as rivals for the same man, when the truth is that we're actually allies, just trying to stay alive. Emotionally, I mean. I've never seen Victor become physically violent."

"Strange to me, that he could be verbally abusive but not physically."

Eliza shrugged. "Thank God. That's all I have to say. Thank God. It's bad enough to be called terrible names and to hear the kind of language he uses." She shivered. "The first time it happened, I thought I was having an out-of-body experience. I'd never had anyone talk to me like that. And then the controlling started. I'm sure it's nothing in comparison to what he's doing to Betty, but

I'm always at such a loss to know what to do to help her. I can't even seem to help myself."

"I'm going to suggest something, Eliza, and I hope you don't take it the wrong way."

"What's that?"

"That day I was in your office, I happened to notice a therapist just down the hall a bit."

"You think I need therapy?" Her eyes narrowed.

"I think we all need therapy, to be honest. It helps to have someone to talk to. After my husband died I met with the pastor of our church. Sometimes I think it helps to see a neutral party, someone outside of the situation, to get a balanced perspective. You've been through quite a shaking with Victor. In many ways, you're as traumatized as his wife. So why not go ahead and see someone who can help you let go of whatever pain he's caused so you can be free to move forward?"

"You're a wise woman, Priscilla."

"I'm just as likely to do something goofy as to make wise choices, but at least I try. There's something to be said for that."

"It will be hard to open up and share some of these things I've kept locked up inside of me."

"You've done a pretty good job of sharing with me." Priscilla shrugged. "It's a start."

"Well, you're easy to talk to." Eliza gave her an admiring look. "Maybe you should've been a therapist, Priscilla."

Priscilla laughed. "That's so funny. Gary used to tell me all the time that I dished out advice too freely. Maybe I just missed my calling." She paused and gave her new friend a compassionate look. "Just take care of yourself, Eliza. That's all I'm saying. You're the only you there is."

"I will. I'm a lot like this old car, Priscilla—in need of restoring."

"Good thing God's in the restoration business, then." Priscilla crossed behind the car and gave Eliza a warm hug.

Standing there, with her arms wrapped around a woman who, only hours ago, had been a chief suspect, Priscilla had to admit the truth: God truly was in the business of restoring lives, and she couldn't wait to see what He would do with this one. No doubt Eliza Jamison would come through this a brand-new woman.

CHAPTER TWENTY-ONE

On the morning after her one-on-one visit with Eliza Jamison, Priscilla awoke to a quiet solitude. Well, until Jake realized she was awake and started a yap-fest. Apparently he wanted to go outside. She slipped on her robe and made her way to the door.

Once outside, Priscilla noticed the newspaper at the end of her driveway. She pulled the robe a bit tighter, just in case anyone happened by, and ventured out to pick up the paper. What she wouldn't give to have a dog who could fetch the paper right about now.

Thank goodness, no one passed by. She retrieved the newspaper and called the dog back inside, where she whipped up some pancakes and sausage. These days she rarely troubled herself with such hearty morning meals, but pancakes sounded good.

Once she settled into her chair, Priscilla opened the paper. She gasped as she read the headline: *McClaren Moves Ahead in Polls*.

She scanned the article, which was written by a local female reporter. According to the article, women around the island had their sights on a new commissioner, one who resonated with their views.

Perhaps that brochure had done the trick, after all. Or maybe it had more to do with the article. Had Tony's comments about Victor turned voters against the other man?

For a few moments, Priscilla lost herself to her thoughts. Maybe it had something to do with the smell of pancakes and maple syrup, but her thoughts drifted back to Wheatfield. How comfortable and familiar the farmhouse had felt. To live in the same home for so many years. Not everyone had that blessing. How many pancake breakfasts had she fixed for Gary and Rachel? How many sweet conversations had they shared over a breakfast like the one she'd just eaten—alone?

Kansas held a piece of her heart, even now. Some days it tugged at her, encouraging her to return to her roots. Other days it drifted through her memories, a place of the distant past, not the hopeful present. This was one of those mornings, thanks to a plateful of pancakes.

Oh, but she wouldn't trade her current life, would she? Martha's Vineyard had won her over with its weathered buildings and winding roads, with its coastal views and delicious breezes. Most of all, she'd fallen in love with the water, that sparkling masterpiece. Sometimes the sunlight hit the water with such intensity that she found herself blinded by a dazzling light display. Other times the tranquility served to calm her troubled nerves and remind her of the scripture, "Peace, be still."

And how wonderful to have gained so many new friendships. She wouldn't trade one of them, not for all the wheat fields in Kansas. Folks in Martha's Vineyard had welcomed her. And, on some level, they seemed to need her as much as she needed them.

In the middle of her ponderings, Priscilla's cell phone rang. She glanced at it, not at all surprised to see Tony's number.

"You did it!" he said, the moment she answered. "You've worked your magic, Priscilla."

"I don't really think it had much to do with my brochures, Tony."

"Sure it did. And the women of Vineyard Haven have decided they're not going to let Victor Fox bully them into voting for him any longer. I'm proud of them. And you."

"Thank you. Happy to be of service."

"Are you coming into the office today? I was hoping you could help me update the website."

"I don't know, Tony. I have a lot to do around here." She glanced around her living room. "I never finished with my spring cleaning."

"Come if you can. No pressure, though. Just know how much I appreciate you, Priscilla. Thanks for everything."

"You're welcome."

She ended the call and leaned back against the sofa, her thoughts in a whirl. Victor was falling behind in the polls. That was a good thing. She decided a meeting of the minds was in order, so she called her cousins and Mildred. They all agreed to gather at the museum at ten o'clock.

When she arrived, Priscilla quickly filled the others in on her conversation with Eliza. The ladies listened in silence, but she could tell they were stunned by the information.

"So, let me get this straight." Mildred rose and paced the room. "Victor wasn't just bad to his wife, he's controlling Eliza too?"

"Yes."

"And they aren't having an affair?" Trudy asked.

"Eliza denies it, and judging from the fear in her voice, I have to say I believe her." Priscilla leaned back in her chair. "To make matters worse, Victor was tracking both ladies through their phones."

"Huh?" Trudy shook her head. "I'm not tech-savvy, so you're going to have to explain that one to me."

"Most phones have a 'find my phone' feature," Priscilla explained. "What lots of people don't realize is this—that feature can be used to track someone's whereabouts at all times. Easier than putting a tracking device on a car, because these days most people take their phones with them everywhere they go."

"True. I always do," Mildred said.

"So he did know she was on the ferry that day?"

"Eliza said she left her phone at home, but here's why I suspect he still knew. I think Victor had a tracking device on her Suburban. That's probably why he never let her take it in to have the bumper fixed while she was driving it. Maybe he was worried the mechanic would find it and tell her. The minute she went missing, he removed the device and got the bumper fixed. I'm speculating here, but I believe this is a real possibility. I've checked out those devices online, and they're so easy to buy and install."

"Kind of like a GPS?" Mildred asked. "I have a subscription service on my car. I call in for directions, and they guide me. I think they can track my whereabouts, wherever I go."

"Yes, it is a GPS. But while those services are handy, according to what I read online, this one was the sort you would use to keep track of someone's whereabouts. One guy commented online that he put one on his teenage son's car to make sure he wasn't going places he shouldn't."

"Wow. You'd have to really mistrust someone to stoop that low. Right?" Trudy sipped her drink. "I mean, it's a clear invasion of privacy."

"In some cases, sure. One woman commented that she used it on her elderly mother's car because she was starting to show signs of memory loss but didn't want to admit it. It was a good way to make sure Mama didn't go missing."

"I can almost see keeping tabs on an unruly teenager," Mildred said, "or a senior citizen with memory loss. But who in the world would put such a thing on an ordinary housewife's car?" She leaned back against the seat and pondered the notion. "Just the idea that someone might be tracking me gives me the creeps."

"He wasn't only tracking them. He was gaslighting them."

"Gaslighting?" Joan's brow wrinkled. "What's that?"

"Wasn't there a movie with that word in it?" Gail asked.

"Yes." Mildred snapped her fingers. "*Gaslight.* Made way back in the '40s. Ingrid Bergman. Great movie."

"I still don't know what the word means, though, Priscilla," Joan threw in. "You'll have to enlighten us."

"After talking to Eliza, I did a lot of research online. I kept coming across this word: gaslighting. It's a technique that abusers use to make their victims think they're going insane."

Trudy's eyes widened. "Do tell."

"Basically, the abuser will manipulate things around the victim so the person can't believe her own eyes or ears anymore. For instance, in the movie, the wife sees the gaslights in the bedroom dim, but the husband tells her she's imagining it, when all the while he's the one making it happen."

"So gaslighters are men?" Joan asked.

"No, they can be women too, but in this case Victor was the one controlling and manipulating. Based on what I learned from Eliza, I'd be very surprised if Victor wasn't doing this to Betty as well as Eliza."

"This sounds pretty extreme, Priscilla." Joan looked as if she couldn't quite fathom such a notion. "I mean, Victor's a jerk. A hypocrite. But an abuser?"

Priscilla nodded. "I know it sounds extreme. But it would explain why Betty was such a recluse. Not only did he control her movements, he probably had her convinced that she was losing her grip on reality."

"I guess the puzzle pieces are starting to fit," Trudy said. "But it's so frightening."

"So sad, but it does make sense." Mildred sighed. "It is rather strange that someone who's married to a man in the public eye rarely attended social events, never showed up at women's meetings at church, never got close to any of the ladies in town. It's almost as if—"

"She wasn't allowed to?" Trudy's brows furrowed. "Gosh, I always just thought she was standoffish. I never dreamed she might be a victim."

Priscilla scooted her chair back. "Mildred, can I use your computer?"

"Of course."

Priscilla moved to the computer and browsed the Web until she found an article that might prove helpful. "Just look at this, okay? And try to picture Betty Fox through the lens of this information."

Joan read aloud from the article. As the various qualities of abusers were voiced aloud, the other women began to look more and more concerned.

"Whoa," Mildred said.

"It makes perfect sense," Trudy echoed.

"I think that article is a match for this situation," Joan said, when she finished reading. "He's a narcissist, for sure."

"Yeah, he only ever talks about himself," Gail agreed.

"And in the third person too." Trudy squared her shoulders and spoke in a deep, manly voice: "'A vote for Victor is a vote for Victory for the Vineyard!'" Her shoulders slumped forward, and she went back to her normal voice. "I have never understood why politicians talk about themselves in third person. Kind of creepy, now that I think of it."

Priscilla nodded. "Agreed. But in this case, I believe it's because he sees himself as an entity—more than just a human."

"Ooh, like a god-man?" Trudy asked.

"I don't know that I would've phrased it like that, but yes. Narcissists think they're above others, that only their opinions, their plans matter. They think everyone should go along with them, no matter what."

Trudy snorted. "Then half the men I've ever met are narcissists."

"No, they're just men. A true narcissist completely overpowers the woman in his life. And she gets so used to being subjected that she learns to go along with him no matter what."

"Until she snaps and dives off the edge of a ferry into the Vineyard Sound." Trudy's eyes widened. "Ooh, is that what you think happened, Priscilla? Did Betty do away with herself to escape, once and for all?"

"I don't know. The ferry's cameras didn't catch anything. And I can't be sure she was running from him, though everything points to it."

Trudy snapped her fingers. "Maybe he *suspected* she was about to bolt, so he arranged to kill her once she did. If he couldn't have her, no one could—that sort of thing."

"This is getting really creepy." Joan shivered. "Can't we just go back to thinking the guy is a jerk? A hypocrite? That was enough to make me walk on the other side of the road as he went by. The rest of this is just freaking me out."

Priscilla had to admit the whole thing was creepy. But seeing Betty Fox as the victim of domestic abuse certainly gave her a lot more to go on. There was one more topic she wanted to cover with her cousins before they parted ways, but she didn't know quite how to broach the subject.

She started with the words, "I've been thinking about Tony a lot."

"Right." Trudy laughed. "That's obvious."

Priscilla shook her head, wishing she'd phrased things differently. "Not like that."

"Really? 'Cause I know plenty of women who do think of him like that, but he hasn't reciprocated those feelings as he's done for you." Trudy crossed her arms and gave Priscilla a knowing look.

"I think he's just confused. But I've settled the issue once and for all—he had nothing to do with Betty's disappearance. He's too overwhelmed with the campaign."

"True."

"But the most random idea entered my head. You'll laugh when I tell you."

"No, please do." This time it was Gail who spoke. "Your instincts are usually spot-on, Priscilla."

"I've noticed that Teresa would do anything to get Tony elected."

"She would," Trudy agreed, then her eyes widened. "Do you think she . . . " She clamped a hand over her mouth, then pulled it away. "Our own Teresa?"

"I told you, it was just a random thought. But doesn't it seem odd to you that she cares so much about him winning?"

"I think she cares about him. Period." Joan shrugged.

"But would she go to such lengths to see him win? To sabotage the opposition, I mean?" Trudy paused to think it through. "It doesn't make much sense. She wasn't even on the ferry, right? And the police haven't brought her in for questioning."

"That I know of." Priscilla pursed her lips. "When you're looking for clues, anyone and everyone is a suspect."

"Hey, just because I happened to be on the ferry doesn't mean I'm a suspect." Trudy put her hands up in the air. "Don't arrest me, officer. I'm innocent!"

They all had a good laugh. "That'll be the day, Trudy, when I point fingers at you." Priscilla gave her cousin a hug. "If they ever threw you in jail, who would keep us entertained?"

"Who, indeed?" Trudy said with a wink. "Who, indeed?"

CHAPTER TWENTY-TWO

That day Priscilla did little but work with Tony at the campaign office. Teresa came and went. Except for the way she hovered around Tony, nothing about her seemed suspicious. Then again, they were all swamped with work, especially during the final week before the election. Priscilla barely had time for a conversation with friends or relatives. So when she received a phone call on Friday morning from Trudy letting her know that Tilly Snyder had been hospitalized, she jumped up and ran.

"Everything okay?" Tony asked as she bounded from her chair at his campaign office.

"No. It's Tilly. She's been taken by ambulance to the hospital. I need to go. It must be really bad. Trudy was in tears."

"I'm coming with you." Tony's words were comforting. Firm. "In fact, I'm driving you there. You're in no shape to go by yourself."

Before she could say no, Priscilla found herself in the passenger seat of Tony's car.

"Any idea what's wrong with her?" he asked as he rounded the corner toward the hospital.

"Trudy said something about her breathing. I guess she's struggling to breathe."

"Is Tilly asthmatic?"

"Not that I know of. But to be honest, Trudy was crying so hard, I could barely make out what she was saying. I know there's some sort of upper respiratory thing going around. April can't seem to shake it."

"We'll pray, then." And that's exactly what he did. While driving. Tony poured out his heart to the Lord in a prayer filled with passion. Priscilla was somewhat astounded at his boldness. She hadn't seen this side of him before. When he finished, she managed a quiet thank-you, her heart twisting.

When they got to the emergency room entrance, Tony let Priscilla off at the door. She bounded into the ER and was directed by a very kind nurse to Tilly's room. When she got to the room, Priscilla heard wailing coming from inside. It sounded like Trudy. Things must've gotten worse. Priscilla's heart raced as she tapped on the door, and moments later, a doctor in a white coat pushed it open.

"Sorry to interrupt." Priscilla's words came out breathless. "I just heard that a good friend—" Her gaze shifted to the hospital bed where Tilly sat, her face swollen almost beyond recognition. She wore an oxygen mask over both nose and mouth, but it did little to cover the redness and swelling. "Oh my goodness." Priscilla pushed her way into the room. "I heard you were having trouble breathing, but..." She hardly knew what to say as she stared at Tilly's current state. "What happened?"

"We're trying to get to the bottom of that." The doctor approached Tilly's bedside and checked the monitor. "A terrible reaction, I'd say."

Trudy sat in a chair next to Tilly's bed, her face nearly as red as Tilly's. Tears rolled down her cheeks. "I had just finished eating breakfast at the Colonial Inn when Tilly came in. She sat across from me at the table to talk. You know…girl stuff. Makeup and such. Things quickly went south. One minute we were talking about how much we loved our new primer, and the next I was calling 911."

"She was in anaphylactic shock when she came in," the doctor explained. "Clearly in distress and suffering an allergic reaction to something. We're trying to figure out what she might have eaten— or used—to trigger such a violent response. My first guess is seafood."

Tilly began to cry. She pulled off the oxygen mask. "Doctor Ames, I've worked around seafood my entire life. If you tell me I'm allergic, it will be the end of me and the end of my restaurant." She snapped the mask back in place.

"If you're allergic, it really will be the end of you if you make it part of your routine. You have to take these life-threatening allergies seriously, Ms. Snyder." Tilly began to cry in earnest. The doctor turned to her and offered words of comfort. "We'll get you through this, I promise. The medicine appears to be working, so I'm confident this episode will be behind you soon. But I'm sending you to an allergist, and I want you to take whatever he says very seriously. You will have to carry an EpiPen for the rest of your life. Everywhere you go. Don't even go to bed at night unless it's on the bedside table."

Tilly pulled the mask away from her face again. "Well, for pity's sake. Am I supposed to take it into the shower with me too?"

"I'm not saying that." He crossed his arms. "You know what I mean. It's important that you have it handy, just in case."

"Are you springing her loose, Doc?" Trudy dried her eyes and offered a strained smile.

"I can't go back to the restaurant looking like this," Tilly moaned, her words barely understandable from underneath the mask.

"No. You're not going anywhere except to a private room on the second floor of this hospital. You need time for your body to recover, and I want to keep an eye on that blood pressure while we're pumping more meds into you. You're safe here with us, Ms. Snyder."

Trudy sighed. "It's for the best, Tilly. Do what the doctor says."

Tilly pulled the mask back and glared at Trudy. "Easy for you to say."

"We don't want you back in the restaurant until we're sure this isn't a seafood allergy." The doctor checked the monitor as the blood pressure cuff registered a reading. "Better safe than sorry. It looks like your pressures are better. I'm going back to the desk to see about getting you into a room."

And just like that, he disappeared.

Priscilla turned to face her friends, unsure of what to say. "I'm—I'm so sorry this happened to you, Tilly."

"One minute she was fine, the next—" Trudy blanched, and tears rolled down her cheeks. "Scared me to death."

Tilly pulled the mask away from her face and muttered, "No talking about death, if you please. I'm still very much alive over here."

"And thank God for it."

"We have Gerald to thank too," Trudy explained. "He was at the restaurant having breakfast, and he jumped into action the minute it happened. He's the one who called 911, not me. I'm of no use in a crisis. I just freeze in place."

"God bless Gerald," Tilly said.

Yes, God bless Gerald, indeed.

Priscilla stayed until an orderly showed up to wheel Tilly to a room. At that point, she headed to the waiting room to look for Tony. He'd been texting her all along, but responding seemed inconsiderate to Tilly.

Unfortunately, the hallway had been freshly mopped, so she was forced to take the long way—down a lengthy hall, past the surgery center, then back around to the ER waiting room. Priscilla didn't mind. She needed to clear her thoughts.

As she passed the surgical entrance, nurses wheeled a man by on a gurney. She wouldn't have thought a thing about it, except she heard the nurse mention a familiar name. "You're doing a wonderful thing for your daughter, Mr. Fletcher. Such a gift. I'm sure the surgery will go well, so just rest easy."

Fletcher? Priscilla paused and leaned back against the wall as the nurses pushed the gurney through the doorway. Sure enough, Carson Fletcher was being wheeled to surgery. But why? And what was all of that about his daughter?

Priscilla made her way down the long hallway, turned left, and then headed back to the waiting room, where she found Tony on his phone. He looked frustrated by something.

He rose the moment he saw her. "Is she okay?"

"She's going to be. It was an allergic reaction to something. They suspect seafood."

"Oh no." His eyes widened. "That's horrible. What will she do, if that turns out to be the case? Her whole business is built around seafood."

"I know." Priscilla sighed. "I guess she'll cross that bridge when she comes to it. They're admitting her for further treatment and allergy testing." She watched as he shoved his phone into his pocket. "Everything okay on your end?"

Tony shook his head. "I wasn't going to say anything, but since you asked... Victor got a write-up in the paper. He called me insensitive."

"Ah." Should she tell him that his recent article in the *Gazette* had been a little too rough?

"I know, I know." He sighed. "I hit below the belt in that article. But it wasn't really my fault. That reporter asked me pointed questions. All I did was answer them. And the next thing you know, I was putting my foot in my mouth. I felt horrible about it afterward, but it was too late. They took it to print."

"Happens to all of us." She shrugged. "Well, not the 'took it to print' part. I'm awfully glad some of my dumb comments over the years didn't make the papers. But let's just forget about it and move forward. Sound good?"

"Yes." He nodded in agreement. "I just hope Victor's piece doesn't do too much damage to my campaign. The election's Tuesday. I'm hoping I can hold my head above water until then."

"You're doing just fine. Hang in there." Priscilla glanced at her watch. "I hate to rush you, but I have to get back to the office to wrap up that update for your website. Then I need to head home and take Jake out for a while. Poor guy's been spending far too much time inside."

"This election will be over soon. Then you'll have more time on your hands." Tony caught her gaze. "I'm hoping you'll still spend a little time with me, Priscilla. It's gonna be pretty lonely in my office when this is said and done."

With the wave of a hand, Priscilla tried to dismiss any concerns he might have. "When you win this election, and you will, you'll be so busy, you won't have time to hang out."

"I hope that's not the case." He gave her a look so sweet, she could've melted right there in the ER waiting room.

Tony led the way out to the parking lot. Just as they reached his vehicle, another car pulled in—Eliza's red Corvette. Victor climbed out of the driver's seat. He approached, his eyes narrowing when he saw them together. Strange. Eliza was nowhere to be seen.

"Tony." Victor stopped cold.

"Victor." Tony extended his hand, but his opponent did not take it.

"I heard about Tilly. I thought she might benefit from a visit from her commissioner." His words came out slick and rehearsed.

"Any word about your wife, Victor?" Priscilla wasn't sure where she came up with the courage to speak those words, but there they were.

His eyes narrowed to slits. "No. But I'll never give up. The police will find her. My wife was—is—the joy of my life."

"Of course." *Referring to her in the past tense, though?* That was certainly alarming.

His jaw flinched, and his eyes blazed with emotion. "No one will ever know how much my wife has meant to me. She's been my rock, my safe place. Not a day has gone by that she hasn't known my love, my admiration. Trust me when I say these ridiculous rumors are completely unfounded and vicious... a clear attempt by my opponent to sway voters away from me." He glared at Tony, who walked to his vehicle and opened the passenger door for Priscilla to get in.

"You think Tony is behind the rumors?" Priscilla asked. She wanted to add that Vineyard Haven's citizens had been speculating about Victor and Betty's marriage for years but didn't go there. Their relationship was none of her business, and talking with him about it just felt awkward. Besides, he didn't appear to be in an amiable frame of mind.

"Well, of course Tony is behind the rumors. I read his article in the *Gazette*. Who else would stoop to such a level, if not a politician?" Victor's eyes widened a second later when he realized what he'd said. "Well, you know what I mean."

Yes. She knew what he meant, all right. But it didn't make her feel any better about the situation with Betty. Where was she? Would she ever come back to the island? It was starting to look like she had simply vanished into thin air.

CHAPTER TWENTY-THREE

Priscilla tossed and turned all night long. So many questions tugged at her that she found it hard to doze off. When she finally did fall asleep, she dreamed of Betty Fox, who stood at the railing on the side deck of the ferry. The poor woman couldn't stop weeping.

Then the dream shifted, and Priscilla was walking down the corridor in the hospital. She passed by a gurney and glanced down to find Carson Fletcher writhing in pain.

When she awoke, Priscilla rose from her bed and went straight to her computer. A little digging on social media helped her put things in perspective before she made an impromptu run to Edgartown. She had an uncomfortable suspicion she would find some answers there. She decided to go alone, stopping only to grab a muffin from Candy's bakery on the way. Candy greeted her but was so busy with early morning customers that she couldn't chat long. She did let Priscilla know that all of the brochures had been taken and that local women seemed excited to vote for Tony McClaren.

Priscilla arrived in Edgartown before the Perfect Fit opened. She parked along the street and waited for the owner to show up. The woman—a beautiful platinum blonde with fair skin, who looked to be in her late fifties—arrived at 9:45. She walked to the front of the store, unlocked the door, and stepped inside.

Perfect.

Priscilla wanted a few minutes of the woman's time before other customers arrived. She got out of her car and walked to the door of the shop, pausing to look at the Closed sign on the door. She decided to ignore the sign. She opened the door, and the bell jingled.

She was greeted by the phrase, "We're not open yet." The woman glanced her way, fine lines forming on her brow. "Fifteen more minutes, and then you can shop to your heart's content."

"Yes, I know. Sorry to interrupt." Priscilla took a risk and stepped inside. "I was hoping to speak with the owner before the shop opened."

The woman took several steps in her direction, and for the first time Priscilla took note of her beautiful outfit—a gorgeous white top with fine embroidery and dark slacks. "I'm the owner. Marcia Peterson. How can I help you?"

"I know this is going to sound strange, and please forgive me if I've overstepped in any way, but is it possible that you know—or are acquainted with—a man by the name of Carson Fletcher?"

Marcia released a slow breath, and her bright smile seemed to fade a bit. "I know him, yes."

Priscilla nodded. "I was in the shop the other day, talking with your daughter, Claire, about some clothing tags I found on the ferry the day Betty Fox went missing."

"Oh, yes. She mentioned you. I've gone through our files, and those items were paid for with cash, so there's no way to trace them to anyone in particular." She paused. "But what does this have to do with Carson?"

"Nothing. Well, nothing that I know of. Is—is your daughter here, by any chance?"

"My daughter is in the hospital, recovering from surgery."

This news did not come as a surprise to Priscilla, of course. Her suspicions had led her to this very conclusion. "I'm sorry to hear that. I do hope everything went well."

"As well as can be expected. She just underwent a kidney transplant, so it will be some time before she's back at work. We're just so grateful it's behind us now. She's been ill for some time, and we were praying for a donor for ages."

"I'll be praying for her. And for the person who gave her the gift of life."

Marcia busied herself with the clothes on a nearby rack. "I would give you his name, but I suspect you already know it."

"I suspect I do." Memories of Carson on that gurney tugged at her heartstrings even now. "But just for the record, Carson hasn't spoken to me about any of this. He doesn't even know me. In fact, I feel like I've horned in on personal business here, and I'm sorry. This really just started as a quest to discover why a woman went missing off the ferry."

"A ferry that Carson happened to be on." Marcia moved to another rack of clothes. "I see."

"Yes."

Marcia sighed and then turned back to face Priscilla. "It's my fault he was on the ferry that day. Not that it's really anyone's business, but I'm the one who asked to meet him there."

"Oh?"

"I was headed into Boston to have lunch with an old friend. I needed someplace where Carson and I could talk about the situation with Claire, but not on the island. Too many watching eyes here. You know how it is. People like to talk."

"Sure."

"Not that I needed to be worrying about what people think, but I was. I guess I was afraid folks would judge me. Or worse, they would somehow make things harder on Claire than they already were."

"I'm sure folks would understand."

"Hmm. Anyway, I bought our tickets online. He agreed to walk on board and meet me so we could talk about the plan as we crossed the Sound."

"Were you wearing a pink blouse? One from your shop? With jeweled sunglasses and a brightly colored scarf?"

"No." Marcia shook her head. "I had on a black and white blouse. No scarf."

"I don't remember seeing you at all that day," Priscilla said. "But I guess I didn't know you then, and the ferry was so crowded."

"I never got out of my car. I sat there the whole time, waiting for Carson to join me so we could talk. My purpose in meeting him that day was completely personal." Marcia paused. "I wanted to tell him how badly I felt for not letting him know he had a daughter before, well…"

"Before her health issues sprang up?"

"Yes." Marcia sighed. "This is awful to admit, even to a stranger, but I simply didn't want anyone to know that Claire wasn't my husband's child. She was a toddler when I married Joe. When we moved to the Vineyard, Claire was four years old. By then, Joe and I had another child, a son. So we didn't see any point in letting anyone know about the particulars of our situation. It was no one's business. But I should have told Carson from the very beginning."

Priscilla didn't know what to say in response to that, so she simply nodded.

"We had parted on friendly terms, both agreeing the relationship wasn't meant to be. He was in the military at the time. I didn't even find out I was pregnant until after he was deployed. It was just more convenient…" She hesitated. "Well, to keep it from him, I guess."

"Were you scared he would try to take her away?"

"Maybe deep down, but it would've been impossible, considering his deployments. I just walked away from the situation as if it never happened in the first place."

"So he never had a clue."

"Until four months ago. I tracked him down through Facebook. He was recently widowed and living in Naples, Florida, the same town where we'd met. Same town where I got pregnant with Claire."

"And you told him?"

"The conversation started on Facebook, but I didn't tell him right away." Tears brimmed over Marcia's lashes. "I asked for his number and ended up calling him. My husband Joe was on the line with me. We told him... together."

"How did he take it? If you don't mind my asking."

"He was shocked, of course. And I'm sure he was angry with me too, but he covered well. I think he was at a point in his life where he needed something—or someone—to hang on to. He and his wife never had children. I don't think she was able. And, of course, she passed away less than a year ago, which left him completely alone. So maybe the timing was a good thing. I've been hoping so, anyway."

"And Claire?"

"She started asking questions when she got to her teens. Joe is blond, fair-skinned. Same as me. If you've met Claire, you know that she's got that beautiful olive skin and dark hair."

"Same features as you, though. And such a pretty girl. She could be a model."

"Thank you. I've always thought so too." A smile turned up the edges of Marcia's lips. "But she's a dead ringer for Carson. I'm sure you can see how awkward all of this was. Carson came, never asking anything for himself, not even the plane fare. He met Claire, and they immediately got along. It was almost as if they'd known each other forever."

"That's remarkable."

"Yes. Best of all, he was willing to be typed and matched to see if he could be a kidney donor... and everything checked out perfectly. I don't think we could've asked for a greater miracle, to be honest."

"As if it was meant to be."

"Yes." Marcia smiled. "I don't know what I was so nervous about. Maybe other people's opinions? Maybe that Carson would be angry for all the years he missed out on? That Claire would never forgive me for not telling her the truth?" She dissolved into a haze of tears. "I'm a business owner, a Bible study teacher, a woman who is well thought of. But I had this secret, and I didn't know if people would still accept me after the truth came out."

"We all have a past, Marcia. And sure, there are things you could've done differently, but aren't you glad we serve a God who wants us to pack away our yesterdays and look only at today?"

Marcia's eyes misted. "Today is all about my girl. She's sitting in that hospital room with a new chance for life."

"Which she has because you were brave enough to reach out to her father—to risk your reputation, your pride, your fear. So don't be too hard on yourself."

"I know you're right." Marcia nodded. "I can't go back and change those years. And I'm grateful for that day on the ferry, because that's where I came to grips with what I'd done—to Carson and to Claire. I had to ask for his forgiveness, and he gave it, no questions asked. I sat in my car and blubbered like a baby. He was nothing but gracious and kind, just as he's been ever since." She paused and dried her eyes. "He's a good man. That hasn't changed. He was always a good man."

"Who has a beautiful daughter."

"Yes."

Priscilla shifted her position and suddenly wished she'd chosen more comfortable shoes. "Like you, I'm a woman of faith, Marcia. I truly believe God can use all of this for good."

"He already has. My daughter will recover. I don't have to keep secrets anymore. I want everyone to know what a miracle this is. And Carson is moving here. Did you know? He wants to continue his relationship with her. And he's bringing his business to the island."

"Yes, a friend told me. I heard he's in investments."

"You're a good detective." Marcia smiled. "Yes, he's in investments and will be opening a firm as soon as he has recovered. In the meantime, I owe him a debt I'll never be able to repay."

"Nor would he want you to. I'm sure he's grateful to be included in his daughter's life."

"Yes, and strange as this might sound, he and Joe get along well. I thought it would be awkward between them, but it hasn't been. Just one more God thing, I guess." Marcia's smile returned. "Remarkable, really."

"He smooths troubled waters, for sure."

Priscilla wrapped up the conversation with her new friend and left the shop, her heart full to overflowing. There were still lingering questions, of course. She would get the answers she sought, but first she had a little visit to make—to see a certain father who'd just given his daughter the gift of life.

CHAPTER TWENTY-FOUR

Priscilla pointed her car in the direction of the hospital. She would stop to see Tilly first and then head to Carson's room for a chat.

As she pulled into Vineyard Haven, Priscilla noticed a new sign in front of the hardware store: *Let's Take Victor All the Way to Victory!* His photo was plastered to the left of the words, that fake smile so broad it looked like it had been painted on. *Ugh.* She still couldn't figure out why people voted for him. Did they like his politics? Was he helping the town of Vineyard Haven or simply staying in office to pat himself on the back?

Priscilla noted that Betty Fox was in the photo too. She looked stiff. Awkward. But, boy, was she ever dressed the part, with a gorgeous outfit and designer handbag. As she drove by, Priscilla tried to figure out why Victor would put up such a strange billboard just a few days before the election—and with his wife missing too. So odd.

Then again, nothing about Victor Fox made sense to her.

Priscilla parked and walked into the hospital. When she reached the information desk, they gave her both room numbers. She made her way to the second floor to room 210 to see her friend. Tilly looked to be in good spirits. Much of the swelling and redness in her face had diminished, and she was eating a bagel.

"Well, good morning to you," Priscilla said.

"Hardly." Tilly's nose wrinkled. "They call this stuff food?" She gestured to the tray in front of her. "The eggs are runny, the bagel is hard, and the coffee is cold. These people could learn a thing or two from me about food service."

"You're the best, Tilly. No doubt about that."

At Priscilla's words, her friend's demeanor changed. The grumpy expression shifted to one of pure delight. "Thank you, Priscilla. I'm sorry I'm such a grumbler today. I just got the worst possible news."

"Oh dear. You're allergic to seafood?"

"No, it's even worse." She groaned and pushed the tray aside. "I'm allergic to Heavenly Faces makeup!"

"Oh, no! Have you told Trudy yet?"

"Yes. Poor woman was in shock. I told her it's just one particular chemical in the new powder, so as long as I avoid that, I should be okay. But what a surprise to find out such a thing." Tilly's wrinkled brow ironed itself out as she added, "But, hey, at least it's not shrimp or lobster. Can you even imagine? My life as I know it would be over."

"That would've been tragic, for sure. Half the island would be in mourning if they couldn't have your seafood, Tilly."

"Half?"

Priscilla laughed. "Okay, okay. The entire island would be in mourning."

"That's more like it." Tilly's brows elevated, and she leaned back in the bed. "This is the most uncomfortable bed I've ever slept in. I can't wait till they spring me loose."

Priscilla visited with Tilly until the nurse came to check her vital signs. Then Priscilla headed to the third floor to find Carson Fletcher. She reached room 315 in short order and tapped on the door.

He responded, "Come in."

Priscilla stepped inside, and he glanced up from his spot in the bed. She offered a little wave, as if visiting an old friend. He responded with an easygoing smile.

"I wonder if I could have a few moments of your time, Mr. Fletcher?" Priscilla took a couple of hesitant steps in his direction.

"Sure." He looked perplexed by the visit from a complete stranger but extended his hand. "Who do I have the pleasure of speaking with?"

"Priscilla Grant. I don't believe we've met before." She shook his hand.

He gestured to a chair next to the bed. "Well, I'd offer you a more comfortable place to sit, but all of my nicer furniture is out for reupholstering."

She laughed as she took a seat. Carson had a sense of humor, and a good one, at that.

He shifted in the bed and flinched, and his hand went to his side. "Sorry. Still a little sore. Just went through surgery."

"To help your daughter."

He looked stunned. "How did you know that? I didn't want anyone to know."

"Why is it that the heroes in stories never want people to know they're heroes?" She gave him a knowing look.

"They just don't like to draw attention to themselves, I guess." He rubbed his side again. "Do me a favor, okay? Keep this between us."

"I think a handful of folks already know, so you might be out of luck there."

"Well, don't paint me to be a hero, if you do tell the tale. Claire is going through such a tough time already. I'd like to keep the focus on her. Just ask people to pray that her body doesn't reject the kidney. That's a real possibility."

"I will pray. I promise. But I have every reason to believe she will live a long and healthy life." Priscilla meant those words from the bottom of her heart. She would also commit to pray for that very thing.

"I hope you're right." He offered a genuine smile. "Now, how can I help you, Mrs. Grant?"

Priscilla still flinched when people called her Mrs. Grant, even after all this time. "I wanted to ask you about that day on the ferry when Mrs. Fox went missing."

"Ah." His smile quickly faded. "I feel so awful about that day."

"Why?"

"I don't know." He shifted his position in the bed again, pain registering on his face. "I just feel like maybe I overlooked something. Like maybe I should've noticed something."

"I've felt the same way. I don't know how—or even what—happened to Betty Fox, and it has bothered me ever since."

"Me too."

Maybe she had more in common with this guy than she'd realized.

"Carson, can I ask a question?"

"Sure. I'm an open book."

"Is there any chance, even a small one, that you might be a reporter traveling incognito?"

He laughed so hard he ended up grabbing his side in pain.

"I'm sorry, I'm sorry!" Priscilla rushed to the edge of his bed. "Are you okay?"

"I'll be fine." He chuckled. "I haven't had a laugh like that in ages. What in the world makes you think I might be a reporter?"

"Oh, it was just a thought. When we saw you on the ferry that day, it occurred to us you might've come to town to write an article on Victor Fox and his wife."

"I can assure you, I'm not a writer. No way. So put your mind at ease. And for the record, I didn't even know who Victor Fox was until the news story came out about his wife's disappearance."

"I see. Well, I had to ask," she said. "The ladies would never have let it go if I'd missed that question."

"I hope you can convince them. If not, I will gladly offer writing samples to prove I'm not a wordsmith."

"Oh, I don't know. You're doing pretty well with words today." Priscilla flashed a smile. "I do apologize for being so nosy. I just don't want to leave any stones unturned."

"That one has been duly flipped. Mark it off your list."

"Will do." She paused. "Now, a question about Betty Fox. I was in the vehicle behind hers, and I saw you walk up to her at one point and say something."

"Right. I did." He smoothed the sheets with his palms. "Though I didn't know who she was at the time."

"Ah. Do you mind if I ask what you said to her? She looked very...concerned."

Carson's eyes narrowed, and he appeared to be thinking. After a moment he snapped to attention. "Oh, right. I told her that her left taillight was out. Probably from the dinged bumper. I noticed it as she pulled into the parking lot at Vineyard Sound."

"That's it?"

"Yeah. I'd never met her before, so there was no reason to stay and chat. I just said, 'Thought you'd want to know your left taillight is out' and left it at that."

So, that was all? The concern on Betty's face when she'd spoken with Carson had nothing to do with her personal life. Just her vehicle.

"Women do tend to get worked up when things go wrong with their cars," Priscilla added. "I know I do. Just the other day my oil light came on, and I was at a loss to know what to do."

"I hope you stopped driving," Carson said. "Otherwise you could easily destroy your engine."

"I happened to be in front of a mechanic's shop, so I stopped in."

"Good girl." He paused. "But about that day on the ferry—my perspective is a bit different, because I went on foot, not in a vehicle."

"Yes, I remember seeing you walk on board."

"Are you a detective or something?" His eyes narrowed. "Am I under investigation?"

"No." She shook her head and laughed. "Trust me, I'm no detective. Just observant."

"I was on the ferry to meet a . . . friend." His gaze shifted downward. "Marcia. But I suppose you already know that."

"Yes. She bought your ticket."

"She did. I guess she has some sort of online account, since she goes back and forth so frequently. At any rate, she passed off the ticket to me before I boarded, but it wasn't in my name."

"Right."

"When I got to the Woods Hole landing, I took a cab to pick up my car." His face lit up. "I just bought an older model Jaguar from a guy in Falmouth. Picked it up that same day. It was worth the wait while it was being restored."

"Is it dark blue?" she asked.

"Sure is. Why?"

"I've seen it. I actually thought you were following me one day last week."

He paused and then snapped his fingers. "Oh, right. Do you drive an SUV?"

"I do."

"You won't believe this, but I did follow you from the gas station, because you left your gas cap open. I tried to get your attention, but you were in a hurry to get to the bakery. I finally gave up and decided you'd figure it out."

"Wow. Well, that answers that. Someone must have seen it open and taken pity on an old woman and shut it for me at some point. I thought maybe you were after me."

"Hardly." He chuckled and then groaned at the pain it caused. "To be honest, I was so excited about driving the car on those back roads that I took off in a hurry."

"You're a car guy?"

He beamed. "Yes. I've worked on quite a few over the years. If you asked my wife—God rest her soul—she would tell you that I collect older model sports cars. Drove her crazy, poor woman. It's a real obsession, one I can't seem to shake."

"You need to meet my friend Eliza. She drives the coolest old Corvette."

His eyes widened. "Red?"

"Yes."

"I've seen it around Vineyard Haven. Gorgeous vehicle."

"She's done a great job of maintaining it. It belonged to her brother, but he passed away."

A look of genuine compassion flowed from Carson. "So much grief in this world."

"She's into cars too. Maybe I should introduce you."

He shrugged. "I didn't really come to the island to make friends. Well, outside of the obvious one, I mean."

"Your daughter. I've met her."

"You have?" His face lit with joy as he pulled out his phone to show off pictures. "She's a beauty, isn't she? She's in the next room, if you want to stop by."

"I'll do that before I leave."

"She and her mom have a wonderful shop in Edgartown."

"I know. I saw you outside one day, taking pictures. That's one of the reasons I put two and two together and guessed you were Claire's father."

"Yes." He nodded. "I'm so blown away by what Marcia has done. And so proud of Claire too. She helped design the outside of that building. Did you know?"

"I didn't."

"Yeah. Her mom handles the business side, but Claire's the creative force. She laid out the inside of the store too."

"Did she get that creative side from you?"

"Me?" He laughed. "I'm the least creative person I know. I'm in investments. I have no idea where she gets it from, to be honest. From on high, I guess."

"Guess so. Speaking of investments, rumor has it you're opening a firm on the island."

"I am. Just as soon as the hospital releases me."

"Well then"—Priscilla extended a hand—"let me be the first to welcome you to the neighborhood. I'm pretty new here, myself, but the people are welcoming."

"Unless they think you're someone you're not," he added. "Then they treat you with suspicion and disdain." He shrugged.

"You've passed the test, Mr. Fletcher. I shall spread the word, and all will be well. I do hope your firm gets off to a great start."

"I'm sure it will. Lots of folks on Martha's Vineyard with funds to invest, I would imagine."

"Yes, you've picked the perfect locale for that." Priscilla glanced at the clock on the wall and gasped. "I'd better go. I'm going to stop off in Claire's room and then head back up to the campaign office. I've got a few loose ends to tie up."

"You working for that Fox guy?" Carson's brow wrinkled. "Never met him in person, but something about him just hits me the wrong way."

"No, I don't work for him. I'm assisting his opponent, Tony McClaren."

"Good." Carson shuffled his position in the bed and grimaced.

"I'll let you get some rest, Mr. Fletcher. Would you like me to call the nurse?"

"No. I'm tough. I can take it." He offered a forced smile.

Priscilla rose. "Thanks for the chat. I'll go visit Claire now."

"Good, you do that. And give her a hug from me."

Priscilla walked to the door of his room and then turned back. "Just one more question."

"Sure."

"What does it feel like?"

"What?" Carson gave her a curious look.

"To give part of yourself to someone else so they can live?"

His lips turned up in a smile. "After so many years of not even knowing she existed, it feels wonderful. I was happy to do it."

"Most people wouldn't even consider giving up something so valuable for someone else, especially something that left a permanent scar."

"I've given up nothing." Tears sprang to his eyes, and his voice trembled. "I've gained the whole world. The scar is a reminder of what God has given me. That's all. I will never look at it any other way."

Now she was crying too. "I just want you to know that I really respect you, Carson. And I'm glad to know you."

"Good to know you too. If you ever need help with investments..."

"I will bring my millions to you." She laughed. "Okay, maybe not millions, but I will give thought to changing up my current situation."

"No pressure." He gave her a warm smile. "Just do what's right for you."

"Thank you. I will."

Priscilla opened the door and walked into the hallway, then dissolved into a puddle of tears. Every time she thought about Carson Fletcher—how she'd suspected him without even taking the time to get to know him—she felt guilty.

That was what sleuths did, of course. They suspected people. People like Carson Fletcher. And Eliza Jamison. And Tony McClaren. And Victor Fox.

Priscilla wiped her eyes with the back of her hand and paused to think about Victor more carefully. It looked like he was the only one left on her suspect list. The most obvious suspect of all might just turn out to be the one "whodunit."

CHAPTER TWENTY-FIVE

On Election Day, Priscilla awoke feeling confident Vineyard Haven would soon have a new commissioner—Tony McClaren. It felt good to know that she had helped him all the way to the finish line. Now, if only she could help locate Betty Fox, all would be well. If she could just put an end to the lingering questions about the woman's disappearance, Priscilla could relax and enjoy Tony's victory.

Of course, a victory for Tony would be defeat for Victor Fox. She had to wonder how he would take such a devastating loss on top of Betty's disappearance. Priscilla felt a little sad for him. He was a troubled man who needed help. Perhaps, with free time on his hands, he would get the counseling he so desperately needed.

Priscilla also found herself entertaining wild ideas on the opposite end of the spectrum—that perhaps Betty really had taken her own life to get away from him. If he was really as bad as Eliza said, then she might have been driven to the brink. Stranger things had happened. Or maybe, as some believed, Victor had played a role in getting rid of her. Had he hired someone to do away with her? When her thoughts shifted in this direction, Priscilla stopped feeling sorry for Victor and continued to see him as a suspect.

Would Eliza manage to break free from him and start fresh with a new boss, a new company? Priscilla hoped so. She prayed so.

She spent the morning at home, taking care of some things around the house. Then she cast her vote for Tony. Afterward, she headed into the campaign office, where she was greeted by all three of her cousins and Uncle Hugh, who had arrived to wait for election returns together.

Tony was in fine spirits. He bounded from person to person, place to place, nibbling on sweets that Candy had dropped off earlier that morning. Either he was high on sugar or excited about his upcoming win. Not that he was a shoo-in. According to recent polls, Victor still stood a chance, albeit slight. No one seemed concerned, though.

Just before noon, Priscilla and her family members all settled around a large table in the conference room. Tony joined them moments later after filling his cup with coffee for the umpteenth time. He couldn't seem to stop smiling, but every now and again the smile flickered, and she could read the concern in his eyes.

"Chin up," Uncle Hugh called out from his spot at the end of the table. "You've got this one in the bag. I asked all the fellas in my Rotary Club to vote for you. Most of those guys can't stand Victor Fox, anyway."

"I appreciate you, Hugh," Tony said. He gestured around the table. "In fact, I'm grateful to all of you. In case I haven't said it enough, thank you all so much."

This led to an exciting conversation about the election process on the island.

Priscilla rose and walked over to the coffeepot, where she filled her cup. "This is my very first time to be involved in local elections on Martha's Vineyard, and I've loved the process. I usually think of politics in the fall, not the spring, so this has been a fun diversion."

"I love that you've played a role, Priscilla. I really mean that." Tony's beautiful blue eyes sparkled. Priscilla turned back to her cup of coffee, embarrassed.

"Before long, you will have experienced every season on the Vineyard, Priscilla," Gail said. "In consecutive order, I mean. To see one season give way to the other is just so special."

"Yes, I hate that I missed so much as a child. But I've loved every transition so far." Priscilla glanced out of the window at the blue sky, dotted with puffs of white. "But spring is my favorite. The whole Vineyard is a garden in bloom, colorful, fragrant blossoms bursting forth." Where such flowery words came from, she had no idea. Priscilla took a sip of her coffee and sighed.

"Beautiful description," Joan said. "I love it too. I've never thought to word it in such a magnificent way, though. Maybe you missed your calling as a writer, Priscilla."

"She did a fantastic job on those brochures." Tony gave her an admiring look. "I'd say her writing skills are stellar. And your descriptions are especially good. You should be writing travel articles or something like that."

"You think?" Priscilla paused to think that through. "I could see myself doing that. There's so much to do and see around the Vineyard, I wouldn't even have to go back to the mainland to find material."

"I like to think of the Vineyard as a person," Trudy said. "With plenty of information to offer."

Gail's brow wrinkled. "Male or female?"

"Oh, female, of course. She has many layers and lots of *drama*." Trudy laughed. "And her moods change from village to village. And season to season, of course. In the summer, she's a happy-go-lucky woman, running around in her bikini."

"Now there's a lovely image." Gail rolled her eyes.

"Sounds good to me." Uncle Hugh quirked a brow and then laughed.

"In the fall, she's pumpkin spice and ginger—all things crisp and beautiful. Her leaves change and tumble, and cool winds blow."

"She puts away her bikini, in other words." Tony chuckled. "That's sure to depress the men."

"Yeah, bummer," Uncle Hugh threw in and then shrugged.

Trudy's voice grew more animated as she carried on. "She locks up in winter, like an old woman with arthritis. She has trouble moving her joints."

"If that is an attempt to make fun of me, I resent it," Uncle Hugh grumbled. "And for the record, my arthritis doesn't just act up in wintertime. It's pretty awful right now, thank you very much."

"I'm sorry about the arthritis, Uncle Hugh," Priscilla said. "I have a touch of it, myself, in my hips."

"I should be so lucky that it would just be my hips." He shifted his position in the chair and muttered something under his breath.

"I was going to say that springtime is my favorite because that's when frozen things thaw." Trudy glanced Uncle Hugh's way and rolled her eyes. "Not that there's much chance of some things changing much, no matter how glorious the season."

Uncle Hugh grunted and then eased his way out of his chair to hobble toward the coffee.

Priscilla thought about Trudy's description of the island. Maybe her cousin was the real writer in the family. Before she could give it much thought, Tilly arrived with a tray of seafood hoagies.

"Thought you might need some sustenance, folks," Tilly called out as she hefted the tray over her shoulder. "There's more on the way, so eat up."

Tony thanked her profusely and then grabbed a sandwich.

Teresa entered the room seconds later, all smiles. "I just came from the library. Voters are lined up around the block, and I think most of them are voting for you, Tony."

"They are?" His eyes widened, and he took a bite of the sandwich.

"It didn't hurt that I carried a sign with your photo on it. And I might have touched up the eyes a bit to make them even bluer."

"Good gravy." Uncle Hugh slapped himself on the forehead.

Everyone started laughing.

A few minutes later, they all settled around the conference table to eat and visit. Tilly stuck around and even ate one of the hoagies.

"Sure you're okay to do that?" Gail's eyes grew wide. "Aren't you allergic to seafood?"

"Nope."

"But I thought..." Gail looked perplexed. "It was an allergy, right? That landed you in the hospital, I mean."

"Oh, it was an allergy, all right." Tilly shot a glance at Trudy, who gave her a pleading look.

"What aren't you two saying?" Gail asked.

"Yes, something is definitely up with both of you," Joan added.

"I had an allergic reaction to something." Tilly wiped her lips with a napkin. "But it was non-food related. Thank goodness."

"Well, that is a relief. Eat up, then."

"I will, thank you." Tilly took another bite of her hoagie.

"So if it wasn't food related, then what was it?" Gail asked. "It must've been something horrible."

Trudy coughed.

Tilly set her napkin down, her gaze traveling to Trudy and then back to her hoagie. "Let's just say I'm limited in what I can put on my skin and leave it at that."

Trudy flashed a broad smile. "Speaking of which, have you ever seen anyone's skin look as beautiful as Priscilla's does, since she's been using her new products? I think she looks ten years younger."

Priscilla hardly knew what to make of such a comment. She felt her cheeks warm in embarrassment at the flattery.

"Priscilla looked wonderful all along." Tony gave her an admiring look. "No beauty products required. I think all that makeup is highly overrated."

"Humph." Trudy rose and threw her trash in the garbage can. "Go on talking like that, and you'll end up losing my vote, Tony."

He chuckled. "Didn't you already cast your vote?"

"Oh, right." She paused. "Well, next time, I mean. And just for the record, Tilly's allergic reaction was limited to one product—the powder. So all's well that ends well."

"Could've ended a lot differently, though," Gail said. "Scary."

They wrapped up their lunch, and Gerald arrived. He made a beeline to Priscilla. "Hey, good to see you."

"Good to see you too."

"I wanted to let you know that Carson is officially off the suspect list."

She waved a hand. "Oh, I know. I went to see him the other day."

"You did?" Gerald's brows creased. "When?"

"The day after his surgery. He was still in the hospital. I dropped by unannounced."

"Of course you did. So you knew he donated a kidney to his daughter? I can't tell you anything. You've already got it all figured out."

"I stopped to see Claire as well. Hopefully her body doesn't reject the kidney."

Trudy overheard Priscilla's last comment. "Claire got a new kidney? I've been praying for her for ages now, ever since her mother told me she was ill."

"Yes," Priscilla said. "Her birth father arrived in town and was a perfect match."

"God bless her birth father." Gail paused. "But, wait, Joe isn't her father?"

"And this is why Marcia was so hesitant for people to know the whole story," Priscilla said to Gerald. "She was worried about their reactions and wondered if people would judge her."

"Judge her...for what?" Trudy asked. "I'm so confused. I've met the daughter. I've met the mother. And I felt sure I'd met the father—Joe. But what does this have to do with that guy we saw on the ferry the day Betty disappeared? I felt sure he was the one responsible."

"Nope. He's not responsible," Gerald said.

"Not even close," Priscilla echoed. She spent the next several minutes filling everyone in. She did her best—as Carson had instructed—not to make him out a hero. But how could he come across as anything but?

"So let me get this straight," Gail said after hearing everything Priscilla had to say. "Marcia is connected to Carson, the man we've all been calling a drifter?"

"Speak for yourself," Trudy said. "I've been calling him a reporter, not a drifter."

"He's neither," Priscilla said.

"How do you know all of this?" Gail asked.

"Because she's a super-sleuth, that's how." Gerald gave her an admiring look. "She just has a way of figuring things out."

"Truth is, I was at the hospital seeing you, Tilly, when I got my answer about Carson. When I left your room, I was diverted down a different hallway and saw Carson being wheeled by on a stretcher."

"Wow," Trudy said.

"Yes. I overheard the nurse talking to him, and she said something about how sweet it was that a father would give his own child the gift of life. And that's how I put the pieces together. I remembered Trudy telling me that Claire needed prayer for a health issue, and I also remembered seeing Carson outside of the Perfect Fit, taking pictures. I pieced it all together in my mind and then went back to the shop to talk with Marcia, who bared her soul. Carson, who didn't even know he had a daughter until four months ago, came all the way from Florida to donate a kidney."

"To a child he never knew he had," Gerald added.

"Man. He sounds like a great guy." Trudy sighed. "Now you should all feel bad for thinking he was a murderer. Or a kidnapper."

"He's certainly shifted to hero in my book," Joan added. "Poor guy. He didn't even know he had a daughter, and now he's risked his life for her."

"That's the long and the short of it. The recovery time won't be long, but Claire will have to be on anti-rejection drugs for some time."

Uncle Hugh, who had remained silent until now, cleared his throat. "Don't get any ideas, Gail."

"What do you mean, Pop?" She gave him a curious look.

"I'm old. My body's falling apart. I can't give up any organs. Not now. So don't even ask." He took another bite of his hoagie.

She rolled her eyes. "I know you're kidding, but you can rest assured, I won't be asking."

They spent the rest of the afternoon and evening watching the results come in. Everyone was giddy with delight when Tony was named commissioner. In fact, the noise was so loud in the room, Priscilla could barely hear herself think. This led to a full-out party, as other islanders converged on the campaign office to offer congratulations and to cheer their new commissioner on. Priscilla marveled at how at home she felt. She was truly one of the gang now.

When the festivities died down, Gail headed home with Uncle Hugh. Joan and Trudy stuck around to help Priscilla clean up the room. It took some time before they made a dent. Tony worked alongside them, never losing the smile on his face.

Afterward, Trudy paused in the open doorway to have some final words with Priscilla. "Hey, I keep forgetting to ask if you finished that book I loaned you." She leaned against the doorjamb, looking exhausted.

"I did."

"Did you enjoy it?"

"Very much. It took me longer than usual to read it, though."

"Well, you've been a little busy."

"Yes, but all of this is now behind me, and I can get back to the business of relaxing. I'm long overdue for some quiet time."

"I would join you, but then it wouldn't be quiet." Trudy winked and walked out the door.

A short while later, Tony walked Priscilla out to her car.

"It's been a good day," she said as she turned to face him.

"A very good day."

An awkward pause followed. Tony finally broke the silence. "Priscilla, I was hoping we could go out to dinner tomorrow night. Tonight was so crazy. There were so many people. I'd like to celebrate—just the two of us."

"Oh, I—"

"I was thinking of a nice, romantic place—maybe Aubrey's Steakhouse in Edgartown, something like that?"

Priscilla paused and tried to think of an appropriate answer. "I think you're a great guy, Tony," she said at last.

"Thank you." He took her hand and stared into her eyes. "I think you're great too, Priscilla."

She swallowed hard and then continued. "You're going to be a fantastic representative, and I'm happy to have you as my commissioner."

"That's very kind, Priscilla." He squeezed her hand.

She pulled it back as gently as she could so as not to hurt his feelings. "But, Tony, I need you to know that I'm not interested in anything beyond that. It's been great to work with you and fun helping out with the campaign, but I can't move forward in any sort of personal relationship. Not beyond friendship, anyway."

His smile faded and silence followed.

"You're going to be so busy in your new position, and I'm going to be..." Her words trailed off.

"Seeing someone else?"

"Maybe. To be honest, I'm not sure what's coming around the bend. I'm just trusting the Lord to show me moment by moment. I'm inching my way along to protect my heart. It's the safest way to travel, trust me. I highly recommend it."

He sighed. "I suspected as much but still hoped I might be wrong."

"My life was flipped upside down a couple of years ago when my husband died, so I understand what you're going through. My heart goes out to you. But it takes time for a broken heart to heal, Tony. You've only been widowed a little over a year. Trust me when I say it'll be a while before you're able to care for someone like that again. And when you are, she needs to be the right someone. If you make the wrong choice too soon, you'll be stuck, and both people will be miserable. There are already too many broken relationships out there. No point in setting yourself up for failure."

He released a slow breath. "You're a wise woman, Priscilla. I understand now why people say you're discerning."

"Trust me, I've made a lot of mistakes. I don't always get it right. But I've learned one thing: the very safest place to be is at the center of God's will. When I wander outside of that place, I find myself in trouble every time."

He nodded. "So...I guess God will open that door when the time is right."

"He will. And, as with anything in this life, we'd be foolish to push open doors before the timing is right."

"Truth." He gazed at her with admiration. "So, just to clarify, you won't date me?" He laughed and then said, "I'm kidding. But you can't blame a guy for trying."

"No, you can't. And I have to give you an A+ for your efforts."

"Thanks." He sighed. "Whoever ends up winning your heart will be one lucky guy, Priscilla Grant."

"The only one who truly has it right now is the One who created it."

Even as she spoke the words, Priscilla felt the peace of God flood her heart. How long had it been since she'd acknowledged the fact that she would be perfectly content, perfectly at peace, to live the rest of her days with God as her sole source of comfort and joy? Sure, it would be wonderful to fall in love, to marry again, to enjoy romance. Maybe God would grant her that opportunity. Maybe He'd already started the ball rolling. But to know the kind of romance that could only come with her Creator? She wouldn't trade that for all of the votes in Vineyard Haven.

CHAPTER TWENTY-SIX

The day after Tony won the election, Victor Fox's billboards were removed. Priscilla found herself thinking about him nonstop. How was he taking this loss, especially with his wife still missing? Two blows in a row for Victor. He must be crushed.

Or was he responsible for Betty's disappearance? Priscilla couldn't get the poor woman off her mind. Would she mysteriously reappear now that the election was over? Or had Victor weaseled her away into hiding, once and for all? Only one person would know the answer to that.

Priscilla decided to give Eliza a call. They arranged to meet at the bakery for a midmorning snack and lengthy conversation. She arrived at Candy's half an hour later, ordered a raspberry scone, and settled in at a table to wait for her new friend.

Eliza arrived looking like a new woman. Many of the concerns she'd worn on her brow were now wiped away. She plopped down at the table, released a loud sigh, and proclaimed, "I've been set free!"

"Meaning, you're out of a job?"

"Yep. But I don't care, Priscilla. I really don't. I'm just so relieved to be out of that situation."

"I hate to ask, but how did Victor take the loss?"

"Let me order one of those scones, and then I'll tell you all about it." Eliza walked to the counter, ordered, and returned a couple of minutes later, treat in one hand and a cup of coffee in the other.

She put her goodies down on the table, sat, and pulled her chair close. "Now, where was I?"

"About to tell me how it went last night with Victor."

"Strangely well." She shook her head. "I have no words to describe how he responded. He had a bunch of his guy friends there, and I guess he didn't want to lose face in front of them. Either he was completely faking it, or he was actually okay with not winning. I'm telling you, I hardly knew what to make of it."

"Wow." Priscilla thought for a while before saying more. "Do you think—and I'm just speculating here—that he might be relieved? Maybe he got in the habit of being in the public eye and kept up his persona to win votes, but maybe he's weary with all that. Deep down, I mean. Do you think it's possible?"

"Anything's possible. But I almost felt like I witnessed a miracle last night."

"What will he do?"

Eliza shrugged. "Go back to selling cars, I guess. He used to own one of the biggest lots in town. That was ages ago, though, so who knows."

"And you? What will you do now?" Priscilla asked.

"Guess I'm looking for a job." Eliza shrugged again. "I've got some money socked away, but I'm sure there will be secretarial jobs available if I just look. I'm a fast typist and great on the computer.

I have a ton of other office skills too. At least I walk away from Victor Fox with that."

"You walk away with a lot more than that, my friend. You've got your dignity and your pride. After all you've been through, I'd say that is a lot." Priscilla paused. "Can I ask you a question about Victor's wife?"

"Sure." Eliza took a sip of her coffee. "Not sure I'll be able to answer it, but I'll try."

"Was she a fancy dresser?"

"Betty? No way. Left to her own devices, she would wear jeans and a simple blouse. Why do you ask?"

"The most recent billboard, the one that just went up last week—had a picture of Victor and Betty."

"Yes, I sent that design to the billboard artist myself." Eliza picked up her scone and broke off a piece. She popped it into her mouth, and a delirious look followed. "Oh, wow. This is amazing."

"First time?"

"Mm-hmm." Eliza took another bite.

"My point about Betty's clothing is this: you never see pictures of her looking anything less than perfect. So I suspect she was part of his image."

"Totally Victor." Eliza rolled her eyes. "He dressed her. And took her to the makeup counter at the mall to learn how to do her face. I'm not even kidding."

"That's creepy."

"Tell me about it. He was always after me to wear fancier clothes too. Remember, it's all about the image with him." She paused. "Or it was. When I worked for him." A delighted smile followed, and then she took another bite of the scone.

"Maybe she got tired of being his dress-up doll," Priscilla said. "I would imagine that sort of life would be annoying after a while. I mean, it's one thing for your husband to buy you pretty things, but for him to pick out your clothes and choose your makeup . . . who does that? Most men couldn't care less about such things. On the other hand, she must've really loved designer handbags, because she was carrying one that day on the ferry in spite of her casual clothing, the same bag she was holding in the billboard photo."

"Yes, she always carried a Landelier bag."

"Landelier?" Priscilla let out a little whistle. "Wow. Expensive."

"Yes. They didn't come from Victor, though. He liked nice stuff, but not that nice. She got a new Landelier bag from her daughter every Christmas. The one in the photo was her latest Christmas gift. Victor was very proud of those bags and very grateful he didn't have to pay for them."

"Wait, her daughter?"

"Yes." Eliza paused to take another bite. "Like I said before, Keeley lives in Manhattan. Well, she did. We tried to find her after Betty went missing, but she seems to have moved. Victor was furious. He expected me to wiggle my nose and make her appear, but she's good and truly gone."

"Why didn't he look for her himself?"

"Victor? Search for something on the computer?" Eliza laughed. "That's what he has me for. He doesn't even know his own email address, let alone how to search the web for a missing person."

"I find that hard to believe."

"Think about it, Priscilla. He's always surrounded himself with people who would do his bidding." Eliza sighed. "I wasn't always able to accomplish all he expected, which generated a lot of anger in the office. We'll just leave it at that. He was particularly angry that I couldn't find Keeley."

"Weird, that his own daughter wouldn't let him know where she moved to."

"Not so weird. She's Betty's daughter from her first marriage. And she has never been a fan of Victor, trust me. I heard all about it when she came to visit a couple years back." Eliza paused, and her gaze shifted downward. "I'll be honest...I didn't really bend over backwards to find Keeley after Betty went missing. She's seen Victor's angry side too. I was afraid she'd never forgive me if I gave him information that might lead to her. I did call her company in Manhattan, and they said she no longer worked there. That's all they would tell me."

"I see. And did you say Keeley was a designer of some sort?"

"Yes." She shrugged. "When she worked in Manhattan. I have no idea what she's doing now...or where she's doing it."

Priscilla lost herself to her thoughts for a moment. "Speaking of design, when I saw Betty that day on the ferry, she was wearing jeans and a blue blouse. Is that what you remember?"

Eliza squinted, as if in thought. "She's so beautiful, she looked great in anything. I remember thinking that her jeans were just average looking. But I don't remember a blue blouse—"

Before she could continue, the door of the bakery opened, and Carson Fletcher walked in.

"Well, this is a sweet coincidence." Priscilla lifted her hand and waved, then smiled as Carson waved back. He approached, moving a bit slowly.

"Mrs. Grant." He smiled and extended his hand. "Great to see you again."

"You're recovering nicely, I hope?" Priscilla asked.

"Yes, and so is Claire. She should be released from the hospital soon, Lord willing. No signs of rejection, which is very good news."

"Wonderful."

Carson turned his gaze to Eliza and extended his hand. "Sorry. Didn't mean to exclude you. I'm Carson Fletcher."

Priscilla quickly made introductions. "Carson Fletcher, meet my good friend, Eliza Jamison."

His eyes lit up at once. "The owner of the red Corvette in the parking lot."

"Yes." Eliza grinned. "But how did you know that?"

"Mrs. Grant shared your name when she came to visit me in the hospital. It's great to meet a fellow car enthusiast. I've seen that beautiful red Corvette around town, and I have to say it's in great shape for a '76."

"Thanks. I work hard to keep it that way. It means the world to me."

"I understand that. You'd have a hard time prying me away from my cars too, though I had to leave a few behind in Florida when I moved here."

This led to a lengthy and passionate conversation between the two of them about their love of vehicles and the particular makes and models he'd left in storage in Florida. Priscilla couldn't make sense out of all of it, but these two were clearly a match made in heaven. Before she knew it, Carson was escorting Eliza out to the parking lot to look at his new Jaguar.

"Do you think we'll ever see them again?" Candy asked as she sidled up next to Priscilla.

"Not sure, to be honest. But I guess that's okay. They seem to have a lot in common."

Candy nodded. "That's great. I heard through the grapevine that he's planning to stay, that he's got an office in the building near Ortmann's."

"Yes, so I heard." An idea hit Priscilla at once. "Do you think he'll be hiring?"

"Likely."

Priscilla laughed. "I might have just the person. In fact, he's getting to know her better as we speak."

"Really? Eliza is looking for work?" Candy looked perplexed by this notion.

"She is now that Victor lost the election."

"Oh, right." Candy nodded. "Remarkable turn of events."

"I think the whole thing is pretty remarkable," Priscilla said. "But nothing is quite as remarkable as what God has done for Carson's daughter, is it?"

Candy shook her head. "Can you imagine finding out you had a family member you didn't know about? I'm sure it's a journey Claire is very grateful for."

"I can relate on some level," Priscilla admitted. "I've been here less than a year, but in some ways, I feel like I've discovered family I barely knew. I lived my whole life in Kansas, far removed from family members in Martha's Vineyard. Now I'm here—a place that didn't feel like home at first—and loving every minute. You've all become like family to me."

"Aw, I'm so glad you feel that way." Candy rested her hand on Priscilla's shoulder. "God brought you all the way from Kansas."

"And brought Carson all the way from Florida," Priscilla added. "Distance is nothing to the Lord. When you need some-thing—or someone—badly enough, you cross any number of miles to get to them."

As she spoke, Priscilla's heart rate skipped into overtime. Yes, when you needed someone badly enough, you would cross any number of miles to get to them.

And suddenly, she realized that was exactly what Betty Fox had done.

CHAPTER TWENTY-SEVEN

Priscilla excused herself from the conversation with Candy and barreled toward the parking lot. She found Eliza and Carson standing next to the red Corvette.

Eliza glanced her way and grinned. "Priscilla, you're never going to believe it, but Mr. Fletcher is looking for an assistant at his new office. Isn't that the coolest coincidence?"

"Yes." Priscilla stopped to gasp for breath. "Eliza, I have to ask you a question."

"Sure. What is it?"

"You said—" Priscilla paused to catch her breath once more. "You said you didn't remember Betty Fox wearing a blue blouse. That day on the ferry, I mean."

"She was wearing blue when I saw her," Carson said. "At least I think she was."

"Same here," Priscilla said. "I distinctly remember a blue blouse. So why are your recollections different, Eliza?"

Creases formed between Eliza's brows. "I saw her coming out of the restroom as I headed down to my car. I remember thinking how pretty she looked in that pink blouse she was wearing. It really suited her."

"Bingo." Priscilla blew out a breath. "Tell me once more the name of the bank that Betty uses here on the island?"

"Vineyard First."

"Got it. And you're absolutely sure she always carried a Landelier bag, even on ordinary occasions like ferry crossings?"

"Always. I saw it with my own eyes that day. There was some sort of a special bond between her and her daughter over that particular brand."

"Right. Thanks for confirming." Priscilla paused, knowing she finally had her answer. Victor Fox hadn't harmed his wife.

Yet.

But he might, if he found her.

Priscilla's next words were rushed. "Eliza, I can't thank you enough. I knew you would have the answers to my lingering questions."

"Did I?" Eliza shrugged. "I'm still confused, but I'm glad I could help."

"Oh, you did. More than you know." Priscilla sprinted toward her car, turning back only to holler, "Congrats on the new job, by the way. I think you two are going to enjoy working together."

They both waved as she got into her vehicle and headed toward the museum. She arrived minutes later and asked Mildred to call her cousins for an important meeting.

"Won't you just tell me what this is about, Priscilla?" Mildred asked after making the calls.

"When they get here. I don't want to have to go through it more than once. In the meantime, can I use your computer? I've got a couple of unanswered questions."

"Of course."

Priscilla browsed the web, searching for the name Landelier. As she suspected, the company was located in Manhattan. But they also had a second plant in a place that suddenly sounded very familiar. She then looked up the name of the credit union from the deposit slip she'd seen on the floorboard of Betty's vehicle. No doubt Betty had accidentally left that slip behind. How it had gone unnoticed by the police was another question altogether, one she would ask April or the police chief later. Right now, there were other, more pressing matters.

It took some time for all the ladies to gather, but when they did, Mildred ushered them into the conference room so Priscilla could share her thoughts.

"I'm pretty sure I know where Betty Fox is," she began.

"You—you do?" Trudy looked stunned. "Are you saying she's alive and well?"

"She is. At least I pray my instincts are right and she is." Priscilla rested her hands on the conference table. "I feel the need for a little road trip. Anyone want to join me?"

"How far are we talking?" Gail asked. "Pop's got to have his pills at two."

"And I've got a beauty appointment at three thirty," Trudy said. "My roots are showing,"

"That leaves me," Joan said. "I'm free as a bird, but I'm still recovering from a cold, so I might not be the best candidate. I don't want to sneeze on you."

Mildred frowned. "You haven't even said where you're going yet, Priscilla."

"To the Hartford Credit Union."

Trudy wrinkled her nose. "I didn't realize you banked at a credit union."

"I don't. But I need to swing by Hartford Credit Union—in Hartford, Connecticut."

"Connecticut?" Trudy's eyes widened. "As in, the state?"

"Yep." Priscilla paused and willed her tumbling thoughts to slow down. "It's not where I bank, but it is where Betty Fox banks."

"I thought the Foxes banked at Vineyard First," Gail said.

"Yes. She has an account there too, and I can confirm it. That day at Victor's office, I saw a computer screen loaded with her bank account information on it. The account was at Vineyard First, here on the island. It didn't hit me until this morning when I was talking to Candy. I remembered seeing a deposit slip on the floorboard of Betty's Suburban that day on the ferry. Maybe it fell out of her purse. Maybe it fell out of her pocket. Who knows? But it wasn't a bank at all. It was the Hartford Credit Union. I looked it up online just now, and there's only one listing, in Hartford, Connecticut."

"Wow, Priscilla."

"Something else has been bothering me too. That purse we found in her vehicle. It was a plain purse. Ordinary. Like something you'd buy at a local shop or even at the mall."

"Right," Trudy agreed.

"She always carried Landelier purses. Always. According to Eliza, anyway. Her daughter sends one every Christmas."

"Where do I have to go to get a daughter like that?" Trudy asked and then laughed.

"Right?" Priscilla paused. "If you saw the most recent billboard photo of Betty and Victor, she was carrying a gorgeous new Landelier. It occurred to me that the lady I saw walking off the ferry that day—the one in the pink blouse, sunglasses, and scarf—was carrying a designer purse just like the one in the photo."

Joan gave her an admiring look. "You really have pieced this together. And you think you'll find her in Hartford?"

"I do. And I'll tell you why."

"Why?" they all said in unison.

"Because Keeley Collingsworth, Betty's daughter, is a designer for Landelier. And the company only has two locations: a design studio in Manhattan and a manufacturing plant in—"

"Hartford, Connecticut!" Trudy squealed. "Oh my goodness, I don't know how you do it, Priscilla. I really don't."

"Eliza tried to locate Keeley in Manhattan after Betty went missing, but the company said she no longer worked there. Eliza took that to mean Keeley no longer worked for Landelier at all. But I got to thinking about it and decided maybe she'd misunderstood."

Gail shook her head, as if not quite believing all of this. "Remarkable."

"So what do you say? Are you ready for a drive?" Priscilla asked.

"To Connecticut?" Trudy hesitated. "Well, it sounds like I'd better cancel my beauty appointment. My roots will just have to wait."

"And I'll get Pop's pills ready now. He can take them on his own," Gail agreed.

"I wish I could go," Mildred said, "but I can't leave the museum on such short notice."

"We'll keep you informed, I promise."

The ladies scattered to take care of necessary details, and Priscilla put in a call to Gerald. He seemed stunned by her revelations but filled with admiration as well.

"I should go with you, Priscilla. It's not safe for you to go alone."

"She'll be intimidated if I show up with a man in uniform, Gerald. You know she will. And besides, she's not a suspect."

"True."

"Will you do something for me?"

"Anything." His words were laced with emotion. "As long as you promise to be safe."

"I promise. But I'll need an address for Keeley Collingsworth in Hartford, Connecticut. Do you think you can track that down for me?"

"I'll do my best."

"And Gerald, one more favor? Keep an eye on Victor while we're gone. I don't want him to figure out that we're on Betty's trail. He might try to follow us."

"Trust me, I'm already on my way to his place now. I'll talk to him about…"

"Politics?" She laughed.

"No. From what I understand, he's talking about opening a new car dealership. I'll talk to him about that."

"Thank you." She ended the call, grateful for his help.

Less than an hour later, the ladies were all gathered in Priscilla's SUV, headed for the ferry. She managed to get a ticket—quite a feat without a reservation. As she pulled on board Priscilla replayed the whole incident in her head—every detail about the day Betty had gone missing. The ding in the fender. Betty's face as Carson spoke to her. Betty, in a blue blouse and tan scarf, walking the side deck after the ferry left the landing. Getting back in her car. Finding out that Betty was no longer on board. Looking at the contents of the purse as it fell open. Driving off the ferry. Seeing several pedestrians pass her car. Walking back on board to search for Betty. Finding the clothing tags in the bathroom.

It all added up to just one thing now. Betty Fox had bolted. She'd simply changed into a new blouse, donned sunglasses and a different scarf, and walked off the ferry to a new life, one she had clearly planned for months—possibly even years—with her daughter's help.

Priscilla didn't blame her one little bit. In fact, she would have offered to assist, had Betty asked. And so would any number of people.

But Betty hadn't asked. She'd bravely marched off that ferry and into a new existence, one that did not include Victor Fox.

"I still don't see how we're going to find her." Trudy's words roused Priscilla from her thoughts. Her cousin flipped down the passenger seat visor and stared at her reflection in the mirror. "All you have to go on is the address for a credit union, right?"

"They won't give away a private address for a customer," Gail concurred. "So we can really only go as far as that, right?"

"Maybe. Or maybe not. I called Gerald. He's trying to track down the daughter's home address. I'm not sure if he can manage it, but maybe."

"Do you think he's told the police where we're headed?"

"Probably, if he can't track down the address on his own." Priscilla sighed. "But remember, we can always go to Landelier and ask to speak to Keeley. If she's still in the office by the time we get to Hartford, I mean."

As the ferry pulled away from Vineyard Crossing, the ladies riddled her with questions.

"How did she get off the ferry without anyone noticing her?" Trudy asked.

"Easy. She walked off."

"You're saying she drove on, left her car sitting there, and just walked off the ferry?"

"Sure. Why not? People walk off all the time. She left the ferry wearing a different set of clothes—including sunglasses and scarf. No one was any the wiser."

"Certainly not us," Trudy said.

"But if she left her car on the ferry, what did she do when she got off? How did she get anywhere?" Gail asked.

"Simple," said Priscilla. "My theory is that she caught a cab, took off from Woods Hole, and didn't stop until she arrived in Boston."

"How do you know she landed in Boston?" Joan asked.

"I'm speculating here but would venture a guess she had a flight from Boston to Hartford, booked and paid for by her daughter."

"Maybe she took a cab all the way to Connecticut," Joan suggested. "People with money do that. Take long rides in cabs, I mean."

"I don't doubt she had the money to manage that. I suspect her daughter had been tucking quite a bit of cash into the linings of those purses she was sending. But I don't think Betty would take a cab all that way, because it would be too easy for Victor or the police to track her, if so. I'm guessing she only took the cab as far as Boston, then hopped on a plane. That way, if the cab driver was questioned, he wouldn't have any knowledge of where she was flying."

"Makes sense," Gail said. "But I can't imagine having to sneak around like that just to get away from a husband. It's so awful to think that some women have to live that way."

"Awful, for sure," Priscilla said.

The ladies continued to chat until the ferry arrived at Woods Hole. Then Priscilla asked Gail to serve as navigator. She took Trudy's place in the front seat and guided them all the way from Massachusetts to Hartford, Connecticut, a three-hour drive.

She rambled on about how beautiful Connecticut was in the springtime, but Priscilla only heard half of it. She couldn't stop thinking about Betty Fox. About that bank account. About that Landelier purse. And she prayed she would somehow reach Hartford and locate Betty's address. Then she could finally put the remaining puzzle pieces together, once and for all.

CHAPTER TWENTY-EIGHT

Priscilla made two stops along the way—both for Trudy, who had the smallest bladder of anyone she'd ever known. When they arrived in Hartford, Priscilla stopped at the credit union at the corner of Madison and Vaughn. She stared at the building and sighed. So this was where Betty had been sending her money all these months. God bless the Hartford Credit Union for taking such good care of her.

She pulled into the parking lot and put the car into Park.

"Going inside, Priscilla?" Gail asked.

"No. Checking my phone to see if I missed any messages." Sure enough, she'd missed a couple of texts from April at the police department. Priscilla called her and set the phone to speaker so her cousins could hear the conversation.

April answered with, "Priscilla, Gerald tells me you're in Connecticut."

"Yes. Did you get that address for me?"

She sighed. "Yes, we located Betty's daughter's address. It's a private listing in Weatogue, a suburb of Hartford."

"I knew she must be in the area. Thanks for checking."

April gave her the address, and Gail jotted it down on a scrap of paper.

"Just promise me you won't do anything foolish if you find Betty," April said.

"If?"

"When. *When* you find her." April's voice took on a motherly tone. "And for the record, you really should've asked me to go along, just as a precaution. Not that I could do much in a different state, but I could certainly involve local police, should the need arise."

"Betty Fox is a victim, not a suspect. I have every right in the world to talk woman to woman with someone who might need a friend."

"Right."

"And trust me, if the police swarm her daughter's place, it will crush her. She's been through enough already. I just need you to promise that Victor won't find out where I'm headed. That's key."

"He won't. In fact, Gerald is with him now."

"Good. Please tell him to talk Victor out of that car lot. It's the last thing we need in Vineyard Haven."

"Agreed."

"April, let me ask you a question before we end this call." Priscilla glanced in the rearview mirror at Trudy, who was busy adding blush to her cheeks.

"Sure." April paused. "I guess I've got it coming."

"It's not an accusation, just a question. How did it escape everyone's notice that the deposit slip in Betty's purse was for a credit union in Hartford, not her bank here on the island?"

April sighed. "I guess that's my fault. We found her checkbook in the purse on the seat. It was for an account here on the island. I just didn't look closely enough to realize that the deposit slip was for a completely different institution. In my mind, it had fallen from the checkbook. I simply overlooked it, Priscilla." She sighed. "To be perfectly honest, I shouldn't have gone into work that day at all. I was really sick with that stupid upper respiratory infection and was running a low-grade fever to boot. I should've stayed home in bed, I guess, and let someone else handle the case."

"I'm sorry you weren't feeling well. And I'm not saying this was a glaring mistake. It took me a while to figure it out too. I'm just curious how we all could have looked right at it and not seen it for what it was."

"Isn't that what life is like? We look at people, situations, and so on, thinking we see one thing. Then we dig a little deeper and find out the situation was completely different from the one they painted."

"Well, thanks, April. I'd better hang up so I can swing by Betty's daughter's place. I'll keep you posted on how this goes."

"Please do. And be careful, Priscilla. Gerald is worried about you."

"O-oh?"

"Yes. We are all praying this goes smoothly. Please give Betty our assurances that we're doing all we can to keep Victor from knowing where she is."

"I will."

Priscilla ended the call and shoved her phone into her purse. "Well, there you go."

"I've already pulled up that address on my phone's navigation," Gail said. "Weatogue isn't far from here."

"Can we stop for food first?" Trudy grumbled. "I'm starving, and I need to go to the bathroom."

"I could stand to fill up the gas tank too," Priscilla said. "So, yes. Let's stop for a bite and come up with a strategy. I hate to barge in on Betty during the dinner hour, anyway."

She pulled her vehicle into a fast-food restaurant, and the ladies ate cheeseburgers and fries while they talked through a plan. In the end, they decided to let Priscilla take the lead.

"If we all go to the door, she'll think she's under attack," Joan said. "I know I would feel weird if a group of women showed up at my door."

"Ooh, a group of women showed up at my door once, trying to give me a religious pamphlet," Trudy said. "I sent 'em packing. Groups don't intimidate me."

"Well, you're not like most people, Trudy," Joan countered.

From her spot across the table, Gail looked up and grinned. "You can say that again."

After eating, they drove to the address April had given them. Priscilla pulled the car up to the front of a massive, beautiful home, and Trudy whistled.

"Boy, howdy. I don't know what I was expecting, but not this."

"Keeley works for Landelier. I guess she makes good money."

"Maybe she has a husband who works as a banker or something too," Trudy added.

Priscilla slipped the car into Park and turned to face the others. "Okay, pray for me. I'm going to do this."

"Let's pray right now." Joan's calm voice spoke in a reassuring manner. She began to pray, which calmed Priscilla's spirit.

Afterward, Priscilla got out of the car, squinting as the overhead sun cast its red and gold sunset over her. "Please, God," she whispered. "Let her be home."

She was.

Keeley answered the door. She was just as Priscilla had imagined her, only a bit younger and more casually dressed than someone this well-off might be. Priscilla did her best to explain who she was and why she'd come. When she mentioned Betty's name, Keeley blanched.

"I—I don't know what to say," Keeley offered in response. "I really don't think—I mean, I really..."

"Who is it, Keeley?" a male voice asked from inside.

"Someone from the Vineyard," she responded.

"The Vineyard?" The man, who looked to be in his early forties, arrived at the door in short order. "How can I help you?"

Priscilla went through the speech again, ending with the words, "I know she's here, and I understand why she came. I promise I'm not here to harm her in any way, just to offer assurances that she's loved and cared for."

"Does that husband of hers know you're here?" Keeley's husband put his hands on his hips.

"No. And he won't. The police have assured me of that."

"The police?" Keeley's eyes widened.

"They know I'm here, but they're not coming, either. It's just me." Priscilla gestured to her car. "And a trio of cousins, who are praying women. We wanted to come to ease our minds, to make sure Betty was—is—okay."

"My mother has not been okay for some time." Keeley's eyes flooded with tears. "She has quite a journey ahead of her to get there."

A wave of relief washed over Priscilla. "So she is here?"

"She's here."

"But possibly not for long, now that you people have tracked her down," Keeley's husband said.

"I promise you, 'we people' are only here to make sure she's okay. Nothing more, nothing less. Would you please ask Betty if she would be willing to visit with me?" On second thought, it might be good to add the cousins into the mix, because Betty was familiar with them. "With us?"

"I can ask, but I'm sure she'll say no." Keeley took a step back, and a female voice sounded from behind the door.

"I will see them, Keeley. I can only hide for so long."

Seconds later, Betty Fox stepped into view. She wore the same pink top and a casual pair of jeans. And she looked terrified.

CHAPTER TWENTY-NINE

How did you find me?"

Priscilla reached into her purse and pulled out the clothing tags, ready to explain. "It was a totally random thing, Betty. I found these in the trash can in the ladies' room on the ferry. It took a lot of finagling, but I finally pieced the story together with the help of a few friends."

Betty clamped a hand over her mouth and then pulled it away. "I can't believe I did that. I was being so careful. I should never have thrown those away."

"It's just instinct to throw things away. But I tracked the tags back to the Perfect Fit and eventually realized you must have been the one who bought the items."

"I thought I'd covered all my bases. I even paid for this blouse in cash."

"Yes, and you did a fantastic job. Great blouse, by the way. Very flattering."

"Thanks."

"I like it so much, I might just get one like it." Priscilla chuckled. "But you did a great job of getting off that ferry without being recognized, Betty. If you ever want to work for the CIA, you've already got the skills. Coming on board the ferry in a blue blouse. Wearing a tan scarf. Then changing to something altogether different so that you could walk off…you really put a lot of thought into this."

"I had to. I'm not sure you would believe me if I told you how many months we planned for that day. Even getting a reservation on the ferry was tricky." She glanced toward the car, and Priscilla could read the recognition in her eyes when she saw Trudy, Joan, and Gail. "Keeley and Chris took care of it all."

"Would you mind terribly if I brought in my cousins?" Priscilla asked. "I think you know all of them. I promise we're not here to interrogate or alarm you in any way, just to offer support and comfort."

"You came all this way just to talk to me?"

"We did. We care about you, Betty. We're concerned and want you to know you're being prayed for, even now."

"Thank you. And yes, bring the ladies in." Betty pulled the door open a bit wider. Keeley and her husband, who Priscilla learned was named Chris, headed into another room while Priscilla gestured for Trudy, Gail, and Joan to join them.

A few minutes later, they were all gathered in the spacious living room of the Collingsworth home, drinking sweet tea and eating cookies.

"As I said, we're here to support you, Betty," Priscilla said after taking a drink of her tea. "You don't have to share anything you don't want to."

"Does he know she's here?" Keeley's husband asked.

"No."

"Good." He took a seat near Betty. "He can't ever know."

"He'll come if he knows." Betty's eyes registered fear. "I know it. He'll come to get me, and I'll have to go back."

"He won't. Even if he finds out, the police won't allow him to bother you."

"I hope you're not here to try to talk me into going back to him. I won't do it." Betty began to cry. "I can't do it. I spent too many years begging God for an opportunity to escape. I won't go back."

"No one would expect that of you." Gail rose and walked over to Betty's chair. She rested her hand on the other woman's shoulder. "That's the very opposite of why we're here, in fact."

Betty sniffled, her words sounding as broken as she looked. "He's so g-good at making people think he's s-something he's n-not."

"People are onto him, Betty," Gail said. "And they know what he's been doing to you."

"Yes," Priscilla chimed in. "You can thank Eliza for that."

"Eliza?" Betty's features hardened.

"That woman has done more damage to my mother's marriage than anyone else," Keeley said. "Why would she thank her, of all people?"

Priscilla shook her head and shifted her gaze to Betty. "Trust me when I say she was not having an affair with your husband. In fact, she was just as scared of him as you were."

"She was?" Betty shook her head in disbelief.

"She helped me every step of the way. Did you know that on the ferry that day, she was hoping to speak with you privately? Without Victor's interference."

"I avoided her like the plague." Betty released a slow breath. "I felt her watching me."

"There will come a time when she'll be able to explain all she'd hoped to say that day. But for now, just please trust me that she only wants to make sure you're safe. And she's terribly sorry she didn't try to do more to protect you."

Chris and Keeley looked as if they didn't quite believe all of this. Chris responded with a *humph* and leaned back in his chair.

An odd silence hung over the room for a moment.

"Did you know that he timed my trips to the grocery store?" Betty said at last.

"What?" Joan looked stunned by this notion.

"Yes." Betty nodded. "When I left the house to go grocery shopping, he set the timer for forty-five minutes. If I wasn't back home in that length of time, he would come looking for me. Ask Mrs. Ortmann. I can't tell you how many times he called her, just to check up on me. Of course, the way he did it made her think I was so lucky to have such a caring, sweet husband."

Joan mouthed the word *wow* but remained silent.

"And he used to call me from work—ten or twenty times a day. I'm not exaggerating. Every time we weren't together, he was checking on me." She shivered. "But trust me, that wasn't all. He had weird obsessions, Priscilla."

"Like?"

"He took zillions of pictures of the two of us. Selfies, mostly. I know, I know, lots of husbands do that. But he filled every room with those pictures. It was almost like he was making a shrine. And he went around telling people what a perfect marriage we had, but when doors were closed, it was anything but."

"What was it like at home?"

"Confusing. Scary. For a while he would be fine. Loving. Over-the-top affectionate. Then, out of the blue, he would snap and become someone else altogether. During those times, it would get terrifying. The names he called me were"—she trembled—"horrible. We'll just leave it at that."

"I'm so sorry, Betty." Trudy gave her a compassionate look. "We had no idea."

"No one did," Betty whispered. Her gaze shifted to her daughter. "Except Keeley, of course. And Chris."

"Was he physically violent?" Priscilla asked.

"That's the strange part. He never hit me." She shook her head. "Sometimes I wished he would, just so I would have an excuse to leave."

"Isn't that awful?" Keeley clenched her fists, and Priscilla could read the anger in her eyes. "A woman hoping her husband would beat her so she would have an excuse to leave?"

"Awful," all of the cousins said in unison.

"People are very understanding when a woman leaves because she's being physically abused," Keeley said. "But they aren't as compassionate when the woman is 'just' being verbally abused."

"It's true," Betty explained. "I took a risk and spoke to one of the pastors at our church. He told me to pray and ask God to change Victor's heart. So I did." Her eyes filled with tears. "I prayed for years, and he never changed. I'm not saying that people can't change. I'm not saying that people should run from their marriages because they've had a fight or two. But when a woman is constantly berated and has no one to stand up for her, she ends up leaving because it's the only option she has. Either that or she stays and is terrified for the rest of her life, bound by fear."

"I can't even imagine." Priscilla couldn't, either. Gary had been loving. Gentle. Nothing like the man Betty was describing.

"I've been staying with Keeley and Chris since the first of the month. They moved to a new place, far from where they had lived, so Victor couldn't track us down. That's how worried they were about me. Keeley really has been a rock for me these past few months. I started texting her some time ago. I had to get a separate phone, one Victor didn't know about. He almost saw it one day, and I was scared to death."

"That's awful, Betty," Trudy said. "I would've thrown the first phone out the window and pretended I lost it."

"No, that's just it," Chris interjected. "We told her to keep up appearances with the first phone, to send us occasional messages, as always, so Victor wouldn't suspect we were communicating any other way."

"Man." Trudy shook her head. "Sounds like a lot of work."

"We knew he was reading all of those messages," Keeley explained.

Betty shrugged. "He had my password, of course. And he always knew where I was going. The phone had a tracking feature set up. I had no privacy at all. None."

Joan shook her head. "You poor thing."

"Now you understand why I had to get the new phone. Keeley took care of it for me. She bought it and hid it in my Christmas present."

Priscilla nodded. "The Landelier purse."

"Yes. How did you know?"

"She's a very discerning woman," Trudy said. "That's how she knew."

"Well, I was never so grateful to get that phone, I'll tell you. It was the first step toward my freedom. And I don't want to go back. Not ever. I won't go back."

Priscilla shook her head. "No one is here to ask you to do that, Betty. Your safety is our priority. We've only come to make sure—with our own eyes—that you're alive and well."

"I'm alive." Her eyes took on a new light. "For the first time in years. Truly alive. I feel like a caged bird set free. And it helps that I've been in counseling. Keeley recommended a great therapist, and I've seen her twice already. I think it will be helpful, but it's going to take a while to break free after all I've been through."

"No doubt." Priscilla paused. "Has she mentioned the term gaslighting to you?"

"Gaslighting? I don't think so."

"Look it up. I think you'll find some familiar things there."

"Will do." Betty looked at Priscilla. "So what happens next?"

"With your permission, I'll tell Martha's Vineyard police your situation so they can close the case."

"I read the *Gazette* online," she said, "and saw that the police are trying to figure out what happened to me. They thought I was kidnapped?"

"Or murdered. I don't know if you realize it or not, but a couple of the locals were suspected of harming you or even kidnapping you."

"Oh, my." She clamped a hand over her mouth. "I didn't even think about that. I just drove onto that ferry and took off on foot, never looking back."

"Tell us about that day," Trudy said. "I was there, but I want to hear about it from your perspective."

"A lot of thought and prayer went into that day," Keeley responded. "Trust me when I say I was terrified."

"You have to pay in advance to bring a car on the ferry," Chris explained. "As I'm sure you know. And it has to be done online."

"Keeley paid for it," Betty said. "She made sure I had everything I needed to get out of there."

"I never liked Victor," Keeley explained. "Even though I was just a teen when they first started dating, all I saw were red flags."

"Why didn't I listen to you then?" Betty sighed. "It would've saved us all so much trouble."

"I thought he was creepy, but Mom didn't see it at the time."

"I thought his obsessive behavior was a little odd but endearing." Betty shrugged. "Turned out the daughter was right, and the mother was wrong."

"Well, God bless your daughter for caring enough to make sure you had a safe place to go." Trudy looked admiringly at Keeley.

"Yes, and I hope it stays a safe place." Betty shot a terrified glance Priscilla's way. "Promise me?"

"I promise."

"Anyway, I decided to leave a purse in my Suburban to throw off the police. I figured it would stall them and give me time to slip away."

"In a cab?" Priscilla asked.

"A cab that I was waiting in," Keeley said.

"You were there at the Woods Hole landing?" Priscilla nearly gasped at this revelation.

"In the back seat of the cab. When we left the landing, the driver took us as far as a restaurant in Falmouth, where I'd parked my car. We drove home from there."

"Wow. Good work." Priscilla turned to face Betty head-on. "You've been through so much. Don't you think it's time to file a restraining order against Victor?"

Betty's eyes filled with tears, and she shook her head. "No. In order to do that, we'll have to list this address. Don't you see?"

Ah. She had a point.

"We've looked into all that," Chris said. "It might do more harm than good. For one thing, Victor doesn't even know if she's alive at this point."

"I'd kind of like to keep it that way," Keeley added. "Feels safer."

"I will have to face him sooner or later." Betty wiped at her eyes with the back of her hand. "I'll be filing for divorce, of course."

This did not come as a surprise to Priscilla.

"But I'm hoping to find an excellent attorney first, one who will be tough enough to stand up to him. His acting skills are amazing. He can bluff his way through any situation, so I need someone extraordinary. Once I get all of that settled, I'll have the attorney go ahead and file a restraining order."

"I've been waiting until just the right moment to tell you, Mom, but I think I know someone." Keeley rose from her chair and lifted her tea glass from the side table. "Harrison Bradley represents Landelier. He's the best in business law. But one of his associates works in family law. He's already recommended her."

"Well, there you go," Trudy said. "That was easy."

Priscilla knew it wouldn't be easy. Betty had a long road ahead of her, one that would require courage and tenacity. She would have to strengthen her resolve and stand firm—a tiny David against a seemingly mighty Goliath.

Only this time she would have the women of Martha's Vineyard in her corner. And when you got the ladies of the Vineyard riled up, well, you really didn't stand a chance.

CHAPTER THIRTY

L ess than a week after Priscilla tracked down Betty in Connecticut, she arranged a meeting with the cousins. Instead of gathering at the usual place, they headed to a local ice cream parlor for a sweet treat to cool them down on a hot day. Priscilla also invited Gerald to join them so she could get caught up on the latest regarding the case.

Trudy was the first to arrive. She bounded toward Priscilla's table, a grin on her face. "I've just signed up a new distributor to sell Heavenly Faces makeup! You'll never guess who."

"Eliza Jamison?"

"Nope."

"You finally talked Mildred into it?"

"Nope. That's never going to happen. But I just signed Teresa Claybrook."

"Oh, wow." Priscilla grinned. "Well, I think that's perfect."

"She's been rather lonely, now that the campaign is over. I think she was happy to spend so much time with Tony."

"What's this about Tony?"

Priscilla turned to discover Gerald had entered the ice cream parlor. He was holding a bouquet of roses in his hand. He passed them her way without saying a word. This, naturally, rendered Trudy mute.

"What in the world? What are these for?" Priscilla pulled the bouquet of roses—yellow, red, pink, and white—closer for a lovely sniff. *Mmm.*

"You told me not so long ago that you hadn't received roses in ages. I decided to remedy that."

"Wow." She held them close, the aroma making her giddy. Or maybe it was just the heat making her swoon. If the island was this hot at the end of May, what would temperatures look like over the summer?

He plopped down into the chair next to her. "I didn't do this so you could sing my praises on Facebook, by the way. Just making that clear."

She laughed. "So I guess I'm not posting a picture?"

"Your choice. But that wasn't my motivation." His manner radiated genuine sweetness. "You deserve roses, Priscilla. You really do."

"That's very sweet, Gerald." She ran her fingertips across the petals of one of the pink roses, and a lump grew in her throat. Then her eyes filled with tears as she was struck by a memory of the last time Gary had brought her flowers. They weren't roses—they were wildflowers he'd plucked from the field on the west end of their property. She'd scolded him for pulling them. Now she would give the world to have them once again. To have *him* once again.

The image was almost more than her heart could take.

"You okay over there? Did I strike a nerve?" Gerald's voice roused her from her reminiscing.

"I'm okay." She wiped the moisture from her eyelashes. "Just thinking."

"I think she's overwhelmed," Trudy said. "In a good way. This is a stellar move, O'Bannon. I think you've even topped Tony McClaren this time around. I was starting to think he had the upper hand, if you get my drift."

"Tony." Gerald sighed. "Are we still talking about him? Isn't he busy running the city or something?"

Before Priscilla could respond, the bell above the door jingled, and Gail walked in with Joan following behind. Uncle Hugh dragged in on their heels, grumbling about the heat.

"Don't worry, Pop," Gail called out. "I'll get you some ice cream. That'll cool you down." She paused to acknowledge Priscilla, Gerald, and Trudy, then got in line to order. Uncle Hugh took a seat at the table next to them.

"Why the flowers?" Uncle Hugh jabbed his finger in the direction of the roses. "Someone die?"

"No, Uncle Hugh. They were a gift from Gerald." Priscilla ran her finger along the green wrapping paper. "Aren't they beautiful? I'll put them in a vase as soon as I get home."

"Never understood the point, myself. Why give a woman a gift that's only going to die in a few days?" Uncle Hugh shrugged and reached for the newspaper. "Well, lookee here. Victor's opening a car lot after all. I'd hoped someone would talk him out of it." He glared at Gerald.

"Hey, I did my best. But he's got his heart set on it. And you know what a salesman he is. I guess he couldn't resist."

"Yeah, before long we'll see billboards all over town." Trudy groaned. "Only instead of photos of his wife, it'll be Victor standing in front of some souped-up car, singing the praises of the vehicle."

"More likely singing his own praises." Uncle Hugh sighed and returned his attention to the paper. "And what's this about some famous historian coming to speak at the museum? Jacob something-or-another?"

"Oh, Mildred is probably beside herself," Priscilla said. "She's been trying to get Jacob Lansford here for ages. Good for her."

Trudy got up to order ice cream, but Priscilla remained at the table with Gerald. She was happy to have time alone with him.

"Did you hear that Eliza is working for Carson?" she asked.

"Yep." He nodded.

"And did you hear that she moved her mother into the B&B so she can take care of her?"

"I hadn't heard that, but I'm happy for them."

"It'll be nice to have her mother close by. Eliza needs that, after all she's been through. Her years with Victor have left her rather traumatized, from what I can tell."

"Speaking of Victor, I finally got him to come clean about why he watched Betty so closely," Gerald said. "Why he was afraid to let her out of his sight, I mean."

"Because of his first wife, right?"

Gerald looked stunned. "Yes. But how did you know that?"

"Eliza once said that Victor is the man he is today because of what happened with his first wife. He wasn't there to watch over her. He felt responsible for her death."

"Right. So when he married again, he swung the opposite direction. Never let his wife out of his sight. He was determined nothing would ever happen to her. He overcompensated. And the anger inside his heart was probably rooted in guilt. He never forgave himself."

"But he took it out on Betty."

"Yes, sadly."

"In the end, he smothered her, and she fled." Priscilla paused. "The whole thing is so sad. I feel horrible for Betty, but I suppose I feel bad for Victor too. He's got so many layers that need to be peeled back before he can be fully healed of all that."

"What would you do if I told you that Victor has come to me for advice?"

"What?" Priscilla gazed into Gerald's eyes.

"I'm certainly no counselor, but he asked for my recommendations. I think he's ready to be rid of whatever is troubling him."

"Truly, or is this just some sort of ploy to set himself up for the next election?"

"It's hard to tell with manipulators, but he seemed genuine enough."

"Why did he come to you, Gerald? No offense, but it's not like the two of you are close or anything."

"True, we haven't been. But I mentioned that I saw a counselor for a while after Cathy and I split up."

"You did?" This was news.

"Sure. Nothing wrong with getting help when you need it. And it helps to have someone to talk things out with. Besides, I had the kids to consider. Ian and Aggie were young, just ten and eight at the time. I wanted to be the best possible dad I could be for them."

"And you have, Gerald. You've been a wonderful father and grandfather."

"Thank you."

Priscilla sat for a moment, unable to respond over the lump in her throat. Perhaps she should have sought out a counselor after Gary's death.

"Anyway, Victor's talking about getting help, and that's a good thing."

"Do you think he'll try to win Betty back?"

Gerald shook his head. "Pretty sure he's given up on that at this point. The police have told him that they located her and she's safe, but they've warned him not to try to track her down."

"And you think he'll abide by that?"

Gerald shrugged. "I suggest she file a restraining order. Then he won't have any choice."

"She plans to, as soon as she files for divorce. She called me last night to say that she's already hired an attorney, so the ball's rolling."

"Good to know. But I still think it's a good sign that he's getting help, even if they never see each other again. I'm of the opinion that coming to peace with yourself is ultimately the best gift. When you do that, you stop hurting others, and you're finally able to heal."

"Wow. Maybe you should've been a counselor, Gerald." She smiled.

"Gerald O'Bannon, psychotherapist." He held out his hands as if framing a sign for his new office. A chuckle followed. "I don't think so, Priscilla. I'm content right where the Lord has me."

Priscilla wondered if his words had a double meaning, if such a thing could be judged from the sweetness pouring from his eyes right now.

"I did recommend a great counselor to Victor, one who specializes in grief. That's the driving force here, I believe. Grief has driven him to control."

"Right." Priscilla paused to think that through. "I guess we all grieve differently. When Gary died, I felt like crawling in a hole. Victor took the opposite approach and thrust himself into the public eye."

"You've been digging your way out of that hole since you arrived on the island, Priscilla." Gerald reached over and squeezed her hand. "I've been a witness to that. And, in some ways, you're in the public eye too, now that you've found yourself in the middle of so many mysteries here on the island."

She laughed. "Grieving widow takes up sleuthing."

"Something like that." He chuckled, and the dimple in his right cheek became evident. Priscilla found herself struck by his handsome face. In fact, she could barely look away as he spoke. "But the point is, you're making progress. Victor is not. He's stuck, and I think he knows it, which is why he's overcompensating in front of the public. If he puts on a show, acts like everything is great, he won't have to deal with the pain of losing someone he loved. If you think about it, he's pretty locked up with fear."

"And now he's lost the one person who was the focus of his life, so you can imagine he'll be in a bad place psychologically, especially once those divorce papers are served."

"Maybe that will help him heal. You know? Maybe getting away from the person he obsessed over will give him the time and space he needs to make improvements to his own life. Point is, we all have to come to grips with our grief, no matter how hard."

She watched the sadness in his eyes and realized he must be talking about his own divorce. "It's all so hard, isn't it? If I'd known that being an adult was this tough, I would've opted to stay a kid forever."

"Agreed. And just for the record, I've never once thought of you as a grieving widow. You're no cliché, Priscilla. Your grief is genuine, but you don't wear it on your sleeve. That's not to say people are wrong to grieve openly. I'm just saying you seem to have made some progress in that area."

"Either that, or I'm really good at keeping things inside." She paused, considering. "No, I think you're right. I really have come a long way. There's no denying it."

There was also no denying how much she enjoyed these quiet conversations with Gerald O'Bannon—even with Uncle Hugh grumbling over an article in the newspaper at the next table. What a comfort Gerald had become in her life. What a good man he was.

Trudy, Gail, and Joan returned moments later with their ice cream. They seated themselves at the table with Uncle Hugh, who latched onto his cone and dove right in.

"You ready for ice cream?" Gerald scooted his chair back. "My treat."

"Sure." They rose and walked to the counter.

As they stood in line, Teresa Claybrook passed by the front of the ice cream parlor, likely on her way to her tour guide shop nearby.

"I've been thinking a lot about her," Gerald said as he gestured with his head in Teresa's direction. "She's been single a long time. For as long as I can remember."

"You thinking of dating her?" Priscilla quirked a brow.

"No, no. Not at all. But I think we would all agree she's a good match for Tony McClaren."

"I'm not sure Tony is ready to date yet, though," Priscilla observed. "He's only been widowed a little more than a year."

"Oh, I don't know." Gerald shrugged. "Sometimes it's better for a man to have a woman around. She seems like a great candidate."

"So now you're offering matchmaker services?"

"Only to the needy."

"I see." Priscilla found this discussion rather surprising. "So you're okay with Tony dating Teresa."

"Well, sure. I see no problem with it. They both love the island, they're both passionate about making a difference. Seems like a match made in heaven."

They inched forward in the line, finally arriving at the counter.

"Why were you so suspicious of him before, then?" Priscilla asked.

"Suspicious of him?" Creases formed between Gerald's eyes.

"Yes. Every time he was around, you acted oddly. Did you see him as a suspect in this case because he was Victor's political opponent, or because you felt you had some sort of evidence against him? I never fully understood that."

The young woman behind the counter was ready to take their order, but Gerald seemed distracted. He faced Priscilla and shook his head. "You really don't get it, do you?"

"No." Clearly.

"My concerns about Tony McClaren didn't have anything to do with Betty's disappearance or with his qualifications as commissioner. They ran a little deeper than that." He gave her a knowing look.

"Meaning?"

"Meaning..." Gerald lowered his voice. "I didn't like the idea that he might have designs on you."

"Oh." Priscilla paused before saying more.

"Look, Tony's a great guy," Gerald said. "Maybe a little too great. I know what all the ladies say about him."

"What do they say?"

"He looks like a movie star." These words came from the teenage girl behind the counter. "Just quoting my mom, sorry."

"What she said." Gerald gestured to the girl with the ice cream scoop in her hand. "I guess there really is something about his green eyes that wins the ladies over."

"Blue." Priscilla clamped a hand over her mouth and then pulled it away. "Oops."

"Whatever. Point is, he's got the looks to draw women in. He never needed your help getting the female vote. Half the women in town were already voting for him. The other half were only voting for Victor because their husbands told them to, and they didn't know any better. Victor had all the guys at the club in his pocket."

Gerald stopped talking long enough to order their ice cream cones. Then they moved to the counter, and he paid for them.

When they arrived back at the table, cones in hand, Priscilla picked up where they'd left off. "So, if Tony didn't need my help with his campaign, why go to all the trouble to bring me in?"

"Trust me, he had an agenda." Gerald paused. "And I can't say I blame him for trying. He's been hurting since his wife died. They had a wonderful relationship, and I'm sure he's very lonely."

"It was never about the campaign?" Priscilla asked.

Gerald shook his head. "No. It wasn't. He's putting out all the signals that he's lonely, which is what made me think of Teresa. I do think they would make a good couple. After his heart has time to heal from his wife's loss, I mean. Everything in God's time, of course." He paused. "I never like to get in front of Him."

"Me either. The safest place to be—"

"Is in the center of His will." They spoke the words in unison.

Gerald's eyes widened.

"Wow." Priscilla looked at him. "Have you heard me say that before or something?"

"No." He shook his head. "I say it all the time."

"So do I."

She stared at him, dumbfounded. "Well, there you go. One more thing we have in common."

"Speaking of things we have in common, there's a new movie playing at the Strand Theatre in Oak Bluffs. One of those British flicks that women like so much. I'd be willing to give it a try if you think it sounds like something you would enjoy."

"Well, there's a tempting offer. And you want to go...why?"

"I don't. I'm just trying to win the female vote." He flashed a smile. "Is it working?"

Priscilla's heart skipped a beat as she stared deeply into his eyes. "Um, yes. It's working."

"Good. Because I'd hate to think I'd lost out simply because I didn't understand the mind of the opposite sex."

"If you can figure out the female mind, you'll have the shock and awe of every man on the planet. But don't worry, Gerald, we women don't want to be figured out."

"You don't?"

"Nope. We like being elusive."

"All right, then. Elusive, it is. So, about that movie."

"Just tell me when and where, and I'll meet you."

"You will not meet me. I will pick you up. It will be a proper date with dinner after."

"Okay. Friday night. But let's have dinner first."

"It's a date." He grinned. "I feel like I'm sixteen all over again. Only I would never have agreed to see a British romance back then."

"You're maturing."

"Are you calling me old?"

She laughed. "No, I'm not."

"Well, good."

She was going on a fun date with Gerald O'Bannon. Priscilla's heart warmed as she thought about the evening they would spend together. And she knew just what she would wear—a beautiful pink blouse with embroidered flowers she'd picked up at the Perfect Fit. She might not look like a fashion model in it, but that lovely new blouse might be just the ticket to turn a certain man's head. And right now, she was suddenly interested in doing just that.

AUTHOR LETTER

Dear Reader,

Just a few short weeks into the writing of this story, my beautiful mother passed away. She had battled Alzheimer's for many years, but the final weeks still caught us off guard. We were convinced we would have more time with her.

I was my mother's caregiver until the very end. After she passed, I wasn't sure I would be able to write at all. Grief held me in its grip. Many times, I sat at the computer and tried to force the words to come. They would not. Then God did a remarkable thing: He captivated my imagination with this story. He brought the characters to life in my mind's eye. The story began to tumble out, one scene after another. Now, on the opposite end of writing it, I can honestly say that God used my grief to propel me forward. He also showed me how to use it as a driving force in my story. Several of the characters in *Bridge over Troubled Waters* happen to be dealing with grief. Some, like Priscilla, are handling it well. Others, like a new character named Victor Fox, are not. We all handle grief differently, after all.

Perhaps you're walking through a loss right now. The grief is all-consuming. You've lost a loved one, someone you miss dearly. My prayer, as you read this story, is that you will find comfort in the fact that God will meet you right where you are—in the middle of your grief. He longs to heal your broken heart and bring hope once again.

Thank you so much for reading.
Janice Thompson

ABOUT THE AUTHOR

Author Janice Thompson got her start in the industry writing screenplays and musical comedies for the stage. Janice has published over one hundred books for the Christian market, crossing genre lines to write cozy mysteries, historicals, romances, nonfiction books, devotionals, children's books, and more. She particularly enjoys writing lighthearted, comedic tales because she enjoys making readers laugh.

Janice is passionate about her faith and does all she can to share the joy of the Lord with others, which is why she particularly enjoys writing. Her tagline, "Love, Laughter, and Happily Ever Afters!" sums up her take on life.

She lives in Spring, Texas, where she leads a rich life with her family, a host of writing friends, and two mischievous pups. When she's not busy writing or playing with her eight grandchildren, Janice can be found in the kitchen, baking specialty cakes and cookies for friends and loved ones. No matter what she's cooking up—books, cakes, cookies, or mischief—she does her best to keep the Lord at the center of it all.

AN ARMCHAIR TOUR OF MARTHA'S VINEYARD

Edgartown, Massachusetts

If you enjoy an elegant storybook setting, then Edgartown, Massachusetts, is the place for you. Located just eight miles away from Vineyard Haven on the far east end of the island, this exquisite seaport village is a world apart in look and feel.

Walk the picturesque streets and view some of the island's most magnificent architecture. Enjoy beautifully maintained, centuries-old homes once owned by whaling captains. Venture down to the waterfront for a glimpse of yachts that will take your breath away. Afterward, why not head downtown for a meal at one of Edgartown's many restaurants, where you can enjoy seafood fresh off the boat? Then, when you've eaten your fill, linger a while in one of the shops or art galleries nearby, where the locals will fill your ears with stories about how the movie *Jaws* was filmed in their little village.

Surprises await you around every corner in Edgartown—brightly painted homes with gingerbread trim, quaint inns with expansive porches, grandiose hotels perfect for hosting the ideal wedding, a pristine lighthouse nestled on its own private beach, and a harbor view to rival any other. There's plenty to keep you busy, both day and night.

Oh, and while you're at it, visit the Old Whaling Church while you're in town. Tell 'em Moby Dick sent you.

SOMETHING DELICIOUS FROM OUR SEASIDE FRIENDS

Candy Lane's Cookie Butter Cupcakes

Cupcake Ingredients:

- 1 white cake mix
- ¼ cup crushed Lotus Biscoff cookies
- 1 teaspoon cinnamon
- ½ teaspoon pumpkin pie spice
- 1 stick (½ cup) softened butter
- ½ cup melted cookie butter
- 2 tablespoons brown sugar (or 1 tablespoon maple syrup/pancake syrup)
- 3 eggs
- 1¼ cups milk

Additional crushed Lotus Biscoff cookies (to top off before baking)

Frosting Ingredients:

- 1½ cups softened butter
- ⅓ cup cookie butter
- 1 block softened cream cheese
- 1 tablespoon maple syrup
- 1 teaspoon cinnamon
- ¼ teaspoon pumpkin pie spice
- 5–6 cups powdered sugar
- 1 teaspoon vanilla

CUPCAKES:

Combine cake mix, crushed cookies, and spices and mix thoroughly. Add softened butter, melted cookie butter, and maple syrup, then mix until crumbly. Add eggs, one at a time. Gradually add milk and mix until smooth. Spoon batter into cupcake liners and sprinkle approximately 1 tablespoon crushed Biscoff cookies on top, then bake at 350 degrees for 15 minutes (or until done).

FROSTING:

Mix butter, cookie butter, cream cheese, and maple syrup and beat until creamy. Add remaining ingredients and beat until desired consistency.

When cupcakes are cooled, top with frosting and finish off with drizzles of melted cookie butter and cookie crumbs. Press half a cookie into each cupcake as a decorative topper.

Read on for a sneak peek of another exciting book
in the series Mysteries of Martha's Vineyard!

Smoke on the Water
by Beth Adams

Priscilla braked as the car in front of her slowed down along Beach Road. The marina was spread out in front of them, and the lights on the ends of the docks were just starting to twinkle on. Priscilla saw the passenger stick a phone out the car window and take a picture, and she tried not to let frustration get the best of her.

It was a beautiful sight, there was no denying it. She should be glad that people were enjoying the beauty of the island she got to call home.

She took the opportunity to adjust the air conditioning, cranking up the cool air. The whole region was in the midst of a terrible heat wave, and the cold air felt heavenly. Finally, picture taken, the car sped up, and Priscilla started moving again.

It had already taken twice as long to get home from Joan's house as it did during the winter, but there was nothing to be done about it. It was three days before the Fourth of July, and Martha's Vineyard had swelled with visitors. The sidewalks of Tisbury were choked with tourists window-shopping at the Brown Jug and Maypop Antiques and popping into Candy Lane Confectionery and Murdick's Fudge and Ortmann's Grocery. The beaches were packed too, with lines just to park near the island's most popular stretches, and there was a wait at every restaurant on the island these days. The streets, especially the narrow cobblestone roads that threaded through the historic district, were clogged with cars.

Really, though, as frustrating as the traffic was, she couldn't blame the tourists. This was the best time of year to be on Martha's Vineyard. The days were long and warm, the sunshine was plentiful, the hydrangeas and roses and dahlias were in bloom, and there was an energy here, a sense of life that made the whole place feel alive. Besides, many businesses on the island counted on visitors to make it through the long winter months, when the towns emptied out and even many locals fled to warmer climates.

But sometimes the traffic did get a wee bit frustrating, she thought as she slowed again. The car ahead of her was now pulling off to park along the cliff that overlooked Vineyard Sound. The sun was almost setting, and the whole sky was lit with spectacular shades of orange and red and gold that were quickly fading to lavender and silvery gray. She took it in while the car pulled off, and then continued along Main Street.

Priscilla had enjoyed her evening at her cousin Joan's, even despite the heat. Joan's son Sam and his wife, Alice, had come to stay for the week, and she'd had a family gathering to welcome them. Priscilla had never met Sam and Alice before and was thrilled to get to know the grown son her cousin talked about so often. Sam was funny and jovial, and Priscilla had loved hearing about his job as a producer at a local television station in the Boston area.

Sam's wife, Alice, was petite and whip-smart and had her own business restoring and selling antiques. Priscilla had promised to take her on a tour of her favorite local antique stores in the area on Tuesday morning. And of course, Priscilla had enjoyed spending time with her cousins Trudy and Gail, and Gail's father, Hugh. They'd had a lovely evening, laughing and talking and watching the fireflies come out under the beach plum and laurel at the edges of Joan's yard.

Now that she was out of town, the traffic lessened, and Priscilla was able to go a bit faster. As she drove, she used the time to talk to God, thanking Him for bringing her to this island and for the blessing of family and friends that made it feel like home. When she'd lost her husband, Gary, she wasn't sure she'd ever be happy again, and she'd certainly never imagined that she'd leave behind the farm where she'd spent her whole adult life. She'd loved farming, enjoyed the cycles of the seasons and watching the earth bring forth food year after year. She'd raised her daughter there. Had a life there. But when she'd inherited her aunt Marjorie's cottage, perched on the cliff at the base of the Misty Harbor Lighthouse in Martha's Vineyard, she'd taken a risk and moved here, and she'd never looked back. She thanked God for this new home, for these ancient streets and the quaint village and glorious view and this new life she'd never imagined but loved.

As Priscilla got closer to the lightkeeper's cottage, she realized something felt off. At first, she wasn't sure what made her think it. It was something subliminal, some sense that things weren't right. Then she picked up the hint of an acrid smell in the air. Like someone had been setting off fireworks. Well, there had been plenty of people setting off fireworks here and there in the lead-up to the big show Wednesday night. Doing so was illegal, but that hadn't stopped some people. But would fireworks have caused the sky to take on that reddish glow?

As Priscilla got closer, a sense of dread grew in her gut. The light was all wrong. The sun had slipped below the horizon, and twilight had settled over the area, but there was a definite orange tint in the air. And the acrid smell grew. Something was burning, she realized. Something big.

As Priscilla turned the last curve in the road, she sucked in a breath. Something was burning, all right. She pulled off the road and fumbled in her purse, searching for her cell phone. She tried to make herself believe that what she was seeing was real, but it didn't seem possible. After what felt like hours but was probably no more than a few seconds, she felt her fingers graze the hard plastic of her phone case, and she pulled the phone out and quickly dialed 911.

"911, what's your emergency?"

Priscilla watched the flames lick the wood that surrounded the big windows and tried to get the words out. Smoke billowed out of the flames, sending a hazy black cloud into the night sky.

"This is Priscilla Grant. I'm just south of Misty Harbor Light on Main Street. And—I think I—" She stumbled to get the words out, forcing her tongue to form the sounds. "The lighthouse is on fire!"

A NOTE FROM THE EDITORS

We hope you enjoyed Mysteries of Martha's Vineyard, published by the Books and Inspirational Media Division of Guideposts, a nonprofit organization that touches millions of lives every day through products and services that inspire, encourage, help you grow in your faith, and celebrate God's love.

Thank you for making a difference with your purchase of this book, which helps fund our many outreach programs to military personnel, prisons, hospitals, nursing homes, and educational institutions.

We also create many useful and uplifting online resources. Visit Guideposts.org to read true stories of hope and inspiration, access OurPrayer network, sign up for free newsletters, download free e-books, join our Facebook community, and follow our stimulating blogs.

To learn about other Guideposts publications, including the best-selling devotional *Daily Guideposts*, go to Guideposts.org/Shop, call (800) 932-2145, or write to Guideposts, PO Box 5815, Harlan, Iowa 51593.

Sign up for the
Guideposts Fiction Newsletter
and stay up-to-date on the books you love!

You'll get sneak peeks of new releases, recommendations from other Guideposts readers, and special offers just for you . . .
and it's FREE!

Just go to Guideposts.org/Newsletters today to sign up.

Guideposts®

Visit Guideposts.org/Shop
or call (800) 932-2145

Find more inspiring fiction in these best-loved Guideposts series!

Mysteries of Martha's Vineyard
Come to the shores of this quaint and historic island and dig in to a cozy mystery. When a recent widow inherits a lighthouse just off the coast of Massachusetts, she finds exciting adventures, new friends, and renewed hope.

Tearoom Mysteries
Mix one stately Victorian home, a charming lakeside town in Maine, and two adventurous cousins with a passion for tea and hospitality. Add a large scoop of intriguing mystery and sprinkle generously with faith, family, and friends, and you have the recipe for Tearoom Mysteries.

Sugarcreek Amish Mysteries
Be intrigued by the suspense and joyful "aha!" moments in these delightful stories. Each book in the series brings together two women of vastly different backgrounds and traditions, who realize there's much more to the "simple life" than meets the eye.

Mysteries of Silver Peak
Escape to the historic mining town of Silver Peak, Colorado, and discover how one woman's love of antiques helps her solve mysteries buried deep in the town's checkered past.

Patchwork Mysteries
Discover that life's little mysteries often have a common thread in a series where every novel contains an intriguing whodunit centered around a quilt located in a beautiful New England town.

To learn more about these books, visit Guideposts.org/Shop